ANGER
is an
ACID

Praise for The Patience of a Dead Man—Book One

"This first book sets up the trilogy so well that I've already finished book 2 and now eagerly await the final book in the story…Clark is the real deal…I couldn't put it down."

—Mindi Snyder, *NightWorms*

"…this book knocked it out of the park for me…pulled me in fast and never let go…the activity is constant, harrowing and downright frightening…"

—Well Read Beard, *Booktuber*

"I devoured this book. I simply could not stop reading…a full five stars and a big enthusiastic recommendation."

—Matt Redmon, *NightWorms*

"What struck me most was the meticulous planning that was apparent… This book hooked me. …creepy and unsettling… incredibly tense…you get the sense that Clark was made for this."

—Brennan LaFaro, *Dead Head Reviews*

"…there are no moments that would equate to a jump scare in a movie. …unlike any ghost story I have ever read.

—Keelyfuse85, Instagram, *NightWorms*

"I would be willing to bet that this book is unlike any other haunted house book that readers have experienced…

—*AmiesBookReviews.Wordpress.com*

"…one hell of a ghost story. …readers will surely be as captivated as I was…"

—Andrew The Book Dad *NightWorms*

ANGER

is an

ACID

The Patience of a Dead Man—Book Three

MICHAEL CLARK

Don't fall asleep! Stay in touch:
https://www.michaelclarkbooks.com/
Facebook & Instagram: *@michaelclarkbooks*
Twitter: *@mikeclarkbooks*

CHAPTER 1

Mildred Wells waited several seconds, holding the knife steady in Sheila Palmer Russell's ribs until what little struggle there had been was over. Sheila's two little girls were upstairs sleeping and were now Mildred's—forever. The three of them were finally free of the annoying interruptions and schedule changes Sheila had pulled one-too-many times. It was also an essential milestone toward Mildred's ultimate goal—revenge against their father Tim Russell, who had played a large part in making sure Mildred would never see her son again.

Satisfied that Sheila was dead, Mildred stood and walked through the living room to look up into the stairwell. She half-expected the two girls to be at the top of the stairs, wondering what the ruckus was—but fortunately, they slept on. Now, Mildred had some time to arrange things so that when they passed on their way out the door, they wouldn't see the mess. And then they would leave town.

Mildred turned back for the kitchen. Suddenly Vivian, the youngest daughter, appeared from the darkness of her bedroom, peering down the stairs at the person who was not her mother.

Mildred sensed her presence and turned back to meet her before she could descend, blocking her path. If the little girl saw her mother in a heap in the kitchen, it wouldn't be ideal.

"Who are you?" the seven-year-old asked. Mildred held a finger up to her lips to shush her. If the older sister Olivia could be kept sleeping, it would make things simpler. "Oh, it's you! What are you doing here? I know you from daddy's house. What's your name? I've never seen you at *our* house before. Do you know my mom? Her name is Sheila." Mildred glided up the stairs closing the distance between them swiftly but not so quickly as to threaten. "Something doesn't smell very good," continued Vivian. It was the last thing she uttered that night.

With a quick tap of the finger against the little girl's forehead, Vivian fell into a trance and stopped questioning. Mildred walked past her without breaking stride and into the dark bedroom. Olivia was indeed still sleeping but would have to be awakened soon for travel. Mildred shook her twice. As soon as Olivia's eyes were open, she repeated the forehead tap, and both girls were under Mildred's magickal daze, courtesy of the *Book of Shadows*.

Now there would be no screams that might wake the neighbors and call attention. She just needed to lead them through their Amesbury neighborhood and disappear into the woods without being seen. Mildred found shoes and coats for the girls and marched them down, through the living room and past the kitchen, directly past their mother's lifeless form. The girls' heads didn't even turn to look and remained locked on Mildred's presence.

Taking one last look back, Mildred had nearly forgotten her preferred knife, which was still protruding from Sheila's chest. Using her favorite spell, she called the knife to her hand and just as quickly returned it to the place she'd buried it over a century ago—in the woods of Beverly Farms, Massachusetts, over thirty miles away.

CHAPTER 2

Sugar Hill, New Hampshire

Andrew Vaughn had grown up as the black sheep of his small family. They were *four* up until semi-recently, and after a string of bad luck, it was down to just Andrew. The unofficial truth was that he'd always been a disappointment to his parents, and now that they were dead, there was no making it up to them. When Andrew thought of his father, he recalled being ignored, and when he remembered his mother, he saw the nearly permanent scowl she always wore when she looked at him.

The family history was set in stone, and it could never be changed. There was no chance for him to grow up entirely and become a seasoned adult before final judgment on his character— no chance of redemption in their eyes. Now, not yet twenty-three years old, he had a lot on his mind and a lot on his plate.

His sister Rebecca was dead too—recently—*a month ago,* in fact, and it was almost wholly his fault. The guilt hung over him every day like a wet blanket. Rebecca's death happened only eleven months after his parents were killed by a drunk driver. A man who Andrew had hired without his sister's approval had killed her while robbing the family business—The Foggy Orchard Funeral Home. Andrew had been played the fool.

To make a bad situation even worse, Andrew hated the funeral home business, yet his parents had set things up so that it would be financially impossible to escape. They'd finally found a way to corral the black sheep, knowing that the funeral home paid better than any other job a twenty-three-year-old ex-college-drug-dealer could land. The funeral home had been put in an irrevocable trust. He wasn't permitted to sell it, and the trust was overseen by an uncle who was angrier with him than his late mother.

Now Andrew was all but forced to work every day in a place he hated for fear of dead bodies, and odd noises real or imagined. Every day in the funeral home was torturous—he was the first to come and the last to leave. The home itself was located at the end of a long driveway nearly a half-mile long in a small valley that still served as a working apple orchard. The apple trees covered two medium-sized hills, and in the valley between were three buildings: a farmhouse, a barn, and the Victorian mansion funeral home that featured a short tower protruding out of the center of it.

The official name of the valley was *Whitten Pass*, but the Vaughn family had decided to name the funeral home after the orchard itself. Most people in the area referred to the valley, the funeral home, and the orchard as "Foggy Orchard," so one had to figure out why you wanted to go there by the context of your sentence. You could be going to pick apples—or to bury a loved one.

Every day was torture as Andrew tried to think his way around his problem—how to escape this place and not live in a tent? It was agony as he opened the home, turned on all the lights, and brewed the coffee before the part-time help arrived to assist in the day's duties. Every night was also harrowing as he bid the last employee goodbye and sat in his office for at least another hour finishing paperwork—sometimes with a dead body downstairs chilling in the cooler—and odd creaks and noises out in the hallway.

Every night was nerve-wracking, but tonight, right here in his bedroom, was a living nightmare.

CHAPTER 3

Andrew had a lot to drink before bed per usual; otherwise, he wouldn't sleep and would spend most of the night staring at the ceiling, alone, reflecting on his guilt and his miserable life. Despite his near stupor, he sensed that someone else was in the room with him.

The woman opened the book she held over the bed and loudly clapped it shut. Andrew, wide awake under the t-shirt he'd draped over his eyes, threw it off and sat up straight, heart pounding. Three feet away was a dark figure he couldn't quite make out. He screamed in surprise.

"Who is it!? What do you want?!" he looked to his nightstand for any sort of weapon—but no luck. The figure said nothing, and stepped out of the shadows, dimly illuminated by the dull light that made it through the dark curtains. He looked twice, recognizing her posture—her hair—but the face remained in the shadows. She paused to let him *realize*.

The ghost of Colleen Vaughn stared at her son with the usual disgust. She could smell the alcohol—*same old Andrew*. Colleen was dead but was not finished raising her son.

"Mom?" Andrew thought he might be hallucinating. The budding hangover was enough to remind him he wasn't dreaming, but—he remembered how he felt the morning Rebecca was killed.

This experience was equally hellish—a second self-inflicted nightmare. Perhaps he'd let *himself* down this time, drinking too much, too many nights in a row.

She took a step closer to let him see how angry she was. He could make out her furrowed brow and the edge of a frown. She glared unblinkingly, and he knew exactly why. Andrew had thanked God his mother wasn't alive for his sister's murder—but his mother back from the dead—was unimaginable.

She loomed over him, threatening, staring, stepping closer. He backed up into the headboard. Now she held the book out to him. He froze, wide-eyed in disbelief. *Was this happening?*

The ghost of Colleen Vaughn dropped the book next to his leg and waited, curtains beginning to illuminate with the coming dawn behind her. If he couldn't manage this simple task, figure out this simple clue, she was more than ready to guide him through it the hard way, and it would not be fun for him.

Things were different in the afterlife. Communication wasn't as simple as verbally proclaiming your intentions or even writing them down. It was a struggle to make contact with the living—it took a great deal of effort and emotion, and he damn well better meet her halfway.

Finally, Andrew reached out and retrieved the book.

The first five pages were blank.

On the sixth was written one word—"John."

On the opposing page was the word "Sherman."

Andrew flipped the page again. "George" was the next word. Then "Brown."

He turned the page again—"William,"…and then "Lincoln."

Confused, he paused to look up at her, as much as he dreaded it.

"Mom…you're angry. I know I've let you down. I know you blame me for Rebecca's death—and I'm…" he stumbled on his words, choking up—"But tell me, *please*—what *is* this?"

She said nothing but reached out and took the book back. Andrew recoiled as he felt the cold radiating off of her ghostly hand. She tore the pages he'd already read, then turned deeper and ripped out several more without taking her eyes off him. When she'd finished, she handed it back.

Andrew opened the journal again and began flipping to find her message. Suddenly, something caught his eye in the hallway to his left—a tall figure in the doorway.

Father?

—No, it was not his father.

Andrew was surrounded now—caught between two ghosts, one on each side of the bed. They loomed over him as his eyes darted right to left, and his heart pounded.

His mother pointed to the book, reminding him to continue. He read the name but didn't recognize it. His mother raised her arm, directing him to the man on the other side of the bed, and Andrew slowly turned his head to acknowledge the guest.

The dead man was tall, bearded, and dressed in old fashioned farming clothes. Andrew noticed that his eyes were blue.

His mother spun suddenly and walked away, body language suggesting deep disappointment. She was through—finished, and leaving him alone with the stranger.

She walked directly into the closet, passing between the hanging clothes—gone—for now.

What have you signed me up for, Mom? Andrew wondered.

The tall man stared, and Andrew was at a loss for what to do. He took another look at the name in the book and closed it. Out of ideas, he offered it to the visitor.

Colleen Vaughn's guest ignored the gesture. The "flipbook" was—and *must be again*—a useful communication tool between the living and the dead. It was invented by Annette Smith in the town of Sanborn, unbeknownst to Andrew, and had helped get Elmer to safety—but now it was time to help the others who had once helped him.

Tim Russell and his girlfriend Holly stood no chance against Mildred, and things were about to get much worse for them now that they had her undivided attention. Thomas had been on his way back to Sanborn to help them when suddenly, Andrew Vaughn's services were offered up by his dead mother. Unfortunately, Andrew didn't seem to know he'd been volunteered.

Andrew sat up in bed, deep in shock, a tall bearded ghost standing over him, looking down. He'd never believed in ghosts before despite his fear of noises in the funeral home, but now he'd seen *two—for sure—*in the last five minutes.

In Andrew's lap lay a nearly blank journal, and it went without saying—because no one had uttered the words—that he was supposed to understand what the book meant. Having a supernatural being in his bedroom was harrowing, but more than that, the pressure of having to understand his message was unbearable. A tense moment passed. The ghost lingered, then opened the night table by the bed and pulled out a pen.

A pen? What in the world do you want me to write? thought Andrew.

This was so much more than a bad dream.

Thomas Pike had been dead for over a hundred years before someone came along who could help him. Her name was Annette Smith, and she had lived in his old house on Lancaster Hill Road in Sanborn. Annette didn't know it at the time, but her husband Henry had been murdered by Mildred, and his body had been disguised to make it look like a heart attack.

Annette could have easily picked up and left as soon as she'd seen her first ghost, but very bravely, she stayed, even going the extra mile attempting to communicate with him via her "flipbook" journals. Annette would write singular words in bold print, one per page, and leave the book out for Thomas to flip through. If Annette had left him accurate multiple-choice answers to her questions, Thomas would leave the book open to the correct one.

Thomas' patience had paid off, and his long wait was nearly over—soon perhaps, he could get help moving Elmer's bones away from his sick mother, and the boy could rest. Annette Smith was a one-in-a-million human being.

One day Annette wrote several names across several pages in a blank journal then left it closed on a table for Thomas to find—along with a pen. One of the names in the book was his own—written across two pages. *She'd even figured out who he was!* He pushed the pen aside because he had no use for it. For whatever reason, he was no longer able to maneuver the pen through the intricate process of writing as he could so effortlessly before his death.

Doing the best he could, he opened the book to the "Thomas" and "Pike" pages and left it that way for her to find. It was crude, slow, and the only method they both understood, but it worked for them, up until her murder.

But that was another time and another person. Now he needed Andrew to understand—and quickly.

There was no floating, glow, or transparency to the ghost's form. The tall man looked just like any other living person, yet this *was for sure* a spirit. He knew this because the first ghost of the night—his dead *mother*—had just disappeared into his closet. Her purpose for being there seemed to serve as some sort of introduction between him and the tall man. She'd ripped out a few pages of the journal to simplify it, but they hadn't gotten any further than the ghost's name.

The two words left were *Thomas* and *Pike*, which meant nothing to him. Just why she wanted or needed them to meet, he had no idea, but he was sure this was bad news—some form of punishment. It was apparent that Mother was back, and she was angry.

Andrew reached up and took the pen from Thomas Pike. It was cold to the touch—Andrew wondered for a moment if the ink would even flow, but he could think of nothing to write, so he attempted verbal communication.

"Hello, Thomas. My name is Andrew. Why are you here?" The man said nothing. Andrew was confused on top of being frightened. *How does this end?* he wondered. He looked once more at the blank pages of the journal, unsure of what to write. He had no questions—and only wanted him gone. The pressure of the moment became too much.

In a spontaneous burst of nervous energy, Andrew bolted from the bed and bounded down the stairs three at a time, nearly twisting an ankle on the way. He ran right through the kitchen, past the key rack, and out the front door. In the parking lot between the residence and the funeral home, he realized the fix he'd put himself in.

The Foggy Orchard Funeral Home loomed large and dark over the parking lot between the two buildings. Andrew stood in no-man's-land with a decision to make. *Where to?* The house held a confirmed ghost, and the funeral home had scared him ever since he was a boy. The body of Mrs. Agnes Shephard lay downstairs prepped and ready for tomorrow's burial this very moment, and she somewhat resembled a witch. He looked back at the residence, calculating the time it would take to go back in and fetch his car keys. *No way,* he concluded.

He hated the funeral home and always had, but chose the lesser of two evils for now. He swallowed hard as he realized he might even have to spend the night there—and that's if things went *well.* As he crossed the parking lot, he pivoted every few steps to see if Thomas Pike followed.

He found the hidden key and opened the front door. The Vaughn family never even used to lock the doors until they found out kids were using embalming fluid to get high. Kids... and dealers like Jeremy Clary, the man who had killed his sister while stealing the shit. Reaching in, he flipped the light switches illuminating the small foyer and the stairway up to the main floor. *Was it possible the ghost could have already beaten him here?* Andrew could guess the answer, yet only hoped it wouldn't be true.

He hated the smell of this building, which was the work-in-progress-never-ending search for something that did the best job of masking the odor of...so many things that no one ever wanted to smell. He surmised that the average visitor (or even employee) would never pick up on it, but for Andrew, who had almost grown up in the embalming room—he knew why they bought the chemicals.

He knew the odd whiff and the lingering stink. He would forever be sensitive to them. Every odor took him back to the first time he smelled it. The worst was the day he walked in on his father preparing a corpse for burial and inadvertently saw his first dead body. Andrew was eleven years old.

It was a man on the table, and he was naked. His skin was abnormally pale (not for a corpse, but it took Andrew a few seconds to realize), and there was a long bruise down the entire side of his body. The man looked fake, plastic even, but deep down, even as a little boy, Andrew knew that he was real—or, had been real, or living, until recently. The shock of seeing a dead man, never mind a *naked* dead man was something he didn't recover from until he became an adult—if then.

Andrew stood at the bottom of the foyer stairs breathing heavily, checking in front and behind incessantly. Up ahead on the second floor, the hallway was dark. He closed the front door behind him after taking a final look for the potential tail—and all seemed clear. With nowhere to go but up the stairs, he marched quickly and quietly, his next goal the hallway light switch.

The silence was deafening, the only noise, the muffled hum of distant refrigerators—the basement—the same coolers keeping Mrs. Shephard cold. Those rooms in the cellar—Andrew's least favorite, were accessible from a separate staircase that led to the basement at the back of the building—a part of the building patrons never saw, and of course, would never want to.

There was no way in hell he would be going anywhere near that part of the home right now. The plan was to get to the office and lock himself in—then wait for daylight. The office was a small room with only one door; therefore, he could at least lock it, lean up against the outside wall, and try to get some sleep before tomorrow's service. Hopefully, Thomas Pike had given up and would let him be.

The hall before him was long and disappeared into darkness—something that had always bothered him about the design of the building. In winter months, when days were short, his parents would come and go from work in total darkness. On occasion, he would be there when the lights were flicked on in the morning or snapped off in the evening.

Those moments had always stirred anxiety in him. As a young man, he pictured heads peeking around door jambs, leering. There had been so many dead people here that it made it extremely easy to imagine. Now, with his parents and sister gone, he had to live this moment every day, both times. Alone.

Finally, he reached the light switch and lit the hallway to reveal the red floral patterned carpet and the three small chandelier-like fixtures that ran the length of the long hallway. Thankfully, Mrs. Shephard was not standing there naked and pale, ready to greet him. Wasting no time, he entered the first doorway on the right, hit the lights inside, then shut and locked the door.

Andrew moved a chair to block the door and then peered out the office window to check his house across the parking lot. It appeared as dark and motionless as he'd left it a few minutes ago. Andrew exhaled slowly, feeling trapped. There was half a bottle of bourbon in his desk drawer, so he fetched it and took a long pull. For a second, the direct heat of the alcohol spiked his courage just enough to ignite his pride, making him consider marching right back across the parking lot to confront his fears. Two seconds later, of course, the temporary fire went out, and he thought better of it. *What were you going to do when you found him?* He asked himself.

Just then, the office doorknob began to jiggle.

Andrew spun immediately and choked on the second mouthful of bourbon, frozen in fear. He turned the lights off in a lame attempt to even the odds, throwing himself into darkness— but now he could at least see under the door. No feet blocked the light from the hallway. The knob shook again. *Ghosts don't block the light, Andy.* He turned the office light back on, thinking frantically. His options were few.

"Thomas—I'm not interested. I don't understand what you want, and I don't know what my mother has to do with this, or who you are, but…"

Thomas Pike, a patient and reasonable man during his life, began to pound on the door, clearly unhappy with having to pursue Andrew. Andrew took two steps back from the cacophony, fresh out of ideas, bewildered, and freshly inebriated. He heard the wood begin to crack and realized that Thomas Pike would not quit—Andrew would eventually become a part of whatever the ghost wanted, whether he liked it or not.

Andrew fearfully reached out, grabbed the knob, and after hesitating one last second, turned and pulled. Thomas Pike stood in the hallway, glaring as if to say *there's no time for this*. In his hand were the journal and the pen. He raised his arm and held them out to Andrew. *Try again.* Andrew, while terrified by the man standing before him, slumped his shoulders in frustration. Unaware of the ghost's motor-skill limitations, he tried speaking again.

"Mr. Pike, I don't know what you want me to write. *You're* the one who wants something. Why don't *you* write something for *me?*" Thomas Pike opened the journal and put pen to paper for Andrew, but nothing happened. It made no worldly sense. "How is it you can bang on my door, but you can't write?" Thomas Pike said nothing, once more offering the pen and journal.

Andrew took them solemnly and thought for a moment. What

does he want? Words? A picture? A map? More multiple-choice answers to a question I don't even know? Perhaps Thomas Pike couldn't *hear*. Andrew grabbed at straws. It was a longshot, but maybe it was a start. He took the pen and started scribbling. When he was finished, he handed the book back. Thomas Pike read what Andrew wrote.

I'm sorry. I don't understand what you want. Can you even hear me?

CHAPTER 4

Nate Hoginski, the producer of the nationally syndicated TV show *Only If You Dare,* sat in his car a quarter-mile down the road from Tim Russell's supposedly haunted Sanborn, New Hampshire farmhouse. Things were happening fast and furious on the show now with the deaths of his cameraman David Bonnette and Sanborn police officer Robert Simmons.

This story had caught fire with the general public, and Nathan had been in the business long enough to know that when you had a good thing going, you rode it for all it was worth. He would fan the flames of this red-hot "Legend of Mildred Wells" story all he could, and that meant keeping eyes ready at more than one location.

Hoginski couldn't give two shits about the dead cop Simmons, but Bonnette had shown promise as an up-and-coming tabloid television producer. In memoriam, before this story ran its course, Hoginski would make him a legend, and perhaps even milk an extra show or two out of it for the man. Now they could interview their *own people* and eat up countless minutes of airtime saying what a pleasure it had been to work with him, what a great guy he was, a family man, etcetera. In the end, Bonnette had provided *content.* In essence, he'd taken one for the team.

The odd thing about the "Mildred Wells" storyline was,

however, that it appeared as though a ghost *could* have killed the two men. There was little to no traditional physical evidence left at the scene. Hoginski even found himself wondering in off moments if he might be in danger. Was he a believer in *Mildred Wells?* He had to think about his answer for a second, but in the end, settled on *not really*.

When push came to shove, he downplayed it, figuring there were a million reasons how the men could have died—but he would do his damndest to keep any of those theories from being broadcast, at least on *his* show. *The Legend of Mildred Wells* storyline was ratings gold, and he would do anything to protect his bread and butter. Just then, his CB radio crackled to life:

"Bossman, this is Satellite. We have scanner activity. It looks like big stuff. Send the truck ASAP." Hoginski almost spilled his coffee as a million questions entered his brain all at once—but there was no time to ask them now.

"Ten-Four. Truck is on the way." Hoginski scrambled out of his car and ran back to the second passenger van parked directly behind him. "Did you hear that? Get your ass down to Amesbury and don't stop for anything, not even gas. If you have to piss, piss in a bottle. If you fuck this up, your ass is mine. You have the address, right?"

"Got it, boss. We have a map too." The driver of the van full of filming equipment started the engine and threw it into gear.

"Go then! And McDonough, you'd better know how to read a map. If you get him lost, I'll kill you. Do you hear me?" The van spit gravel from under its tires as it headed too fast down Lancaster Hill Road. They hit one of the near-permanent potholes a hundred yards later, and the rear end of the vehicle bounced up and into the air, then kept going. The car who had radioed from Amesbury didn't have a video camera, only a 35mm camera with a telephoto lens.

Hoginski was nervous. They had more than an hour's drive to Sheila Russell's house, and that's if they didn't miss a turn. He prayed they wouldn't lose out on any essential filming opportunities, not that he was a religious man in any sense of the word. He gave himself a pat on the back however, for stationing a car at the two daughters' house just in case something happened.

Now that the boys were on their way to Massachusetts, he got back in his vehicle and had the Amesbury car fill him in on some of the finer details they'd heard on the scanner. It was grim as hell, but he found himself smiling at the apparent death of Tim Russell's ex-wife and the fact that his girls were missing. It was nothing personal—business was business.

CHAPTER 5

Four hours later, Nate Hoginski combed his hair and prepped himself to conduct an impromptu on-camera interview. It wasn't his forte, but the *beautiful people*—what he called on-camera talent—were not in the budget for this trip—he'd have to do the questioning himself, and he was nervous. They'd blown so much money on wasteful international episodes that *The Legend of Mildred Wells* had to suffer. No worries, he thought; the *beautiful people* were mostly pains-in-the-asses anyway, and, as well as saving money, this might be a chance to shine.

"Are you ready, McDonough?" McDonough, the map reader who had successfully found his way to Amesbury, was back in town—as McDonough, the cameraman.

Exhaling one final time, clearing his throat and spitting in the gulley, Hoginski walked up the incline of Tim Russell's driveway and knocked on the front door. Russell had not taken too kindly to the last time *Only If You Dare* knocked on his door—and he would certainly not appreciate this episode either. McDonough hefted the heavy camera onto his shoulder and prepared to film. Tim came to the door.

"Can I help—? Oh, for crying out…" Tim saw the camera and was already noticeably upset. He'd been hoping for a miracle—that someone might still be interested in buying the house. The presence of a camera betrayed this hope. *What the hell do they want now?*

"Mr. Russell, sorry to bother you. I'm Nathan Hoginski from the TV show *Only If You Dare*. Would you have time for a few questions?" McDonough pushed the button and began to film, and because the camera's light had been purposefully disabled, Tim had no idea.

"No. You guys are the worst. I just want to sell this place, and all you want to do is—"

"Mr. Russell, do you have any comments about what happened in Amesbury last night?"

Tim froze.

"What are you talking about?" His face went pale. Hoginski wasn't sure if Tim had heard the bad news yet or not. He'd figured the odds at around 50/50, but now he knew for sure that Tim had no idea. Aware of the intense notification he was about to deliver, Hoginski stammered on for a brief moment, appreciating the grace that the *beautiful people* possessed on camera at a moment like this.

"Uh, well—I'm sorry, you haven't heard. I apologize, but ah— Your ex-wife Sheila was found dead late this morning by one of her neighbors. We aren't sure, but it looks like she was stabbed. Do you know where your daughters are?"

Tim saw red immediately—and grabbed the camera off of the taller man's shoulder, smashing it into the porch. McDonough did nothing to challenge him. Then he turned to face Hoginski.

"What else do you know? Tell me now before I drive you through the fucking Earth." McDonough was wise to hang back, but he would lose his job in the coming weeks because of it. Hoginski, subconsciously relieved that the camera was no longer filming, spilled his guts, all bravado aside. He was more than nervous now, face to face with the wounded father.

"We heard it on the scanner in Amesbury. Some of it we had to guess, but we saw—a body taken out of the house all covered up. It sounded like they were looking for the girls. You might want to check in with the authorities. They might think you did it, and that you took the girls." There was no question in Hoginski's mind that Tim did not have the girls. No sooner did he finish his sentence, a Sanborn Police car rambled up the road and pulled into the driveway. Tim ignored Hoginski and ran to the vehicle.

CHAPTER 6

Sanborn police Chief Lloyd Galluzzo, along with Detective Ron DaSilva of the Amesbury police department, quickly dismissed Tim Russell as the murderer of his ex-wife and kidnapper of his children. Holly Burns—Tim's girlfriend—was also interviewed, and her alibi also checked out. The next logical step was to launch a search party both in Amesbury and in Sanborn for the two young girls.

Dogs were brought in with little success, becoming bogged down by an excessive amount of dead wildlife (birds and squirrels) littering the forest. The only thing the police were able to determine was that the girls' first hundred yards or so seemed to go in the general direction of Sanborn, New Hampshire, where their father lived.

The Sanborn search produced precisely nothing. There was no sign that Mildred or the girls had been in the area at all. The police weren't even sure if they should even try to look for a "Mildred." Did Mildred Wells even *exist*? Should they concentrate on the girls and girls alone—as if they had wandered off by themselves? Or were they kidnapped by a "legend" of whom nobody from the area had ever heard?

Holly Burns with some questions of her own saw the police searching the Sanborn property. Could the girls have made it from

Amesbury to Sanborn on their own so soon? *Most likely, no.* Was this a sign that the police doubted Tim's story? Holly wondered. It had been a nightmare of a month on Lancaster Hill Road—what, with the discovery of Officer Robert Simmons' (Tim's closest neighbor) badly decomposed body found under Tim's willow tree by the pond, and now...*this.* Holly knew the root cause of all these problems. She knew in her heart that it was all because of Mildred Wells.

Asking the police to buy that a ghost—or in this case—a *revenant* (something no one she knew had ever heard of) was responsible for all these things was a fool's errand if you wanted your story to be believed. One had to *see* Mildred to believe in Mildred, and Holly had seen her up close and personal. She hoped she would never lay eyes on her again. Tim and Holly stood in the kitchen, where they were told to remain until the police had finished their preliminary search. Tim was nervous, frustrated, and beyond angry.

"These guys are morons. This is the same Chief who allowed Bob Simmons to be fifty-percent of his police force! I don't even know who the other six guys are. Franklin cops? *Northfield* maybe? I want to go looking myself, but they still think I might have done this! *Fuck!*"

"Did you put the restraining order on the TV show?" asked Holly.

"Not yet. I don't dare slow these guys down any more than they already are! What time is it anyway? Are they almost done?"

CHAPTER 7

At dusk, Galluzzo and his patchwork bunch of cops finished their search and reported that they had found precisely nothing. They packed their things and left for the evening, promising to return in the morning, most likely with police forces higher up the missing-persons food chain. Holly went to the living room to call her mother, who was worried about the girls and, of course, Holly's well-being.

With no desire to get into a debate with Holly about his dangerous plans, Tim saw his window of opportunity and left the house carrying his highly-illegal sawed-off shotgun.

He jogged out to the grove, hoping to see her, daring Mildred to show herself—but what might happen next was something he hadn't allowed himself to think through. As the grove grew closer, doubts crept in. He couldn't shoot her, at least if she were alone. If he did, he'd most likely never find the girls. He also couldn't shoot at her if the girls were anywhere near—the spray from the sawed-off was dangerously wide. But as the only remaining parent—and hope—of his two innocent little girls, he pressed on.

Tim cursed the police under his breath once more for taking way too long to get absolutely nothing done. The precious daylight hours of the first critical day were almost over, and the poor kids must be so *scared*. Just the thought of it began to make Tim angry again.

The hidden grove exploded before him as it always did, but this time he did not take time to appreciate the transformation from the random trees of the wild forest to symmetric rows. He jogged on, beginning to break a sweat, looking down each hallway, praying to see the ghostly white face of the woman he'd helped betray.

Thomas Fucking Pike was indirectly to blame for his daughters' kidnapping. Why had Tim trusted him? He didn't know the man (the ghost) from a hole in the wall: He could have been a Jack-the-Ripper for all Tim knew. But none of this excused Mildred from anything she'd done. They did, after all, witness her drown her son.

The rows of trees zipped past until he came to the very last one—the row that used to be the home of two headstones in the far corner. This place had been Ground Zero for all of Tim's problems—but that was last year. There was nothing to see here now in the twilight. He slowed to a walk—his history with this part of the forest was still fresh in his mind. When he arrived at the now rototilled spot (Tim had turned the soil and made a garden out of it recently), his feeling of dread passed. Mildred wasn't here.

Nobody was here.

Tim turned back to look. The sun had set, and tiny bits of an orange sky peeked between the spruce needles. In frustration, he picked up and ran, leaving the grove to head deeper into the wild woods than he'd ever been.

"Olivia! Vivian! Yell, if you can hear me!" Frustration turned to desperation as he felt the time crunch and the helplessness of not being able to do anything for his two young girls. He jogged another hundred yards then tripped on a root. While he was down, he choked back a cry, then stifled the tears and screamed again.

"OLIVIA! VIVIAN!"

Nothing. And Tim's anger, with nowhere to go, boiled within him as he turned back for the house.

Tim, gathering his wits, suddenly realized he couldn't see more than fifty feet in any direction. He began to think of Holly, and how she would be more than annoyed that he'd bolted into the woods without telling her—the deep dark woods, haunted by a murderous revenant. He hadn't asked for permission, and now he would have to beg forgiveness. Quickly, he picked up the pace and ran back from the direction he came. The sun was completely gone now, and so was his foolish bravado. Now all he could imagine was the wraith named Mildred Wells surprising him from any angle at any time. He was running blind.

Finally, the trees lined up for him—the grove. He booked it through and rumbled down the trail to the driveway, completely breathless. As his shoes touched the asphalt, he looked back for the first time. A yawning dark hole in the trees marked the beginning of the trail, and thankfully no one followed. He realized then and there that he was standing in the exact spot the home's previous owner, Annette Smith, had stood when Mildred ended her life with a spade.

Shaken and demeaned by his poor performance after the sun had set, he jogged the last twenty feet to the side door of the house and let himself in, ill-prepared mentally for Holly's inevitable disappointment.

CHAPTER 8

With the doors locked and Tim's apologies exhausted, he and Holly exchanged concerns.

"Yes, I know it was her. I'm sure she has the girls too. You don't have to tell me, Holly. I'm scared shitless. They could be..." He couldn't bring himself to finish the sentence.

"Well, we can't think that way yet. She left Sheila's body behind. She would have left theirs too. I think they're alive." Holly had other fears, but she didn't finish her thoughts out loud.

"How the hell did she know where they live? Amesbury is seventy miles from here!" Holly felt a chill climb her back as he finished his sentence.

"She seems to come and go from this house as she pleases, Tim. She knows this place as well as if not better than we do. I've told you a hundred times—*I hate staying here! Please*, let's go to my place. Even if she knows where I live, I'll feel a little better. At least I don't think she's ever been there, but this place...she could be anywhere. I don't even want to think about it."

"I can't leave, Holly. As backward as it may sound, I *need* to see her. I'm afraid I'll never see her again! Imagine that? And don't forget that Thomas Pike had no problem finding your place when he dropped off the Simmons scrapbook. Remember?" Holly nodded, unhappy that Tim had a point.

"Oh, you'll see her again, Tim. You can bet on that. At least *once* anyway. It won't be a sneak attack either. She wants you to know she's coming and probably wants you to die long and slow. She wants revenge. That's what revenants *do*, remember? We just never thought that she'd go for the girls. And that—changes everything." Holly's sigh was heavy with dread as she stared blankly at the wall, defeated. There was an unintentional moment of silence.

"How the hell does she get in here?" Tim finally wondered aloud, rousing them both from their separate thoughts. "Does she have a fucking key or something? Secret entrance? The roof?"

"The turret. It's got to be the turret." Holly suddenly seemed extra awake and even afraid. She subconsciously looked up at the ceiling where the turret would be. The stairway to it was only two rooms away. They both rose to investigate, flicking the dining room light on along the way. Tim listened outside the door for a moment, then fetched his baseball bat from the kitchen before opening it.

They climbed the stairs slowly. Holly was relieved to find the turret was empty, but it left Tim with a lack of answers and a growing level of frustration. Mildred had decided to let them worry and wonder about the girls for at least an evening—the very first evening of their captivity. Was it by design, meant to heighten the anguish? Or was she busy looking for a place to *hole them up?*

The girls were trapped with the dead woman and most likely terrified. Tim wished he could trade places with them—they were too young for such terror. Tim rested the bat against the wall and tried the windows. There were eight of them ringing the octagonal room, and much to Tim's surprise, one of them was unlocked.

"What the hell! I locked these—I'm sure I locked them."

"Yes, but you don't check them every night, Tim. All she had to do is get in here once during the day to get up here and unlock it. And look, your papers are all sitting right there." Holly motioned to Tim's box in the corner. "That's how she knew where

Sheila lived. Now we know—and it creeps me out—I can't tell you how much." Tim saw where the conversation was headed and changed the subject.

"I need to boobytrap this place. Get her right here in this room, and then set a trap, like a bear trap or…"

"You don't think she'll see a bear trap in the middle of the floor? That's just going to piss her off, Tim. And you're liable to hurt yourself with the damn thing. Same with knives or fire or whatever else you're thinking." Holly's stress did all the talking.

"I wasn't thinking about *knives or fire,* come on, give me a little bit of credit." Tim lied about the knives. "I was thinking something along the lines of a warning system. Something to make her fall down the stairs. A bag of marbles—I don't fucking know…" Holly giggled, then the giggle turned into laughter. Tim saw that she genuinely thought it was funny and was not making fun of him, so he joined in for a moment—yet the gravity of their problem hung in the room like a cloud of poison dust.

"How about a simple tripwire with a little bell on it?" Holly offered. "One at the bottom of the turret stairs, one in front of the sliding glass door in the breakfast area and one at the bottom of the bedroom stairs? We set it up every night. In the morning, unhook it, so we're not tripping over it ourselves." Tim looked up at her.

"That's an idea. Better than we have now. And like you said—'we're gonna see her again.' We have to. Oh God, I hope and pray she's greedy and wants to see me again. But—" Tim got quiet and put his balled fist under his nose. Holly saw he was getting emotional.

"Honey, we're doing all we can, let's just—"

"But if she's already done—if this is her revenge—and she's never coming back, then she's really good at it." Tim's last three words were nearly inaudible as he choked up, worried sick about his daughters. Holly hugged him, trying to hold back tears of her own.

CHAPTER 9

Holly had one important signing to attend at the real estate agency the next day and left the house early worried for Tim—but she had a plan. She knew he'd go into the woods looking again, and there wasn't anything she could do about it, nor could she blame him.

Tim indeed rechecked the woods, roaming for nearly two hours after Holly left. It was much better with the sun up. His courage returned for the most part, yet he still found himself checking behind him with every sound nature threw at him. He went so far into the woods that he eventually came to a farmhouse with an old collapsed barn more than a mile in, on an old dirt road similar to his own.

The woods had come to an end, and he'd crossed the town line into the town of Belmont. Begrudgingly, he turned back, hoping he hadn't missed any *visits* or *opportunities* back home. When he emerged from the path and crossed the driveway, he called Johnny Upson, his longtime employee and best friend back in Massachusetts, who had been instrumental in keeping Tim afloat financially.

Johnny was a whiz at small projects and kitchen re-do's, and Russell Construction was getting by on Johnny's hard work. *Thank you, my brother*, thought Tim. *I owe you, man*. Johnny volunteered to come up to Sanborn and help, but Tim told him to stay in Massachusetts—Nothing was going on, unfortunately. Not even any supernatural visits this time—*of course!* Now that you *wanted one…*

"If you see her, boss, call me. One of my buddies is back from Vietnam, Purple Heart, but he's a badass, and he would love to hunt that bitch."

"If I want her dead—uh, extra-dead I mean, I'll call you." Tim thanked Johnny for his "kind" offer, and they said their goodbyes. Tim stared at the pond and the field from inside the living room. Now, they were just—a simple pond and an average field. There was no boat floating on it, no kite flying itself, and nobody staring at the house. *Would she come?*

The unique sound of a Volkswagen engine broke the silence. Holly's car came slowly down the cratered Lancaster Hill Road, and Tim checked his watch—it was 3 pm. *She's early*, he thought. It was nice to have her home, but he was beginning to feel the urge to recheck the woods, and she might protest. As the Bug pulled up the driveway, he walked out to the lawn to greet her. Holly put the brakes on and stopped in front rather than pulling around the corner. She had a passenger.

"Who the hell is that?" asked Tim.

"Hi honey, I want you to meet someone. His name is *Neptune*. Neptune, meet your new dad." A large mellow-looking German Shepherd stared at him from the back seat. He was handsome and intimidating but had no problem with Tim's approach. He smelled his hand and let him pat his head.

"A dog? That's not a bad idea. Why didn't we think of that last night?"

"I *did*, I just didn't say anything because I didn't want you to say no. Kind of like how you go into the woods without checking, you know?" Holly teased. "So you're okay with the idea?"

"Yeah, my parents used to have dogs. I like dogs. I just hope he…" Tim trailed off. Holly instinctively followed his gaze to the field, but Mildred was not there.

"Jeez, don't do that! You scared me. 'I just hope he' what?"

"I just hope he doesn't get hurt." Holly's face became serious; the fun of her rescue purchase looked at from a new and negative perspective. Tim could tell she was already attached and changed the subject. "How the hell did he get the name *Neptune* anyway?" Holly was grateful to get off the topic.

"Previous owners, I guess. The shelter didn't say, and I didn't think to ask. He's handsome, isn't he? Tim, I *needed* this big boy. I didn't sleep at all last night. You know how I feel about the house and all that… I think he can help us—as an early warning at the very least. I don't want him hurt. I think I'm already attached."

"You are! I can see it. Do you…want to take him for a walk with me and show him around the property?" Tim was testing her to see if she'd be more protective of the dog than she was of him. Holly saw it coming.

"Yes, I suppose so. Bring that shotgun, though." Neptune was a brand new member of the family—and the family needed his help. In turn, they would do all they could to protect him back.

The dog adored the pond and the field, even taking the opportunity to chase his first squirrel. Tim and Holly let him go free as they passed the pond. There were hardly ever cars on Lancaster Hill Road. The poor dog had lived in a cage for nearly a year and was elated with his newfound freedom. Suddenly he stopped halfway to the treeline and perked his ears. Holly watched nervously.

"Neptune…Neptune, come here, boy!" She began to jog in his direction. Just then, the big Shepherd bolted for the woods, disappearing between the trees. Holly's heart rose in her throat. "Oh my God—Tim!"

"Neptune!" Tim followed his bellow with a shrill whistle, but the dog did not listen. Four minutes of "family time" was not enough to get the dog to listen to his new masters. Holly broke into a run, and Tim followed close behind. "Neptune!" Tim called again.

Just before they reached the trees, he popped out of the woods, the body of a fat gray squirrel hanging from his jaws.

"Damn, that didn't take long," said Holly. "Come here, Neptune." The dog did as he was told, but needed a few extra minutes of coaxing to give the squirrel up.

CHAPTER 10

As much as he hated the idea, Tim knew the right thing to do was attend Sheila's funeral. He did it for the sake of the girls' future and in the name of extended family harmony during this difficult time. Sheila's parents were loved by Olivia and Vivian, and they had always been fair to Tim as well, despite the programming Sheila had subjected them to during the divorce. If all went according to plan, the girls would be rescued, and the maternal side of their family would not be their grandparents, Ted and Linda Palmer.

Tim had felt a coolness whenever they occasionally bumped elbows at one of the girls' sporting events and figured it was most likely due to Sheila's "spin" on her divorce updates. She would have no doubt made him look bad so that no one would blame her for leaving him, and that's just the way divorce worked.

Now, as he arrived at the funeral home, Tim caught Ted's glare from across the room, which was exponentially more intense than usual. When the brief service was over, Tim made his way across the room to break the ice. The idea was to attempt to console them over the loss of their daughter, despite how nasty things had gotten—a neat trick if he could pull it off. The Palmer's made no effort to meet him halfway.

"Hello, Linda, hello, Ted. I have no words—except to say

I'm sorry for your loss." Linda ignored his opener and nearly interrupted him with thoughts of her own.

"We wanted to bury her even though the girls haven't been found. It's the Godly thing to do. I wanted you to know that in case you thought we should have waited." Linda's tone was aloof.

"I hadn't thought about it that deeply, Linda, but I agree with your decision." In truth, it was the farthest thing from his mind. Ted decided he couldn't hold his tongue anymore.

"You know, I thought you did it at first. I wanted the police to nail you to the wall. And I wish they'd take a second look because the shoe seems to fit from where I'm standing—after all you put her through." He was visibly angry, even shaking. Ted was near seventy-five years old and in poor health.

"Look, Ted… I don't know what you heard, but there's a fair chance it was exaggerated. Remember, you only heard one side of the story." Ted lifted his index finger as if to interject, but Tim cut him off. "But I'm not here to talk about that. We need to work together. Your granddaughters are going to want to be a part of your lives as soon as we get them back. I'm not here to speak ill of anyone—this is not the time or place, but if you ever want to talk about things—anything at all, at any time—you have my number." Ted Palmer seemed to remember where he was and lowered his voice. He continued, however, in a low whisper.

"What's this malarkey about a *ghost?* How the hell is this making the papers? Not the rags mind you, but some of the respectable newspapers…and that TV show…*they've got people talking!*" Tim shifted awkwardly on his feet. He was hoping they had somehow missed the media circus, but no such luck. It was time to stretch some truths.

"I don't know what to tell you except that TV show you're talking about has a lot to do with it. They're trying to string together some things that happened in other towns. Things I don't want to talk about right here or right now—you'll understand.

But you might have already heard some of them." Linda nodded her head.

"I haven't seen the TV show yet, but I know about the boy in the woods," she said. Tim tried to discern whether or not that was all they'd heard. If they hadn't watched *Only If You Dare,* they might not have heard about Bob Simmons or David Bonnette. In any case, Tim didn't want to spend his day bringing them up to speed, even in the name of familial harmony.

"But they don't have any legitimate suspects either, do they?" Ted seemed to be looking at Tim again as if he were not yet entirely inside the circle of trust. Ted would probably not be scratching Tim off his list of suspects until the "real killer was apprehended," so to speak. *And how was that going to work?* Somehow Tim couldn't picture Mildred Wells in the back of a police cruiser.

"No, they don't. I've searched my property, and I'm going back to Amesbury after this. I…have a meeting with the police. It's more than frustrating—I don't know what else to say."

Ted Palmer scowled.

CHAPTER 11

Tim pulled into the driveway of Sheila's empty house and parked behind an unmarked police car. A detective named Markus Castro got out and met Tim at the top of the porch stairs. Tim couldn't help but remember the countless confrontations he'd had with Sheila close to these steps. So many stressful Sunday nights, after dropping the kids from a weekend of visitation. Those times were over, and things were different now—but they weren't any better.

"Good afternoon Mr. Russell. Just remember not to touch anything, please, as we talked about." Tim nodded and prepared for an emotional nightmare. The only positive was that the police seemed to have more confidence that Tim was innocent than Ted Palmer did. Together they climbed the steps to a door that opened into a small mudroom directly off the kitchen. *This would be ugly, early.*

Everything was left as it had been discovered, minus Sheila's body, of course. One of the chairs that surrounded the breakfast table was upended, and another was three feet from the table. There was no chalk outline of Sheila's body as he had guessed there would be, but there was a beer-can sized puddle of dried blood under the table where the far chair should be. Tim could easily picture how Sheila's violent death played out, and it gave him no pleasure, despite their tumultuous history. Mildred had no doubt traveled quickly from right to left, pushing Sheila to the floor, upending and scattering the chairs, stabbing Sheila while she was backed up under the table. *No way to go.*

"So, that's where she was?" He swallowed dryly. It was eerie in here and cold. Maybe the police had turned the heat off—*to get rid of the flies*, he thought. There were odd reminders here and there that the girls did indeed call this place home, but without the girls themselves, it was a shell of a building, and the props—the toy, the Barbie drinking glass, and the pile of folded laundry—were only lifeless inanimate objects.

Tim had little to say. Detective Castro, who was there to listen to Tim's point of view and to make sure he didn't touch anything, nodded. Tim stepped carefully around the murder scene and moved on from the kitchen to explore the rest of the downstairs. Tim had lived here until the divorce, so everything was familiar— yet different. The experience was more than surreal. Sheila made lots of changes to the place, perhaps in an attempt to erase as much "Tim" as possible.

Under Castro's supervision, he opened the hall closet and flipped through assorted coats and rain slickers. He wasn't sure (because it could be elsewhere in the house), but he thought Vivian's red three-season jacket was missing. Looking down at the floor of the closet, he saw a pair of Sheila's hiking boots. There was no footwear for the girls.

"There might be some coats and boots missing from this closet," he remarked.

"I'll make a note of it," said the detective. Tim then went upstairs with Castro on his heel. Other than the girls' unmade beds, nothing seemed out of order. Tim dropped his chin to his chest as he broke down emotionally, keeping his back to the detective. He couldn't hold the tears in anymore.

"I'm sorry, Mr. Russell. I have a daughter myself. We'll find them." Tim nodded as he pulled a Kleenex from the box on

Olivia's night table. He also swept the room one last time with his eyes looking for any sort of clue. A single corn husk doll lay on Olivia's dresser. He remembered seeing the girls with them at his house some months back but for whatever reason never commented.

He walked over to the dresser and picked it up. The handiwork was fairly intricate—had the girls made them? He didn't recall Holly making arts and crafts with the girls, and it was undoubtedly not Sheila's thing either. Tim wondered for a second if Mildred had made the doll. He lifted it to his nose, expecting to smell a hint of death, but there was little smell at all.

"Uh, please don't touch anything just yet, Mr. Russell," said Castro.

"Right," said Tim, and put the doll back where it had been.

At that moment, a single fly buzzed against the bedroom window.

CHAPTER 12

Miles from both Amesbury and Sanborn, Mildred Wells, walked the forest in ever-widening circles, the girls safely back in the coyote den with the *Book of Shadows* in a somewhat sedated state. They had been through a lot, and it would take time—naturally, for them to come around. The Book of Shadows would help them over the hump, and they would find a way—together, to become a family.

Mildred trudged through the dead leaves, pointing at every squirrel or bird she saw, dropping them to the forest floor until near every living creature in a half-mile radius was killed. The local fauna was beginning to get the message—this was her third day on the beat, and nature was adapting. Fewer and fewer animals dared enter Mildred's circle of death. Still, there was enough meat on the ground in various states of decay to slow any dogs they might send—and if the bait didn't work, she could always take matters into her own hands.

Twenty minutes later, she arrived back at the den and removed the logs blocking the entrance. The girls lay there in the dark. Vivian slept soundly, but Olivia, the older one, stirred. Mildred could tell she was fighting the Book's influence, whether intentionally or unintentionally, but that would all change soon.

Even with her plan moving ahead smoothly, Mildred still

couldn't help but feel that something had changed—something within. It was hard to put her finger on, but the next step, returning to Sanborn to put a bow on everything, seemed more like a chore than a passion. She missed the zeal and wondered momentarily if her edge was gone—was she merely tired?

Mildred forced it out of her mind—there was much to be done. *Motivation* was the weak cousin of *discipline*. She had faith that as she got closer to Sanborn, and she reviewed in her mind what they had done, that the anger would take over again and sharpen the edge. She'd been tricked, and Elmer was gone forever. It was all unforgivable. *The passion would have to come back.*

CHAPTER 13

The next night, the television show *Only If You Dare* aired the episode announcing the death of Sheila Russell. The big reveal didn't come until the half-hour mark because the first thirty minutes were devoted to the deaths of Bob Simmons, David Bonnette, the Enrico boy in Hampstead, and the fire in Beverly Farms. Anyone who had followed the show from the very beginning several weeks ago got to see the same slow-panning photographs played to ominous music for the umpteenth time.

But no one changed the channel on this night, because the news had broken that there were two missing little girls now and that they were "most likely" kidnapped by the ghost of Mildred Wells. There was a newly dead person, too, their mother. All were related in some way to the home's current resident, Tim Russell. Nate Hoginski had sent six of his employees undercover to local establishments in both Sanborn and Amesbury spreading their version of the story, and it was working.

Now tonight, the broadcast backed it all up, and the cult of Mildred Wells caught fire. The show closed with an emotional scene, the blurred out face of Tim Russell being notified of his daughters' disappearance. Nate Hoginski made sure to mention that Tim had been cleared of any suspicion.

CHAPTER 14

Tim got up from the bed and shut the television off. He wasn't happy, but at least the show made sure to mention that he was not a suspect.

"Maybe Hoginski isn't such a sleaze. I mean, at least for a tabloid journalist," said Holly.

"Yeah," Tim paused in thought. He didn't know what to think anymore. His world was crashing down around him. His daughters, his house, his money—Holly was the only bright spot. "I feel burnt—I am burned out. It's so surreal. Nothing is in my control anymore, and I've never felt this way—ever. I'm tired. I need to sleep more than anything."

Holly cringed. She'd been keeping them up at night intentionally because she was afraid to turn out the lights. Tim was worried too, but of course, he *wanted* Mildred to show up, and that was something on which he and Holly couldn't agree. She *understood*, but she couldn't consent—and now once again it was bedtime—the worst part of the day. Her stomach sank, and she reached down to pet Neptune, her new security blanket. Tim left the bedroom and went down the hallway to brush his teeth.

Neptune was tired, but his tall Shepherd ears were still up and alert, and this made her feel a tiny bit better. Holly could hear Tim's toothbrush beginning to scrub, but she tried to listen further down the stairs to other parts of the house. She wondered if Neptune could hear that far. Perhaps he could hear down into the living room, but could he listen to things in the kitchen or the turret? Was that possible? The turret was down the bedroom stairs, across three rooms, and up its own stairs.

Against her better judgment, Holly got up and crossed the hallway into the guest bedroom. She walked past the hallway window that looked over the front yard and, eventually, the pond and the meadow. There was an eerie fog hovering over the ground, reminding Holly that every night on Lancaster Hill Road found its own unique way to get to her. As she crossed the hallway, she passed directly over the spot that David Bonnette had *allegedly* been murdered.

Tim called it an "alleged murder," and the police did too. There was a conspiracy theory floating that the segment that aired was a fake, filmed on a Hollywood set. Besides all that, Bonnette's body was discovered on the hood of Bob Simmons's cruiser, nearly a mile down the road. But somehow, Holly knew in her gut that the *alleged* story was true.

She stepped through the threshold to the guest bedroom and looked through the window facing the dark turret. She couldn't hear that far through the house, but now at least she could see it. Mildred had obviously broken in and read Tim's papers at some point...what would stop her from doing it again?

The lights were out over there, and there was no one on the roof between them. Holly got a little nervous and turned quickly to return to Neptune. Looking at the turret only made her feel worse. What if Mildred was already in there looking straight back at her, but she couldn't see back? What if a candle was suddenly lit, revealing the dead woman's face? Holly wouldn't be able to handle it.

Holly rubbed Neptune's ears as she waited for Tim to finish in the bathroom—then realized she should have brushed her teeth at the same time. She hated the bathroom at the top of the stairs.

This old house had been built with absolutely none of the modern conveniences of today's homes. She would kill for a bathroom off the master bedroom right now. Tim entered the room, ready for bed, and she envied that his turn at the top of the stairs was over. He didn't seem afraid. He even looked tired…how could he sleep well in a house like this? Tim lay down, and Holly got up.

The upstairs consisted of four bedrooms, two at the front of the house, and two at the back. In between the back bedrooms at the top of the stairs was the only bathroom. A balcony railing surrounding the staircase ran the depth of the house, and she couldn't help but look down the length of it as she approached the bathroom. It was dark downstairs, naturally. Holly wondered for a second if they shouldn't leave the lights on for safety—they might at least see a shadow coming if they heard something.

Holly reached the bathroom and began brushing rapidly to get it over with. She felt vulnerable in here as if someone could come up the stairs, or even more terrifyingly from one of the bedrooms on either side with zero notice. Not having to pee immediately, she skipped it. Holly wanted nothing more than to be back in the master bedroom with Tim and Neptune.

When Holly finished in the bathroom, she had a decision to make. Leave the light on, or turn it off? If she shut it off, she would be blind for a few seconds as her eyes adjusted to the dark. She could eyeball her path along the balcony, flick the switch and go quickly using the rail as her guide until her vision adjusted, … which would most likely be right at the bedroom doorway. Or she could just leave the light on all night—and watch it bleed through the crack of the doorway all night long, sleeplessly, hoping nothing broke the beam. Standing at the top of the stairs, she looked down at the front door and decided to leave it on.

When she finally arrived in the bedroom, Tim was already asleep. *Maybe his life is so upside-down he doesn't fear death like I do,* she thought. Neptune raised his head to acknowledge her presence and then put it right back down again. *If they can do it, so can I,* she thought, and crawled into bed next to Tim, Neptune, on the floor beside her. She stared at the bathroom light leaking in around the doorframe until her eyes closed themselves.

Three hours later, she woke to forget where she was, then saw the light coming between the cracks and remembered all too well. Fear awakened her for the day, and her heart began to beat harder, from sleeping pace to awakened pace, and on to *agitated* pace. *I guess I'm up*, she lamented.

Then Holly realized what had woken her—her bladder. She immediately lamented the rush job in the bathroom before bed. *Why the hell didn't I take care of that?* she thought. Holly looked down at Neptune, who had repositioned onto his side. The house was quiet—surely Neptune would notice any strange noises? She took the fact that he was resting soundly as a good sign. After another moment of procrastination, Holly threw back the covers and swung her legs out over the dog and stepped out of bed.

Every board creaked in this Godforsaken house, she thought. *Why hadn't Tim fixed that?* She studied the floor, trying to recall which floorboards made the most racket. Before standing completely, she watched the ring of light around the door, making sure it was bright and uninterrupted. Slowly she turned the knob and looked across the hall into the guest bedroom. The window facing the turret was out of view, so Holly put it out of her mind and peered around the doorjamb fifteen feet down the hall toward the lit bathroom.

The light blazed, yet the doorway to the right of it was open and dark. Holly couldn't see the fourth bedroom doorway because of her angle. Torturously, she padded down the hallway, ripping the band-aid quickly to finish her business. Stressfully, she bolted back out of the bathroom, passing the dark doorways as swiftly and quietly as possible. As she passed the halfway mark down the hallway, she spun to make sure Mildred hadn't followed.

With the relative safety of the master bedroom at her back and the lit bathroom on the other side of the stairwell, she half-crossed the hallway to look straight through the second bedroom across the roof to the turret, which was thankfully—still dark. *The coast was seemingly clear.* As relieved as was possible, she turned back to join Tim and Neptune—but something caught her eye out the front window to her right. Way out past the pond, in the middle of the meadow and passing through the fog, someone walked. Holly blinked to be sure it wasn't an illusion in the moonlight—and upon second glance, it wasn't. Her heart began to beat like a drum.

"Tim! Tim, get up! Get up! She's coming! She's in the field!" Tim sat bolt upright and scrambled for his pants. Neptune stood and watched them, wondering what all the fuss was. They huddled around the window in the hallway. *There she was,* now parallel to the pond, heading toward the grove. Tim looked at Holly in disbelief.

"I have to go," he said. Holly blinked in fear but didn't question, and quickly moved for Neptune's leash. Tim rushed downstairs and fetched a flashlight and the sawed-off shotgun. He was out the door first, but Holly bounded out after him pulled by Neptune, who wondered why in the world he needed a leash this time. Tim entered the pond area through the break in the stone wall then headed left, bypassing the pond for the meadow. The shape disappeared into the trees. Sensing he might lose her, Tim called out.

"Hey! *HEY!*"

The figure stopped and turned. Mildred seemed to have something slung over her shoulder, and as Tim closed the distance, he began to make out her features. The first thing he noticed was… she was not wearing a farm dress. She turned and began to meet him. Tim stopped, raising the shotgun.

"Don't shoot! Don't shoot! I'm here to help!" It was a man's voice. Holly arrived at Tim's side, struggling mightily with the big dog.

"It's not her, it's not Mildred!" she said. Just then, Neptune broke free, yanking the leash from Holly's grip, rushing the man. "Neptune, NO!" The dog didn't listen, and the trespassing man braced for teeth and fury—but Neptune ran right past him and into the grove.

"NEPTUNE!"

Holly continued to shout, but Tim let the dog go, instead, focusing on the stranger who was now within thirty yards, something substantial and rolled-up on his shoulder. He did not appear to be threatening.

"Don't shoot… I'm sorry to alarm you—I…I thought I was quiet. I figured I'd grab a prime spot in the woods before everyone else showed up. I'm here to help. My name's Ed Bodwell. You… you two scared me there—everything was so quiet, and then…" The man was old and sported a bushy gray beard. He wore a red plaid flannel coat and dungarees. The cylindrical thing on his shoulder appeared to be a rolled-up tent.

"What are you doing here?" Tim asked skeptically.

"Well, I'm here to help. I…"

"You said that, Ed. What does that mean? Why are you here at 3 am marching across my property?

"There's a bunch of us coming. We want to help you get your kids back. Those are two beautiful girls you've got there, and we all want to see them back with you."

"Who the hell is 'we' Ed?" asked Tim.

"A bunch of us at the Elks. And some of the Lions too. And the Rotary. It's more than that even. We've been following your story on TV. We want to help you get that Mildred Wells." Tim lowered the shotgun and exhaled in frustration.

"You've been watching 'Only If You Dare.'"

"That's right. That, and the local news. I live in Northfield. This is all 'local' news for me, all of it. A bunch of us have been talking—especially last night after the show was over. I just got a jump on the rest of 'em. I want to get the best spot. Do you mind? Can I get a place right behind the pond over there?"

"Wait, wait. What's the big plan, Ed?"

"Well, we want to help call attention to your cause. That, and sort of be ready in case *she* shows up. You're going to need help if *she* shows, am I right?" Tim looked at Ed sideways as if the man's question was also a test.

"Do you believe in Mildred Wells, Ed?"

"Sure, I do. Are you saying you don't? Tell me now, brother. Is it bullshit or what? I figured you'd know better than anyone. A lot of people died here...even some things that the TV show hasn't figured out yet—like Annette and Henry Smith. We locals *remember that stuff.* It all fits, doesn't it?" Ed Bodwell looked Tim right in the eye as he talked, and Tim lost control of the moment. There was no way he could fake convincingly he didn't believe that there was a "Mildred Wells" haunting his property and his entire life.

"Who's coming here, Ed?" asked Tim.

"I'm not supposed to spoil it, but the plan was to have a vigil here in the field for your daughters until they're rescued. With your permission, of course. I might have blown the surprise."

"What's that slung over your shoulder? You don't have a rifle wrapped up in that tent, do you? I don't want any guns here, Ed. 'Mildred Wells'...if she exists...might show up, and she alone would know where my daughters are. If anyone gets trigger happy—the girls might never make it back." Tim couldn't believe how much he was admitting to the well-meaning trespasser—a sure sign of how desperate he was.

"Nope, I don't have a rifle. We're here to support, Mr. Russell. Support, prayer, and attention. We thought you folks would need it. How could you not need help at a time like this?" Tim had to admit that other eyes on the property would make the nights easier on Holly at the very least.

"Where do you want to set up your tent?"

"Well, now that you know I'm here and I have your permission, I thought I might set up right over there. That way, she has less of a chance of sneaking up on me." Tim took the opportunity to mask his feelings one more time.

"Ed, do you *really* believe there's a 'Mildred Wells'…like she's a ghost or something?" Ed Bodwell swung the tent off of his shoulder and planted one end in the grass, then rested an elbow atop the other.

"I do, and I think you do too. Bob Simmons, God rest his soul, probably did too. And so does Dick L'Heureux." Tim took the bait as it hung in the air.

"Who is Dick L'Heureux?" Ed Bodwell seemed to take pleasure in Tim's naivete.

"Dick is one of the *Benevolent Protective Order*, just like me." Ed referred to the Elks' slogan *B.P.O.E. –Benevolent Protective Order of Elks*. "He's the nerdy one, but don't tell him I told you that if he shows up. He's into genealogy—family trees and shit. *Whoops!* Sorry, I didn't mean to cuss in front of a lady." Holly hadn't paid attention to nearly half of the conversation. Instead, she stepped forward and began to move toward the forest. Neptune had not returned as yet.

"Holly, what are you doing? You aren't going to the woods, are you?" interrupted Tim.

"Neptune went in there. I need to get him back."

"Hold on, no. Wait a minute. I'll help you. Don't go in there alone. There…are *coyotes*. Give him a minute." Holly slumped her shoulders, nervous for her dog, tired, and frustrated with the entire setting and situation. Tim continued. "What were you saying about genealogy, Ed?"

"Oh, right. Dick L'Heureux is into genealogy, and he found some things about Mildred Wells that even the TV show doesn't know. She came out of nowhere, basically. Showed up in Sanborn, a complete mystery. And Bob Simmons wasn't the only Simmons to die mysteriously. She's been haunting that family for years." Tim knew all about *Mildred Wells vs. The Family Simmons* thanks to the *Simmons Family Scrapbook*—but he was surprised that others were now waking up to the legend. Perhaps he and Holly indeed weren't alone anymore.

Neptune ran through the woods, stealing a rare moment of freedom. He was a smart dog, smart enough to know that it was much too early to commit to Holly and Tim completely. He'd been returned to the shelter twice before…once as a puppy, and then again at age two, after only a four-day tryout with a young family.

There were no squirrels awake yet, but there might be rabbits, and he kept his eyes and ears perked for any critters whatsoever. As he cut through the rows of the grove, he kept his nose low to the ground. Something smelled good. Something smelled *ripe*. Perhaps he could roll in it, and wear it like a badge of honor when he got it all out of his system and decided to return to Holly and Tim.

As Neptune broke through to the next row of trees, he stopped dead in his tracks as the presence of a woman standing in his path surprised him. She didn't share his surprise and didn't move an inch. He felt his bladder let go involuntarily as a full-strength whiff hit his nose—it came from *her*, and there was something wrong about that. His rear legs backpedaled instinctively as his front paws dug in, trying to halt all forward momentum. Neptune cowered.

Mildred Wells had seen the dog leave the front door of the house and, because of this, had turned back into the woods to avoid the early attention. When the dog broke free of Holly's grasp, Mildred retreated even further—but of course, he found her anyway. Now that the dog's curiosity was more than satisfied, he wisely scrambled to get out of her way, a spray of urine wetting the ground beneath him.

Mildred called the knife in case he started barking, but surprisingly, he didn't. The dog whined once, then took a half-dozen steps back and laid down—not what she had expected. He looked at her, and she studied him for a moment, then took four steps toward him—and he didn't move except to lower his head submissively and twitch the tip of his tail as if to ask for affection.

Mildred had never owned a pet or been in close contact with one except for Bob Simmons' dog, King. That confrontation had ended much differently. She sent the rusty blade back to where it came from and turned to walk away. For the first time in as long as she could remember, she decided to let something live.

CHAPTER 15

Neptune eventually returned unharmed, thankfully, and Tim, Holly and Ed Bodwell all went to bed in their respective bedrooms and tents. Holly surprised herself by waking late—nearly 9 am—perhaps because she no longer felt that they were in this alone. Someone else—another pair of eyes—was watching on the front line now—and it was an older man named Ed Bodwell, a naïve but welcomed soul who dared put his life on the line and sleep in the shadow of the overgrown grove. *Maybe he and Neptune would be enough?*

Holly wouldn't attempt such a feat for all the money in the world, but she sure was glad that Ed had volunteered. Surely if something went wrong, there would be an extra layer of—*commotion?* Some screaming perhaps if he were attacked—at the very least? *Not necessarily,* Holly knew. Mildred could kill him in his sleep, or—She caught herself in the middle of her morbid thought and stopped it cold.

She didn't want Ed Bodwell dead or anyone else for that matter. It was healthier to put that sort of thinking out of her mind. She stretched, feeling slightly better rested, after the best night's sleep since the kidnapping, despite the early-morning interruption. To say that was her best night's sleep in a while said it all—she and Tim were both running on fumes.

Tim was already up and out of the bedroom, most likely unable to rest with his daughters missing. She'd better join him to see what he was up to before he followed his desperation through the woods once again. She rose and walked to the front bedroom window to take a look at Ed Bodwell's tent, and was astonished at what she saw.

Ed Bodwell's green tent was there alright, but there were eight other tents as well, some still in the process of being assembled. A row of cars lined Lancaster Hill Road, parked in the gulley just past the property-line stone wall. It was virtually the beginnings of a tent city, and she picked Tim out of the crowd, talking to some of the newcomers. Holly couldn't help but feel a little more hopeful.

She dressed and made her way out into the field, an unforced smile across her face, even feeling a little choked up—this was an overwhelming display of community, led by good samaritans. It was heartwarming, and there was no better way to put it. As she closed in on the heart of the little tent city, she noticed that the young man Tim was talking to had camouflage pants, and a compound bow slung over his shoulder.

"…back from Vietnam. They gave me a Purple Heart because my leg's pretty messed up, but all that means is—I can't run—but believe me, I won't need to run. I've been bow-hunting my whole life. I figured you wouldn't want firearms on your property, but this thing…" Tim interrupted him.

"Look, Corporal, I understand, and I appreciate what you can do, but we can't kill the—*person* who has them—especially if she…uh, *they* show up without the girls. We can't have guns, and for the very same reason, we can't have bows either…"

Holly quietly wished that Tim might relax this rule, at least for this man. He was tall and strong and looked like he might give Mildred problems, especially with the bow. What if he could at least wound her or slow her down? But that was wishful thinking, and deep down, Holly knew this. She interrupted, hopefully, to free Tim from the conversation.

"Good morning! Wow, Mr. Bodwell was right. Looks like he called in the Cavalry!" Her eyes met Tim's, and she saw how tired they looked, how bloodshot. He most likely hadn't fallen back to sleep last night. Tim introduced her to the folks he had already met, and they chatted with Ed Bodwell again for a bit. A few of the vigil-goers were already making themselves at home, combing the property, entering the woods and grove, and getting the lay of the land. Even though the girls were still missing, Holly couldn't help but breathe a sigh of relief. Maybe this was the help that they needed.

A few more cars pulled up to the stone wall, and people poured out of them carrying tents and coolers. They stepped over the knee-high wall and into the meadow to join the mob, and Tim made a move to intercept them and repeat his anti-weapon spiel. Just then, a white van pulled up and parked at the end of the row. Nate Hoginski stepped out of the passenger side, looking sheepishly at Tim. Holly could see Tim's shoulders tense, and she jogged to catch up to him before things got ugly.

"You aren't allowed in, Hoginski. Take your van and your TV show and get the hell out of here."

"Mr. Russell...Tim, please, hear me out. We can help you, in fact, we already have. Take a look behind you. These people are here in large part due to the light we've shined on—your problem. You're going to want people to know. But I want you to know that I'm here to apologize, first and foremost, and I promise we will not film you or your family again without your express permission." Tim was caught off guard somewhat but maintained his defiant pose on the property side of the stone wall.

"You don't give a shit about us. You trespassed in my grove. You also claim David Bonnette was murdered in my house after breaking into it."

"Bonnette came here on his own without our knowledge. I'll take responsibility for that, but I swear I had no idea. If he broke in, it was of his own accord. I thought he was coming to check up on Officer Simmons, who we did admittedly hire—but we did not tell him to trespass either. What I am directly responsible for—and I deeply regret it—is filming your reaction to—the latest news—your daughters. I haven't slept very well since then, and I mean that sincerely. " Holly watched Tim's shoulders relax somewhat.

"Tim, can I have a minute with you alone? Just a quick minute," Holly interjected. Both men were grateful for the intermission. Holly walked twenty feet into an open patch of meadow and began to speak. "We could use the attention, don't you think? This crowd that's gathering is a good thing. *You're exhausted. I'm exhausted. We need help. The girls need help.* Extra eyes and ears at the very least." Tim blinked and nodded. He made some small talk with Holly, made Hoginski wait a few minutes, then marched back over.

"Okay, Hoginski. My girls could use the attention—but I have some rules." Tim cleared his throat, turned, and yelled over the buzzing crowd. "EVERYONE—COULD I GET YOUR ATTENTION FOR A MOMENT? GATHER AROUND PLEASE." When everyone had complied, Tim began. "First, no guns. It's a bad idea for a group this size, and besides, if we kill the kidnapper or kidnappers, we may never see the girls again. I doubt if she, or if they, or if whoever shows up, would be dumb enough to bring them along.

Second, you can camp in the field, but I don't want you to be close to the house or on the other side of the pond. We still need privacy. I don't want anyone in or around my house. Does everyone understand? Please relay this information to any newcomers that may show up from here on out. Does anyone have any questions?"

No one spoke up. When his speech was over, Tim walked directly over to Nate Hoginski for a semi-private conversation.

"You can stay as long as you agree to rent three portable toilets and set them up over in the corner by the *road*—not by the woods." Hoginski held out his hand, and the two men shook.

Hoginski then barked some orders to his men, who quickly began to unload the van. Another car approached. As it came closer, Tim saw that it had lights on the roof. Chief Galluzzo of the Sanborn Police had come to check out the talk of the town.

"What's all this?" he asked.

"The TV show 'Only If You Dare' is running an ongoing story about…about my girls, and this house, and the history of it. They're calling it 'The Legend of Mildred Wells.'" Galluzzo stared at Tim in disbelief.

"Ah, yes—the show that glamorized Bob Simmons' death—turned that into a bullshit ghost story too. You know, at first, I was impressed, just like you are, but now I think they're only making fools of us small-town country folk. And now you're entertaining the rumors too? Throwing fuel on the fire?" Tim had to choose his words carefully.

"We…we appreciate the company in this difficult time. It's a distraction from the reality of my girls being missing, especially for Holly. And nobody can seem to figure out who took them anyway." Chief Galluzzo took Tim's words as a dig.

"Yeah, well, I know we've given you several passes, Russell. *Several.* But it sure seems odd to me that Bob Simmons was found under *your* willow tree, and *your* ex-wife is now dead, and *your* children are missing. Not to mention, we had to get a warrant to look around your place. *'Gardening in the woods.'* Give me a break, Russell. Some would say your garden was in the shape of a *grave.* And I haven't even brought up the dead cameraman rumors. Now you're trying to blame it on a *ghost?* If I were you, I wouldn't be surprised if your name gets dragged right back into the spotlight soon."

CHAPTER 16

Hollywood movie producer Jordan Block landed at Boston's Logan Airport then drove himself the hour-and-a-half to the Lakes Region. He was single again and relieved to have his latest divorce over and done. The newest *ex-Mrs. Block* had taken what she was given in the prenuptial agreement and ran.

All in all, she'd done two years and walked away with a cool one-point-five million dollars. Not too shabby. *She was a smart girl,* he thought. He hadn't even seen the end coming until the papers were delivered.

Jordan Block was here to get away from Hollywood as he did every October, alone, or with a female. He was grateful to the Barrymores for having introduced him to this peaceful part of the country several years back. Who knew that New Hampshire had such a world-class vacation spot?

Compared to most places, it was relatively undiscovered, and for that, he was grateful. Sure, there were some big houses on the lake that were owned by the CEOs of large corporations, but it wasn't dripping with money like the Hamptons or the Vineyard. Around here, all you had to do was put on a fishing hat when you bought your groceries, and you'd blend right in. Jordan Block even rented a Ford every time he came to avoid the unwanted attention a Mercedes or a Jaguar would invite.

At times, he found himself wondering what it would be like to have been born here. The locals always seemed to complain about the winters, but then again, they complained about *every* season. Summers were too hot, he'd heard. "Black flies were the state bird" was another old joke. But Jordan Block didn't have to worry about those things, as he was only in love with New Hampshire *Octobers*, and he didn't have time to visit during the other months anyway.

Block parked the Ford by the house and pulled out the keys, anticipating the smell that always greeted him as he opened the door. It was the smell of more than thirty pine-stuffed pillows scattered throughout the house that he'd fallen in love with his first time visiting. John Barrymore had taken him to a general store in Moultonborough one day, and ever since then, he'd been collecting the damn things. Small little pillows, from golf-ball-sized to as big as your hand, usually with the screen print of a chickadee or a pine cone emblazoned on them. They were slightly kitschy, and the ex had hated them (the last two exes in fact), but their smell was all-natural, and every time he put one up to his nose, it brought him back to his first day on the lake.

Once inside the house, he unpacked the groceries, including the handle of scotch he'd just purchased at the state liquor store. *Cheapest scotch in the country*, he thought—another reason to love New Hampshire. After putting the food away, he took his rocks glass and the several newspapers he'd bought and sat in the chair next to the window overlooking the lake, losing himself in the first precious moments of his vacation.

He wanted to immerse himself and learn about the fishing tournaments and the foliage calendar and the maple sugar farms and the penny sales. *Well, maybe not the penny sales yet, better give those thirty years or so.* For a moment, he wondered if he was an older man at heart, then took another sip of scotch and decided he didn't give a shit.

When he finished flipping through the *Manchester Union*

Leader, he picked up the *Laconia Evening Citizen.* The *Citizen* was a much smaller paper but covered things much closer to Wolfeboro. Some of the headlines were repeats, which he skipped over, but at the bottom of page two, he saw an article that caught his eye.

There had been a kidnapping of two young girls in Massachusetts, but the father was from Sanborn, less than an hour away. The townspeople had rallied around him and had organized a vigil on his property. Jordan read on. The article went on to interview several of the vigil-goers, many of whom— to his delight—shockingly blamed a supernatural being for the disappearances. A television show was involved now too, one he hadn't heard of because he was too damn busy to watch television—a show called *Only If You Dare.*

Jordan's studio had some success in the horror genre a few years back when they produced *Rosemary's Baby,* and Jordan had been a part of the team credited with making it happen. Ever since then, he'd been asked countless times if he had anything else scary up his sleeve—a question he usually dismissed because nothing had caught his eye. He put down the newspaper for a second to think, and a rush of goosebumps climbed his neck. He took it as a sign. Maybe there was something to this article. His instincts were usually spot-on, so he picked up the phone.

"Barry, it's Jordan. Yeah, I just got here, I'm still settling in. What do you know about a TV show called 'Only If You Dare'?— Oh, really?—So you've heard of it?—Is it any good?—Ah… okay.—Right.—Who's show is it?—Alan Lundburg? I've never heard of him.—Yeah, yeah, I know it's because I make movies and he makes TV shows. Do you know when it airs?—Tuesdays? Shit, that's three days from now. Listen, Barry—I need you to get me some tapes of that show, let's say the last half-dozen episodes. Call them if you have to. Then ship them to me here. Super 8 is fine. Oh, and try to keep it low-key—I don't want to be fighting these bastards for rights later on. Don't tell them it's for me. Send one of our reporters or something.—Good. Remember, send it *express mail* or whatever's fastest. Okay, bye."

After another quick slug of scotch, Jordan Block went to the closet and fetched his fishing hat, then grabbed his keys on his way to the door. Before he touched the knob, he grabbed hold of a fist-sized pine pillow and put it to his nose, taking a long pull through his nostrils. *Home again*, he thought. Then he climbed in the car and pulled out a map looking for the podunk town of Sanborn.

CHAPTER 17

Tim sat in the turret paying bills, and it was the same old story—the money tank was near empty. Johnny Upson had been kicking ass—for one man—but Tim's forced hiatus and his inability to sell the house were financially crippling, and he began to wonder if he should look for work locally. There was no way he wanted to leave the house while the girls were missing—whether they were found with or without Mildred.

He pushed away from the desk and spun around to look at the circus that had grown to fill three-quarters of his meadow. It was no longer just hunters, Elks Club members, and soldiers-of-fortune. Now, also there were partiers, musicians and hippies, and even people dressed as their interpretation of *Mildred Wells*. It was still orderly, but Tim sensed that things were on the brink of losing control.

There was no way the crowd knew what they were in for if the monster they were "celebrating" showed up. This concern, on top of all his other worries, made him feel his head might explode. It was overwhelming—too much to be responsible for—all at once, so again, he shoved it aside. Suddenly he heard his name being shouted from down on the lawn.

"Mr. Russell—Mr. Russell! Is that you up there?"

Jordan Block stood below the turret on the front lawn, dressed as a native New Englander. Tim opened the turret window and called down to him.

"Yes, that's me. What can I do for you?"

"I was wondering if you might show me your house. I'm up from Connecticut and looking to relocate. They tell me your house is for sale." Tim was immediately dubious.

"Uh…actually, my real estate agent is in charge of setting those things up. Have you spoken to her?"

"I tried, but she wasn't available. I went to her office in Laconia, and she was out. I ended up leaving a message. Since I had nothing to do, I thought I'd take a ride out myself and see what I could learn about this fabulous property. I, uh—have I interrupted a party or a festival of some sort?" Jordan turned and gestured toward the mob in the meadow. "I can come back later if this is not a good time…"

Tim found himself surprised. Everything the man had said sounded legitimate and made sense. Holly did indeed have a showing this morning and said she would be out of the office. The man also knew that she worked in Laconia. So far, it seemed as if he had gone through all the proper channels.

For a quick moment, Tim felt a ray of warmth—of hope. Then, just as quickly, the hope melted away. The truth was, he couldn't sell right now even if he wanted to…and he would let bankruptcy come long before he left this property as long as his daughters were out there somewhere. He had to be here if and when Mildred returned, and in his bones, he felt it would not be long.

"I'll be right down," he said, and defeatedly descended the stairs to go meet the man on the front lawn. Jordan offered his hand to Tim, and they shook.

"My name's Jordan Banks. I'm a salesman from Connecticut, as I said, and the wife and I are looking for a change of pace—a new life. We were up here this summer and just fell in love with the area. We're only forty minutes outside the city, and…well, it just wears on you after a while."

"Nice to meet you, Mr. Banks, but I have to be honest with you, and it pains me to say it—but I can't sell right now. This... festival you're looking at isn't a festival, or at least it shouldn't be. Do...do you know the story, by any chance?" Jordan Block pretended he didn't, and Tim very painfully recanted his sad tale for four minutes. Block feigned shock and horror.

"I'm so sorry, Mr. Russell. I had no idea. This must be so tough on you. Are you alone in this? You said the mother was dead—I wish I... I want to help if I can. Maybe we could work out a deal?" Tim had no idea what sort of deal he might be hinting at and had little brain-power to devote to figuring it out.

"Uh... I'm not sure, Jordan. It's...been hectic around here. Terrible."

"How are you holding it all together? Are these people donating to your cause? How are you able to work? People need people in times like this! Who's helping you, Mr. Russell?" Tim blinked his eyes as he stared off at a section of lawn, shaking his head.

"We're taking it one day at a time." Jordan looked at the house itself and recognized the new clapboards and gutters, then changed the subject somewhat.

"How long have you lived here, Mr. Russell, if you don't mind me asking?"

"About a year and a half."

"Did you do all this work?" He gestured to the house.

"I did. I own a small construction company in Massachusetts. This is an investment property for me—post-divorce—long story. I guess it just wasn't meant to be." Jordan smiled within, feeling a distant kinship with the man. They shared *divorce* in common, except that Block had plenty of money to recover, and Tim most likely did not.

"Mr. Russell, I...own a place in Wolfeboro that could use some exterior work. I'd like to help you—I've recently divorced myself. Work at my place for a few hours a day, then come back and wait for your daughters."

"Wolfeboro, huh? What's that, an hour away? Maybe a little less?"

"I think it took me about forty minutes. I don't need an answer today on the exterior work, but please consider it. I'd like to help if money is an issue."

"Excuse me for asking, but…if you're from Connecticut, and you already have a place in the Lakes Region, why are you looking in Sanborn?" Block seemed stymied for a second.

"Uh, oh yeah. I forgot to mention that I'm looking for my folks. They live in Connecticut too, and they're looking for a nice place to retire. But please, call me if you're interested in helping me out."

Tim nodded with sincerity, confirming he would. Jordan Block took another long look at the crowd that had gathered in the field. Two more cars had shown up since he'd arrived. There was something very *sticky* about this story—something that caught people's attention—and attention was always right in Hollywood, where attention meant money.

CHAPTER 18

It was the end of another long Foggy Orchard Funeral Home workday, and Andrew Vaughn braced himself as he flicked the switch at the end of his least favorite hallway in the world. It had been a long day because he was currently the only full-time employee, and he was still learning parts of the business Rebecca used to take care of. Only three part-timers had punched-in that week to help with Mrs. Shephard's and then Mr. Keene's funerals, and while there were a few blunders during each of them, the attendees thankfully didn't seem to notice.

Andrew felt like he was juggling professionally, and that he would eventually drop the ball if he couldn't find more substantial help, and soon. His days were jam-packed and his nights—His nights were abysmal. Now, as the lights went out in the long hallway, he was almost too tired to care if something might use the blanket of darkness to come creeping quietly out of one of the rooms to accost him.

Almost too tired.

Now that the hallway was dark, all he had to do was turn quickly, walk briskly about twenty feet and exit the front door, then lock it and descend the stairs to the outer door. After that, cross the parking lot and reverse the process for entering his house. In short, there were no breaks and no safe zones—no haven, home base, or place to relax entirely. It was going to happen again—he just didn't know when or where.

He hadn't slept more than a couple of hours for three straight days. Thomas Pike came every night, and it was still all about the damned *journal and the pen*. Andrew had tried everything. He'd written "answers" about his mother, and his father, and his sister. He even tried writing the names from the last fifteen or so funerals that he had overseen. Every time the ghost closed the book and handed it back. Who the hell did Thomas want to talk about?

The ghost seemed agitated, yet it was almost to the point that Andrew didn't fear him anymore due to fatigue, …but the *anticipation* of every meeting continued to be agonizing. He needed eyes in the back of his head because that was where Thomas liked to appear. It might be the kitchen, the bedroom, the hallway— Andrew never knew. Suddenly, there he'd be, a flicker or a shadow at first—something that made Andrew doubt he saw something, and soon after, a second startle and the ghost would be in his face. There was no such thing as a regular entrance.

He didn't worry so much during the workdays because they were so busy and there were other people around, but after work had become the least relaxing part of the day by far. There were no employees to break the tension, no grieving customers to soothe, and no daylight to brighten the rooms. At a minimum, it amounted to about eleven hours of haunted solitude each day, with Thomas picking one randomly to try to get his "answers." It might be dinnertime, or it might be four in the morning. Andrew never knew.

It was impossible not to turn his back to the rest of the kitchen as he cooked, or the hallway outside the bathroom as he brushed his teeth. After those chores, there was the darkness of his bedroom to contend with, especially the closet. His mother had disappeared in there—would she be coming back out to hold his feet to the fire and try harder?

Andrew rearranged the living room, so the chair had its back to the wall, and the TV was on the other side of the room. Now the problem was his tired eyes darting every few seconds to the open archway that led to the hall and the rest of the house. A few seconds of television that he couldn't absorb followed by a few seconds of mind games, picturing a ghost's face in the hallway. His nerves were shot, and there was no foreseeable end to it.

He caught his eyelids closing and snapped to attention. To fall asleep in the open living room was something he never wanted to do. Although it was a given that the ghost would return, he needed the false sense of security that the locked bedroom door provided, whether he was fooling himself or not. Now temporarily awake, he shut off the television and headed upstairs, checking each room and doorway on the way up.

He brushed his teeth while trying to keep an eye on both ends of the hallway, then leaped to the bedroom with his flashlight (in case the lights went out), made sure the room was clear, and shut the door. His heart beat profoundly right before bed, which was not ideal, yet he prayed for at least an hour's sleep before *the awakening*. Dimming his nightstand light, he laid down and fell asleep within twenty minutes, dog tired.

At 2:51 am, Andrew's eyes opened involuntarily. He glanced right and left, but no one stood over him on either side of the bed. He exhaled halfway, believing for a second it was a false alarm, then noticed a bluish light under the door.

He tried to ignore it, but it seemed to pulse, and he began to question it as a potential fire. It could not be ignored. Getting up, he padded to the door and cracked it as quietly as possible. The distant blue light bounced off the white walls as it moved. Someone spoke downstairs—was it the television? Hadn't he shut it off? *Yes, he had*—for sure.

Andrew waited five full minutes while listening and weighing his options, almost hoping the Pike ghost would make the first move so he could at least know where he was. Leaving the fool's safe-haven of the bedroom seemed uncomfortable and risky, but he knew deep down, there were no good options, and he was at risk no matter what he did. Reluctantly, yet far too tired to calculate risk accurately, he marched down the hallway toward the stairs.

He paused at the top to listen to the room below. His view was obscured from this angle. The only sound was the repeat broadcast of the eleven o'clock news. Exhausted, and with a brand new booming headache, he began his descent, partially hoping his body would collapse so he could skip the upcoming festivities and rest for the first time in days.

When he got to the television, he was alone in the living room. The repeated news signed off and immediately began to promo the upcoming program. He reached for the TV to shut it off so that he could hear better and adequately investigate the downstairs when he heard the hook:

"Coming up next: A ghostly woman terrorizes a small New England town. Two young girls go missing, and their mother is murdered. Stay tuned…'Only If You Dare!'"

This time a real commercial began *(plop, plop, fizz, fizz… oh, what a relief it is)*, and Andrew needed the noise to be gone. He reached for the on/off button but felt a sharp squeeze on his shoulder—then pulled his hand back. From out of nowhere, Thomas Pike stood behind him, putting a steady pressure at the base of Andrew's neck.

"Ow! Let go, let go of me!" Andrew cried out, and the ghost let go. They stood there awkwardly in front of the blaring television. *Here he was again.* This time Andrew was flat out annoyed by the pain of the squeeze. Not threatened, however, because Thomas had stopped when told. Andrew didn't like the ghost so close behind him and quick-stepped across the room—Thomas didn't seem to care. Another minute passed, and the commercials ended.

"Tonight on 'Only If You Dare'—Murder in Massachusetts. Two girls are missing. At least four are dead. Is a sleepy New Hampshire town in the crosshairs of a murderous—ghost? Don't turn that dial. 'Only If You Dare' is next!"

The theme song for the TV show played, and Andrew's eyes remained fixed on Thomas Pike, who stared back, making sure Andrew didn't leave. Thomas had never laid hands on Andrew before, which raised questions. His glare said it all, however—it was different this time. There was more confidence behind it than there was with the journal and the pen. Attempting to run would no doubt be a mistake. The staredown continued.

"Mildred Wells—remember that name, ladies and gentlemen. She's accused of kidnapping two girls and murdering as many as four people in New Hampshire and Massachusetts, …but there's something undeniably odd about that. You see, Mildred Wells has been dead for over one hundred years."

Thomas Pike flicked his eyes over to the television. Then he lifted his arm and pointed at the TV, then looked back at Andrew.

"The townspeople of Sanborn, New Hampshire, are haunted, but nobody wants to admit it. Welcome to 'Only If You Dare.' This unassuming farmhouse was built in 1860 by a young couple named Thomas and Mildred Pike. They had it all, according to local historians, including a young son named Elmer. Everything seemed fine and dandy until Thomas felt the call of duty, signing up to fight for Abraham Lincoln and the Union Army."

The show went on to recite the entire *"Legend of Mildred Wells,"* including Thomas' death during training exercises, then Elmer's drowning, and everything leading up to the kidnapping of Tim's girls. Andrew watched the whole thing, relieved that the television was doing the talking, and they could forget about Thomas' pen and journal. As soon as the show ended, Thomas turned and disappeared down the hallway. Would he be back? Andrew waited until the network went off the air before moving from his spot.

He clicked off the television and watched the test pattern disappear. The adrenalin had subsided, and debilitating fatigue washed over him. He'd gotten the message, and Thomas would let him sleep now, at least for a few more hours. He would be called to duty soon, however—now that he knew the whole story or at least the TV show's version. There was no doubt in his mind things were about to get even busier.

What that entailed, he had no idea, but he knew he'd better get to Sanborn or Thomas would be back, perhaps even with his mother if he waited too long. He would never sleep again if he didn't act now. But what would happen to the funeral home? There was a service Saturday, and much to be done—but now was not the time. Stumbling down the hallway, he nearly tripped as he dove onto the bed, falling immediately unconscious on top of the covers with the door wide open.

CHAPTER 19

Mildred cut off the head and pulled until the skin peeled off clean, then slid the squirrel onto a homemade skewer. There were three in total, which should be enough. The girls hadn't eaten in two days and when they woke they'd be hungry. Before she put them over the fire, she stirred the tea, which would help her get them over the first hump. She stared into the pot daydreaming—and it was impossible not to think of the man from whom the recipe came.

It was Gideon Walker's. The monster, or—*one of the monsters*—responsible for the state she was currently in…a state of permanent *unrest*. Here she was, even after his death, living his damned legacy—as a hypocrite to some degree, utilizing some of his despicable practices. *But even a broken clock was right twice a day*, she rationalized, and despite her aversion to anything Gideon Walker ever did, he…might have been right about some things. She had to believe it. It was that, or live alone virtually forever.

The squirrel meat was a switch from his methods, however. Mildred offered far more protein than he ever did. She remembered her hunger as a girl in the shed, even more than a century later. There was and never would be a *shed* here—or even the equivalent of a shed. They'd make it through this initial rough patch and settle in nicely.

Olivia twitched and called out as she slept. It was another nightmare, and Mildred took it as a bad sign. The older girl knew more—*felt* more—than her younger sister—and the dreams might mean she was fighting the process. Suddenly Olivia sat up.

"*Mommy!*" she shouted, but her eyes were glazed over, and she would mostly not remember the moment. Mildred grabbed her forehead gently and pushed her back down to sleep. The squirrels would have to be discarded, as the girls were simply not ready to be awake yet. Perhaps tomorrow.

Across the room lay the Book of Shadows. Things would be so much quicker if she used it, but the Book was so powerful, and it was so *early*—their bond would be completely artificial. It would be premature. Mildred knew firsthand, for she had not been handled so delicately.

Without taking her eyes off the Book, she walked around Olivia's sleeping form and picked it up. This was the same book she had risked everything in her pathetic former life to come and read as a young girl. The pages had long-since stopped growing by themselves now, and everything there was to know, lay between the two covers.

CHAPTER 20

Tim had nothing to do but wait, and the waiting was getting old. Jordan—the guy from Connecticut who had put an informal offer on his house—had left. Tim wondered if he should have accepted his proposal on the spot. What the hell was his last name? Tim decided in his head to refer to him as Jordan *Almond* before he forgot the first name too. Feeling restless, he decided to take Neptune for a walk.

Neptune smelled the never-ending barbeque coming from the meadow and led Tim toward it, and Tim didn't mind. He'd been sitting in the house all alone, overthinking, and thought it would be good to take a break to talk to someone—anyone. He sought out Ed Bodwell. Bodwell saw him approaching and announced it to the crowd.

"Hey, here he is. The reason we're all here. Mr. Tim Russell, everybody!" Tim was surprised by the amount of applause the throng provided him. He brushed it off sheepishly and struck up a conversation. Neptune found a nearby dog lover to rub his ears.

"I'm going stir-crazy in there, Ed. This whole thing—is eating me alive. I know you're pretty much a stranger to me, but..." Ed Bodwell saw where this might be headed and stood up to offer a brotherly hug.

"That's why we're here, Tim. That's why we're here. Be strong.

We'll find them. We're taking shifts. Duncan and Hightower are out there right now searching for your girls. My shift is around 4:30. What do you say we start a little earlier than that, take a walk together, look for your girls, and burn off some of that nervous energy, kill two birds with one stone? I'm a bit stir-crazy myself right now. I could use a walk. Come on, bring your dog."

Tim, Ed, Neptune, and two others took a walk in the woods. Together they canvassed the immediate area and a bit further. They were gone for three hours. By the end of it, Tim's nervous energy was spent, and beyond that, he was just plain tired. The mental exhaustion, coupled with the exercise left him drained. As they exited the grove, Neptune followed Ed Bodwell toward the eternal barbeque, and Tim let it happen. He was too tired to stop him and was understandably depressed. No doubt, Holly would fetch him when she got home.

CHAPTER 21

Tim looked at his watch—it was 5:27 pm. Holly would be home soon. It was a happy accident, but the search had ended at just the right time. It was better that he'd be back for her when she arrived than still out searching, leaving her not only alone in the house but also wondering where he was. It was better for everyone—fewer questions. He began to think about dinner—for Holly mostly, because he had trouble eating and had lost almost ten pounds since the whole ordeal had begun. He was beyond upset and would eat at *most* maybe one-and-a-half meals a day.

Tim stepped through the porch and entered the front door. Things were normal in the dining room, but the odor hit him hard as soon as he crossed into the kitchen. There, against the far wall in the breakfast area, lost in the shadows of dusk—*stood Mildred Wells.*

Tim dropped the flashlight he'd carried onto the floor. He gasped, his heart suddenly in his throat. He was surprised to be sure, but also realized he must make the most of this moment—if he lived. Why was she here right now? What was her plan? He didn't know what to say, but the words would have to come—and come quickly.

Mildred glared, her face nestled in the shadows the room had accumulated. Tim had never gotten a good, clear look at her and now was no different. He squinted hard to try and read her face.

"Mildred… I'm sorry. We're sorry. My girls are everything to me. Are they alright? Please tell me…they're alive. How can we make this right?" In the end, all that escaped his lips was begging, and she hadn't moved since he'd seen her. She was enjoying his misery. The flies were the only thing proving that time had not stopped.

Mildred Wells absorbed his pain just as she knew she would, and it did indeed feel good. *There would be begging, there would be pleading, and there would be a gnashing of teeth*—as expected—all part of the plan.

Suddenly Tim's concentration broke, and the moment Mildred had waited for was interrupted. He lost focus and spun his head as the sound of an engine pulled up the driveway. When the Volkswagen drove by the picture window, the pleading tone left his eyes, and he became worried…*protective*—*w*hich was exasperating, but far from the end of the party.

CHAPTER 22

Tim took his eyes off of Mildred for less than a second as Holly pulled past the window and around the corner in front of the barn. She parked almost directly on the other side of the breakfast nook wall behind Mildred, and would for sure be coming in through the side door—much closer to Mildred than he was. He had to do something.

"Hey, Mildred. We want to make peace. I know you just saw Holly drive up. I can't—let you hurt her." Mildred didn't budge, allowing his simmer to become a boil, enjoying his anguish, his pain, and his fear. It was but an appetizer of things to come.

Tim moved toward her, his aim, to distract. He already knew how fast Mildred could be. To see Holly in her grasp like a bird in a cat's jaws would be too much—He'd lost enough, and there was no guarantee the girls were ever coming back—he had to focus on the here and now. As Holly unknowingly came in through the side door, he had little choice but to rush at Mildred, commanding her attention—and getting it.

Tim threw a punch, and Mildred caught his arm mid-swing, stopping his fist cold. Tim felt her strength immediately and knew the fight was already over. She held him rock steady as Holly entered the building, seconds from realizing the nightmare in the breakfast area. Flies swarmed Tim's head as Mildred pulled him in close. Her arms were like iron bands, and there was nothing he could do even to slow them. Despite his predicament, he was thankful to not be in this death grip, receiving her full attention. Holly, still unaware, opened the sliding glass door, recognized that Tim was in the jaws of death, and screamed.

"Holly—go. Run…" She couldn't even begin to process his words.

"Let him go," she commanded. Holly's voice was calm, yet determined. "Where are the girls?" Mildred eyed Holly carefully, surprised, yet enjoying every word. She called the rusty knife into her hand for shock value. Tim froze, fearing that his time had come to an end. If this was it, he had no say in the matter—at Mildred's mercy, wholly and utterly. He felt for Holly, who would have to witness the bloodbath, then most likely die a similar death.

"Where are his daughters, Mildred?" Holly repeated. Mildred ignored the question, mildly annoyed that Holly had not begun with panic and begging as Tim had. Holding the knife to Tim's throat wasn't as fun if it was ignored. With a flick of the wrist, the knife went away, and she pushed Tim hard to the floor. He landed audibly and slid to a stop halfway across the kitchen. The three of them were now equidistant, and Mildred turned back to face Holly—to put the proper fear into her and sap the rebellious attitude. Holly took two steps back but persisted.

"Where are Olivia and Vivian, Mildred? Are they alive? *You can talk.* I *know* you can talk. *Tell* me. Tell *us.* Are you going to kill them the way you killed your son?" Mildred called the knife back a second time, and Holly's mouth went dry. Perhaps she had said too much—but Mildred's lack of response had pushed her to the edge. Holly had no option now but to run. Turning quickly, she burst through the side door of the house out into the driveway, knowing full-well she had abandoned Tim.

With Holly gone, Mildred turned back to Tim, who had yet to pick himself up. She approached with the rusty blade, and Tim had to wonder once more if this was the end. Mildred approached and towered over him, letting him think—and realize—the danger he was in—the life he had ruined.

He looked up as she stared him down, flies touching down and taking off in chaotic rhythm. He dug his heels into the floor as best he could and pushed away, clamoring to put precious space between them, praying to at least be able to deflect her attack when it came.

Suddenly Holly burst through the front porch door behind Tim, hefting a pitchfork from the barn. Mildred held her ground, and the three of them stood considering each other for a short moment. Holly wondered if the presence of the pitchfork had given Mildred pause. *Is she thinking about what it could do to her heart?*

Tim kicked backward until he had the space to stand. Eight feet separated them: eight feet and one pitchfork. Holly broke the silence.

"Where are the girls, Mildred? Tell us where and we'll get them—Or bring them back yourself. We won't hunt you. We want peace. We don't want to fight anymore. " Mildred held her tongue, building tension on purpose, forcing Holly and Tim to consider their next move.

Ed Bodwell and the vigil-goers in the meadow had no idea what was happening in the kitchen, but a well-armed mob might just be a revenant's worst fear. Holly wished for a moment that they had not implemented the *"no guns"* policy. She also wished she had a police whistle on her person. Maybe she would scream to call their attention. *Yes.* But then Tim broke the silence.

"Mildred, if you…"

Mildred pumped her arm once, and Holly's pitchfork was suddenly hers. Tim halted, terrified, realizing the gravity of the situation. Holly stood aghast, as exposed and vulnerable as the night Mildred caught them stealing Elmer's bones.

Mildred held the pitchfork out from her body between waist

and chest high, threateningly. Tim and Holly separately began to calculate time and distance to the front door.

But Mildred moved first.

With a mighty thrust, she jammed the pitchfork into the kitchen floor, then slowly turned away and walked in the direction of the side door. *Enough for now*, she thought. Tim, a second ago expecting to run for his life, realized her cruelty—a far harsher punishment than death.

"Wait! Where are my daughters?" Mildred ignored him and walked on, leaving the building and crossing the driveway in the direction of the forest path. It was near dark now, and it was hard to see more than a dozen yards with any clarity. Tim, now desperate, barreled out behind her recklessly as she headed for the trees.

"Mildred!" He lowered his voice so the vigil-goers wouldn't come. He desperately wanted to negotiate, but icily—she continued to walk away. All of a sudden, living or dying didn't matter so much, and Tim lost his temper.

"For fuck's sake, listen!" He charged at her in desperation with no regard to the impotence of his attack. Once more, she read him flawlessly and deftly pinned him to the grass. Holly came bursting out of the house and saw him fall again as if a jungle cat had taken down a helpless calf.

"No!" Holly screamed. The blade flashed again, and Mildred held it to Tim's throat, his hands flailing at hers, which had him choked. Her right knee pinned his chest to the turf.

Holly hung back but continued to yell, scream, and negotiate. Mildred didn't bother to give her the time of day. She was almost finished.

Then she leaned in to share an intimate moment, capturing Tim's full attention, filling his entire line of sight. Her hair hung down around his face blocking the fresh air, filling his nostrils with the redolence of her vile being. It was just the two of them—two parents coming to an understanding.

She spoke for the first time in ages. Mildred's vocal cords sputtered and popped as they were awakened and called into service for a special announcement. She didn't find much use for words anymore, but this was necessary. These words were crafted to cut and cut coarsely—as dangerous and as dull as her rusty knife. But they would hurt more than the blade ever could.

"You took mine…now I take yours."

Mildred was dead, and no longer drew breath, yet the act of talking pushed fetid air out of her chest cavity. The conviction of the words—and the raw anger—amplified by the olfactory punch—went straight through him, as he shuddered at the realization that he could not win. A dark wave of hopelessness washed over him, and he quit his struggle, suddenly hoping it would all end then and there.

Mildred felt his body go limp as she took his hope away. Her words had hit their mark—an essential step in the dismantling of the man beneath her. First, she would take his aspirations, and then his mind, and then, when he could handle no more, she would crumble the husk that remained.

Holly would die too, of course. Most likely first, so he could watch her go. Mildred tapped the knife blade on Tim's Adam's apple gently three times and then let go of his throat. He gasped, and she stood looking back at Holly, who had finally decided to shut her damned mouth, then slipped quietly into the woods.

CHAPTER 23

Holly rushed to Tim's side as he lay on the ground staring blankly at the evening sky. He looked like he didn't care anymore—a beaten man. An Everest climber who was too exhausted to care if he lived or died—a prison-camp survivor who wished he died along with his family. Holly could still smell Mildred on him.

"Tim, what did she say to you? Don't let her win. Don't let her get in your head! Let me help you up. Come on!" Tim raised his arm for Holly's assist, and together they got him to his feet. He was morose and utterly spent. "The first thing you need is a shower. Come on."

"Is everything alright?" Ed Bodwell had heard the yelling and were now standing in the driveway.

"He's—grieving. Maybe we had a little too much to drink, Ed. Rough day. I'm going to get him showered and put him to bed. Thank you for checking." Bodwell studied Tim's exaggerated drunk-act and fell for it.

"Call us if you need anything ma'am."

Holly stayed in the bathroom as he bathed and found a way to talk of positive things avoiding the subject of the horrifying confrontation. They were lucky to be alive. Sure, it was part of Mildred's plan—a "slow death" approach that so far had worked brilliantly—she'd *let* them live—but at least they were not out of *time.* Tim's pride and his *hope* were damaged, however, and he needed to get his confidence back before they could dive headlong into discussions of how to move forward.

As Tim dressed, Holly ran downstairs to pry the pitchfork out of the kitchen floor—a chilling reminder of what had just gone down. He didn't need to see it again. Not now, not ever. As she hid it in the hall closet, she recalled the way it had been effortlessly taken from her—like a parlor trick—as if it had dissolved and appeared across the room instantaneously. *What a terrifying skill,* Holly thought. *We can't win with weapons.*

Tim came downstairs showered and dressed, looking somewhat better. His brow was still furrowed, however, and he was deep in thought. Holly herself would most likely have a breakdown later, as soon as he had his humor back, but for now, her survival instincts had kicked in, and whether she liked it or not—she was the glue holding everything together. Tim spoke up:

"I was thinking while I was getting dressed—I'm probably not—uh, it probably doesn't make sense, but I was wondering if we should tell the police." Holly pretended to be prepping dinner, checking the fridge, and taking out dishes, and as she worked, she pondered his thought. After a short moment of silence, she responded.

"I don't think so, Tim. There were no witnesses. Did you see their eyes when they came running to help? They think you were drunk. I'm so glad we didn't tell them. There was nothing they could have done to help—that trick she has to take your weapon away—*There's no defending that.*

If the mob had arrived before she left, she would have killed them all before they knew what hit them." Tim slowly nodded his head, letting the words sink in. "We have to send them away."

"I need a drink," he said.

"Good idea." Holly opened the cabinet and pulled out the bottle of Jack Daniels that Tim used to keep behind the seat of his truck, thankful that she'd removed it months ago.

Unscrewing the cap and pulling out a drinking glass, she poured an inch of the liquid and handed it to him. He drank half of it immediately.

"Hey, you didn't wait for 'cheers'!"

"Oh, shit. Sorry. Let's try again. Holly refilled Tim's glass and then poured herself one.

"I have to say, though, Tim, I feel safer right now than I have in months. It's like being in the eye of a hurricane. She just left—and she probably won't be back tonight." Tim looked at her sideways. *Don't jinx it.*

But Holly was right—*most likely.* Tim had wanted Mildred to stay. He'd even chased her down in the back driveway. Mildred knew that it hurt him much more to be without his girls indefinitely—*or at least maintain the illusion*—if they were even still alive. He closed his eyes tight and pinched the bridge of his nose. *Here they come,* he thought—and then broke down sobbing.

Deep down, he still thought positively, but the way Mildred had penetrated his psyche was so…invasive…crushing…*skillful.* He'd seen pure darkness and a hopeless future of which he wanted no part. He imagined that depression might feel this way— something he'd been fortunate enough to have avoided his entire life—and it scared him. To allow those thoughts into one's head was to give the enemy the keys to the front door. He would rot from the inside out. Was it some sort of spell she'd cast, or was hatred just one of her skills?

Holly came over and hugged him. He knew that she was nearly as frazzled as he was. They needed each other, and despite this bump in the road, he was not finished.

"She got in my head, Holly. I've never felt that way before. It was awful. We fucked up helping Thomas Pike. I'd take Elmer running around here and Mildred chasing him around any day compared to this."

"No, you wouldn't. You *couldn't.* That was another time with a different set of circumstances. You were sleepwalking out to the grove in the middle of the night for God's sake. The girls were here—in *danger!* You never had a choice." Tim sighed. Thank God she was here to remind him. Thank God they had been through everything together. If they'd met later, she wouldn't have believed him. He rubbed his eyes.

"Yeah, you're right."

"Tim…I don't want to upset you, so you don't have to answer this, but…what did she say to you?" Tim paused for a second, recalling the exact words. His eyes began to water again, but he did not cry this time.

"She said: *'You took mine, now I take yours.'*" Holly's heart sunk in her chest as she let the words hang in the air. *No wonder he reacted the way he did.* Just then, a sharp knock came at the front door. Startled, Tim got up and peered out the kitchen window at the porch. It was Ed Bodwell returning Neptune.

"Did you folks forget somebody? I tried to keep the treats to a minimum, but everybody fell in love with him, and I don't think he's gonna need his dinner tonight!" It was an attempt at humor on Ed's part, but the room wasn't laughing. He noted the somber mood and the empty drinking glasses with no food in sight and realized that Tim was still hitting the sauce, even after his breakdown in the driveway. "Is everybody okay?" he looked directly at Holly to see if she was in any sort of danger.

"Yeah, we're okay. Thanks for bringing Neptune back, Ed—honestly, I think we did forget about him. Don't worry about the treats. Thanks for watching him." Holly nodded in the affirmative as she spoke as if to telegraph to Ed that things were okay, and he need not worry.

"But, um—Ed, I hate to say this, but Tim and I were talking, and we're going to cancel this vigil. We appreciate your support, but—the police are on top of things, and we're feeling like we're wasting your time. I mean, we're all pretty sure that the girls are not in the immediate area, right? You and Tim proved that today. We're guessing now that—they're probably a lot closer to Amesbury." Ed looked at her, dubious—then looked at Tim.

"Really? Jeez, I thought we had a good thing going. Got two guys going out first thing in the morning too—I mean, I think— It wouldn't hurt to take a couple of dogs out there every day and see if they pick up on something new...hey, did I miss something?" Tim sighed, realizing that this was probably the most fun Ed Bodwell had in months, if not years. Although he had never pried into Ed's life, it was becoming apparent that there was most likely no longer a Mrs. Bodwell, and Ed had nothing better to do with his time.

"No. No, you didn't miss anything. We just need some time—and space—as a...family, to perhaps prepare for...an alternate outcome." Tim hemmed and hawed his way through the lie, and it killed him even to suggest his daughters might be gone—but Mildred would shred the vigil if they got in her way, and they needed to be gone for their safety. It was his moral obligation to make them leave.

"Come on, walk with me. I was just about to come out and tell you all."

That's funny. I thought you were just saying that you'd forgotten about Neptune, Ed thought. *You were most definitely NOT coming out to tell us anything any time soon.*

"What, right now? After dark? How about we leave in the morning? Some people are still cooking their dinners," said Ed. Tim looked at Holly as if to say *How sure are you that she's not coming back tonight?*

"That's certainly fair. Sorry for such short notice, Ed. We appreciate you folks and your time and support, but...every time I look at the meadow, I'm reminded of what a mess we're in, and... it's...it's hard to take. I'm sorry, I'm not explaining it very clearly. We're both tired, and..."

"Say no more, Ms. Burns. You don't have to explain anything. I'll make sure we get these folks out first thing tomorrow. I'll tell you what, though—that TV show gang isn't going to take my word for it. I have a feeling you're going to have to tell them yourself. They have recorded a *lot* of film footage since you let them on your property, and they're not going to want to stop." Ed was right. *Only If You Dare*, despite their truce with Tim, would most certainly have to be told face-to-face.

CHAPTER 24

The vigil packed up slowly the next morning, and Tim went out to the meadow and spoke personally with Nathan Hoginski of *Only If You Dare*. Nate protested a bit and even offered Tim a bribe of five hundred dollars to return after the crowd had left, but Holly played the *broken family* card once again, and it worked. Hoginski packed up the crew's tent and retreated to the van, but kept it parked on Lancaster Hill Road—firmly on public property.

The last person to leave the property was Ed Bodwell himself, and he left the way he'd arrived—mysteriously, with no vehicle. As the last car pulled away, he slung his tent over his shoulder and walked down the road toward town. After he'd traveled a quarter-mile and no one was watching, he took a sharp left into the woods and doubled back toward Tim's property. Fifteen minutes later, he'd set himself up a nice little camp in row five of the grove, and had it all to himself.

CHAPTER 25

At precisely 7 am sharp, Andrew woke to a rapping noise coming from downstairs. He was still on his stomach on top of the covers, just as he had plopped himself a few hours before. His sleep had been deep and refreshing, but he needed a lot more, not that he'd expected to be allowed to sleep in all morning. What was that noise? Someone at the door?

He got up quickly and swooned a bit—feeling dizzy from lack of sleep and rising too rapidly. Bracing himself on his bureau, he changed out of his pajama pants and put on some street clothes. It might be a customer at the door—some poor soul who lost a loved one in the middle of the night. Had he slept through a phone call? That was usually how they contacted him after regular business hours.

A second thought crossed his mind that it might be Thomas Pike rousing him, but he quickly dismissed it. Thomas Pike was no stranger to any part of the house, and he most certainly wouldn't knock politely on the front door. He'd be standing over the bed—staring him awake.

Andrew made his way down the stairs to the front door and peeked out of the sidelight. A gaunt older man stood transfixed on the door knocker. He was as pale as a ghost, and in fact, a chill crept up Andrew's neck—he could very well be a ghost—*but a spirit who waits outside and knocks politely?*

Whoever it was, did not notice when he snuck a peek, so Andrew hung back for a second, indecisive. The knocking rattled his nerves one more time, sounding much louder when standing directly behind the door. He jumped out of his skin. Unable to concoct a "Plan B," he grabbed the doorknob, cracked the door, and addressed the mysterious visitor.

"May I help you?"

"I hope so. I've been sent to come for you. My name is George, and I've come up from Hell."

Andrew, already nervous before he'd opened the door, took two quick steps back and closed the door quietly, lifting his right hand to support the left, and lean his body weight into it. *Would this do any good?* He began to breathe heavily—certain the man (ghost?) was still there. He could feel his pulse pounding in his wrists as he put pressure on the door. The knocker struck the door four times—even louder it seemed—and he knew his first instinct had not served him well. *Story of my life*, he noted—and then cracked the door again.

"Why are you here for me? I don't understand. I don't believe in the devil, you know. I'd rather you just left." The old man appeared puzzled.

"Oh, the devil is real. And he's a bargainer—He'll tempt you. He's smart. You won't even realize it's him you're talking to." Andrew shrunk back into the hallway again but did not close the door this time. The man—or the Devil—didn't move, perhaps lulling Andrew into a false sense of security. He's just a little old man, after all—

"Alright. I hear what you're saying. But first, prove it's you. Show me your true form." Once again, the old man raised an eyebrow as if to ask a question, but said nothing.

"How about we skip that and I'll just tell you why I'm here?"

"Because I need proof. You're obviously not a customer, or you would have mentioned it. And nobody drives down my long driveway unless they want a funeral arranged, or they want some apples. Seeing as apple season is over, that can't be it. Show me something that proves who you say you are. Show me a pitchfork or something—your red tail. You know what I mean. *Proof.*" Andrew was manic, now sweating profusely from his armpits. His hands had gone cold, wet, and clammy.

"Well, I'm afraid I can't do that, but I want to tell you that your mother sent me." Andrew froze as his eyes bugged out.

"I knew it. She'll never leave me alone then, will she? She's not interested in me mending my ways, she must be a demon, and this will all end very badly no matter what I do. I'd tell you to tell her to go to Hell, but she's already there, am I right?! Again the old man did not answer directly but pondered Andrew's words and answered very slowly.

"Are…you…alright, Mr. Vaughn?"

"What do you mean? Am I supposed to be feeling ill? Are you killing me right now, as we speak? Did you come to take me to Hell with you?" The man's face was still for a moment, and then very slowly, a smile as wide as the Cheshire cat's spread across his face. Andrew slammed the door and locked it, still unsure what his next move would be. *How do you outrun the devil?*

He couldn't see the man anymore, and it made him nervous, so he climbed the stairs and entered Rebecca's old bedroom at the front of the house to look outside. The man was still under the canopy in front of the door. What's he doing now? There was an older model Cadillac Sedan de Ville in the driveway with Massachusetts plates. *Odd.*

Why go to the trouble of a charade? Massachusetts? If you're the Devil, you probably don't need to hide in an old Caddy, do you? He decided to shout down to the stranger.

"Come out into the parking lot where I can see you." The man strolled out from underneath the canopy and looked up at the window, looking like he couldn't believe what he was seeing. "A little further. Stand by your car." The devil did as he was told. Again, weird. "Now start over. Tell me who you are. 'George' was it?"

"That's right."

"And what does the devil need with a Massachusetts Cadillac, George?"

"I have no idea what you're talking about, Mr. Vaughn."

"Am I taking crazy pills, or did I hear you say that I wouldn't even know if I was talking to the devil or not?" The man shook his head in a sort of respectful disgust.

"Are you?"

"Am I what?"

"Are you taking 'crazy pills'?"

"Are you being a smartass? What's your last name, George?"

"Randall."

"George Randall from—*Hell*, like you said, right?

"Hull."

"What?"

"I'm from Hull."

—Hull? Was that an Irish accent, perhaps?

"Are you Irish, like from Ireland, George?" The "devil" lost his cool.

"Mr. Vaughn, I'm American, like you. I'm from HULL. Hull, Massachusetts. H-U-L-L. The south shore of Massachusetts. Quincy, Weymouth, Hingham, Cohasset, *HULL*. I take it you've never left New Hampshire?"

Suddenly Andrew was extremely embarrassed. *Oh, dear God.* He was hiding in his sister's bedroom from an old man who had driven his ancient Cadillac up from Hull, Massachusetts. He wasn't a ghost, and he wasn't the devil, yet he had told the man he believed he was. *What an ass.*

"So that crap about my mother was all bullshit too?" Now the man seemed taller, healthier, and more fatherly than he had just minutes before.

"Well, I don't know what the hell you were blabbering on about, and I don't know if she's in *Hell* or not—but she came to get me and told me to come get you."

CHAPTER 26

Andrew sheepishly went back downstairs and opened the front door properly this time. He'd never been more embarrassed in his life. He'd made bigger mistakes—but his face had never been so red.

"I'm sorry George, come in, come in. I haven't been sleeping very well lately, I, uh—I won't get into it right now, but..."

"I know more than you think I do, Mr. Vaughn. May I call you Andrew?"

"Yes, of course, sorry." Andrew didn't know why he'd just apologized—he was still embarrassed and off his game. To make him feel even smaller, this little man seemed to be growing more powerful and confident by the second.

"You've got nothing to be sorry for, at least—not in my regard. But let me get you up to speed. I know you're being haunted by a ghost, and he wants you to go to a town called Sanborn. I know you're tired, and that's somewhat understandable."

"*Somewhat* understandable? You have no idea. He's been haunting me for five...six days. See? I can't even remember how long it's been. I'm not tired, George, I'm *exhausted*. And what do you mean you know more than I think you do?"

"Because I'm also haunted, but thankfully only for one day."

"Oh, I'm sorry to hear that—I hate to tell you though, it only

gets worse. You have no idea. Who's haunting you? Let me guess—
my mother." George nodded, but remained surprisingly calm—not
stressed as Andrew had hoped—*Misery loves company* and such.
"She's mean, right? I saw her on my first night too. We're on equal
ground. One day. Are you dreading going to bed? I do. She hates
me. But I have bad news for you—I have no idea how to help."

"Uh...I don't think I need your help—thanks, though. We've
got things figured out on our end. I understood her situation, and
we have a plan in place that I think can work. Oh, and by the
way, I came here to help *you*—at your mother's request." Andrew
was dumbstruck.

"How the hell did you get everything figured out so soon?"

"It was pretty straightforward. Your mother showed me how
in a way that I feel is *ingenious*. Don't get me wrong—I was
shaking in my boots for a couple of hours. I've never seen a ghost
before, and I was a funeral director myself for forty-two years.
And your mother is *direct*. She doesn't beat around the bush even
for a second."

"Only a couple of hours? And yeah, you bet she's *direct*—uh—
but—you use the journal and the pen and that whole deal? With
no problems?"

"'None so far. And I've learned about you and—your sad
history—also your family and the terrible tragedies. And I know
she wants you in Sanborn very quickly. But as for me, I'm retired
and living alone—my wife passed away last year, sadly—and to
be honest, I've been bored lately. What's going to happen is I'm
going to watch the funeral home for you while you're gone. Don't
worry, it's all been arranged, so I've been told. And when you come
back—*if* you come back (she told me to mention)—I'm going to
stay on with you as a full-time employee."

"You got all that out of her—in *one day*—with only a pen and
some blank pages?"

"That's right. She was wondering why it was taking you so
long to understand."

CHAPTER 27

Jordan Block had not heard from Tim Russell and decided to check back. He'd misread the situation entirely. Wasn't Russell hurting for money? He'd expected a desperate call from the handyman, thinking he'd jump at the chance for work in Wolfeboro, but the call never came.

After rolling out of bed at 10 am, he stuck one of his favorite pine pillows and stuffed it good under both nostrils, taking a long pull. Refreshed, he jumped into his rented Ford and drove to Sanborn. The plan was to drive by twice, reassess the situation, then make a decision—but when the meadow was empty of tents and campers (*the mob was gone!*)—he panicked and changed the plan. Block pulled up the driveway and knocked on the door. Tim answered.

"Mr. Russell, hello! I was just driving by and thought I might check back with you. Am I interrupting anything? I, uh—I was wondering if you wanted to take me up on my offer to work on my building in Wolfeboro. If you're busy, that's fine. I can find someone else, just let me know." Tim was skeptical. Something about the man seemed insincere.

"I'm not going to be able to take that job, Mr. Banks. It's crazy around here. Something came up. I'm sorry."

"Hey, that's no problem, I can find somebody else, but uh,

hey, where's the crowd? Where'd everybody go? The last time I was here, your field was full of people. Change of plans? What happened?

"Well, my girls are still missing, Jordan. And I sent everyone home. It's just that nothing was happening with the searches, and we're—focusing on other avenues."

"Ah, well, I'm sorry to hear that, truly, I am… So does this mean that the ghost-woman…is she gone? What'd I miss?"

"Well, for the record, the 'ghost-woman-thing'…was conjecture to begin with, Jordan. Tabloid journalism. Chasing down a *'ghost'* will do nothing to get my girls back, I'm afraid." Jordan Block turned from the front stoop to look down past the pond at the white van parked in the road.

"Who's that in the van? Is that the TV show?" he asked. Tim nodded.

"Some people want to believe a ghost-woman took my daughters. But they're on public property now, and there's not much I can do about it." Jordan Block nodded in mock agreement.

"Do you watch that show, Mr. Russell? Do you watch *Only If You Dare?*"

"I hate to admit it, but of course I do. Only because I want to be kept abreast of what the general public is being fed," Tim said.

"Yeah, me too. Ever since I first heard of your…uh, story though, it kind of captivated me, and I can't explain why. Listen, I'm a real ghost-lover, and this place intrigues me. I'm still interested. Care to show me around?"

"Well, I'd hate to waste your time Jordan. As I said, I can't sell right now. I have to be here, in case my girls return. While there's any sliver of a chance, I have to be here."

"So…you don't believe in the ghost, yet you expect the girls to come walking out of the woods by themselves? Wouldn't a kidnapper simply use the telephone to make ransom arrangements?"

Until this moment, nobody had dared ask such a personal question. Perhaps the questions had been asked of the police, but not the father of the children. Most people had accepted his wish to remain vigilant on-property, no questions asked, and silently gave thanks that they were not in his shoes. Tim, shocked by the question, stumbled badly with his answer.

"I...we don't know who kidnapped them, but since I am the only remaining parent, I'd like to remain by the telephone."

"I see," continued Block. "So your canvassing of the woods with the vigil people was...to stay close to the telephone?" Tim tired quickly of the third-degree.

"Listen, Mr. Banks. I don't want to sell. I can't sell, and that's all you have to—" Jordan Block cut him off.

"I'll give you sixty-thousand dollars, sight-unseen. I haven't even toured the property yet. And you can stay while you wait, up to six months. You'll want to be out of here by then anyway, right?"

"Fuck off, Jordan. Get the hell off of my property."

In truth, Jordan Block wasn't prepared for Tim's reaction. He'd been a Hollywood executive for more than twenty years and was used to calling the shots no matter the circumstances. On the other hand, come to think of it, he'd misread three ex-Mrs. Jordans and did not see Tim's New England *fuck-you* coming. Sensing he had blown it, he scrambled to make things right.

"Wait! –wait. I'm sorry, I've—I've been crass. I want to help you. I want to make this work—for both of us. How does one-hundred-thousand dollars sound...and you get to stay here—for five years—if you need it." Jordan spoke rapidly, shooting from the hip before Tim was able to close the door. And it worked. The door never completely shut as Tim pondered the stellar offer.

"One-hundred-thousand dollars and I can stay here for five years if I want to? I won't be here for nearly that long, but I'll take the deal." Back in control, Block countered with a few demands.

"Hold on, just a few more things. You don't talk to that TV show anymore—and you make sure they stay off-property."

"I can do that." Jordan was back in control. The deal was back on—he'd recovered from his tumble, and rather quickly, at that.

"And you give me a tour of the house—and you answer my questions honestly."

"Who are you, Mr. Banks, and what do you want with this property?"

"My name is Jordan Block, and I produce movies, along with a team of other people. We produced *Rosemary's Baby* as a matter of fact. I want to know everything about this place, and I want to hear it from the horse's mouth. I don't believe in ghosts, but I think you *do*—either that or you're the one responsible for all the murders. But then why would you want to stay here if you killed them? The whole thing is so strange; I'm forced to believe you're innocent."

"Well, you obviously haven't spoken to the police, because my alibi checks out for all of the incidents. How much do you know, anyway? Did you get all of your news from *Only If You Dare?*"

"I stumbled on a story in the *Evening Citizen*, and then I watched the show. That's it. The big crowd in your field confirmed what my gut was telling me. People *believe* this story. What really happened to them, by the way? The crowd. Give me a down payment on my investment. Part of our deal is your whole truth. Why'd you send the tents packing?"

"You haven't paid me yet, Mr. Block. You've already lied to me too, saying your last name was Banks and that you're from Connecticut."

Jordan Block reached into his back pocket and pulled out a fancy checkbook with gold plated trim on the cover. The initials "J.B." were stamped into the leather. In the right front pocket of his fishing pants, he pulled out an equally impressive gold Cross pen and wrote a check for one hundred thousand dollars—just like that. In the upper left-hand corner of the check was written the name "Jordan Block," and underneath that, "Paramount Pictures." The check paper was high quality with a watermark. Tim was impressed…and shocked. As he read the check, Block reached into his wallet and pulled out his California driver's license.

"I'll arrange to have the paperwork signed in the next week or so, but you can cash that check today if you like—but I want your word that you'll tell me everything as truthfully as you can recall. Do we have a deal, Mr. Russell?" Block held out his hand. Tim gripped it and shook.

At least his money troubles were over now.

CHAPTER 28

"**N**ow, where were we? Oh, I remember. Why did you send the campers out in the field packing?" Jordan Block knew there was more to Tim's initial story.

"Because they were in danger. This is all off the record, correct? I don't want to be labeled *a crazy* years down the road. I want to be able to say 'no comment' for the rest of my life."

"That's fine. I see this as a 'based on a true story' movie. Horror-junkies want to be kept guessing anyway. It adds to the urban legend—or in this case, the rural legend, haha. If the movie's good, they'll pay to see it at least twice. Now, what do you mean 'they were in danger'? From what?"

"From *Mildred Wells*. The ghost-woman…except that she's not a ghost." Tim had to smile, not only because he was holding a check for one hundred thousand dollars in his hand, but because the story was so absurd—yet true. He'd forgotten he'd have to explain a "revenant" and how he came to learn the word. For a brief moment, he wondered what else he'd forgotten before accepting the check.

Jordan Block's jaw dropped as Tim was forced to go back to the beginning and start there. He listened and learned about Henry and Annette Smith, and Tim showed him the exact spots on which they died. He showed him where the two headstones used to be in the last row of the grove. They parted the willow's branches pondside and visited the spot where Officer Bob Simmons' badly decomposed body was found.

Block marveled at the spot in front of the upstairs bathroom where cameraman David Bonnette filmed his last frames of the dead woman before being struck down. Finally, Tim took him to the kitchen and recanted a blow-by-blow account of Mildred's dominance there not twenty-four hours before. Block was horrified but had to grin. One hundred thousand dollars for the rights to a story like this was the bargain of a century.

Tim saw Block grinning and knew precisely what the man was thinking. He thought he'd raked Tim over the coals and gotten the better end of the deal. But Tim also knew what Block wasn't considering. He wasn't thinking of Mildred Wells and the dangers she presented. Tim silently prayed that this would all be over soon for everyone involved, including Jordan Block.

Block's smile eventually faded as Tim's recap came to an end, and the new reality sank in. He stooped to the kitchen floor and ran his finger over the holes in the vinyl floor that the pitchfork had made. Three of the tines had penetrated through the wood to the basement below, and he could feel cool air coming up from the cellar. Somehow, everything checked out—felt right. All the evidence pointed to a dead woman covered in flies with superhuman strength. Even if it wasn't real, he could get behind the "Legend."

"I bet you didn't really want to see that mob in the field leave, am I right?"

"Yeah, that's right. A safety-in-numbers type of thing, except in reality, they were just chickens in a henhouse, and Mildred was the fox."

"I'm going to get you a bodyguard in here. Someone who..."

"Jordan, don't. No man can go head to head with her. And you can't use weapons for a couple of reasons—one, we'll never find the girls. Two, she can just take your weapon away—like magic!"

Jordan stared at Tim blankly, wondering if he was serious, then bit his lower lip.

"Relax, I understand. But you do need to sleep, and the guy I will send you will stand watch, so you don't have to worry as much. Plus, he's my cameraman. I want to film everything while I work on putting this project together back in L.A."

Tim couldn't argue. The promise of a bodyguard was a luxury they'd never anticipated. Sleep was a precious commodity that neither he nor Holly had enjoyed enough of recently.

CHAPTER 29

Jordan Block went back to the house in Wolfeboro and made a few calls. It was his house now and his story, and if there was ever going to be a movie made, he sure as hell didn't want to watch it on television first.

CHAPTER 30

Nathan Hoginski sat in the van two hundred yards from the house. He was growing a beard now, and he hadn't showered in a day and a half. The crew was down to sharing one hotel room. The show's budget was sliced almost daily, and they all had to take shifts showering and sleeping in their vehicles.

They desperately needed new material—something exciting to happen. The American public could only take so many slow panning shots of the turret, or the pond, or the grove. His gold mine was in trouble. Suddenly his walkie-talkie crackled to life.

"Boss. It's the studio. We're done. They said to pack it up. Said we could come back if something new happened, but otherwise move on to the next story, or they'll fire you."

Hoginski didn't even respond. He sat there for a second and turned his head to the right, taking one last look across the meadow to the treeline that hid the grove. Nothing moved. Defeated and angry, he reached down and turned the key. The engine came to life, and he turned the van around to head back toward town.

Fuck.

CHAPTER 31

Holly came home to the good news. The money worries were over, and they could breathe easy, at least in that regard. They celebrated half-heartedly with a glass of wine. A security guard was on the way too, courtesy of Jordan Block, but the girls were still missing, and the odds of Mildred coming to visit tonight were much higher than they were the previous night. Holly considered pleading with Tim once more, and she also considered *leaving him*—not forever, but—until it was all over. There were absolutely no right answers, and in the end, she decided to grit her teeth and push through until the security guard/cameraman came.

She didn't sleep at all.

CHAPTER 32

Holly wanted to get out of bed but didn't dare go down to the kitchen alone. Ever since she'd walked in two evenings ago to her worst nightmare, things had changed. Now she had that vivid image burned into her mind, and it wouldn't go away. Her thoughts, like Tim's, were hazy from lack of sleep, and clear-thinking was a thing of the past.

Tim had a rough night, too, of that she was sure. She'd gotten used to his nighttime breathing and his occasional snore, and there had been none of that last night—until around 4 am. At that time, he'd gotten up three times to go to the bathroom, complete with checks of all four bedrooms and the hallway.

Now he was finally sleeping, and she knew that *one* of them rested, was better than *none*. Quietly, she grabbed a magazine off of her nightstand and read as she waited for Tim to wake up. It was 8:13 am.

It was the August edition of *Yankee Magazine*, which was not her cup of tea but better than staring at the ceiling and thinking of Mildred Wells. Faintly, she heard a knocking from somewhere downstairs. Reflexively, she sat bolt upright, waking Tim as she did, just in time to hear the second round of rapping. He was awake immediately, pulling his pants on and looking out the front bedroom window.

There was a strange car in the driveway. Andrew had driven himself the hour-or-so to Sanborn.

"Relax. Someone's here, and it's not *her*. I hope it's not one of Hoginski's crew. I'll go check it out. What time is it?"

"8:15. I'll be right down." Tim left the room headed for the front porch door. He looked out the living room window before getting there and saw a skinny young man who looked as tired as Tim felt. *Who the hell is this?* he thought, then opened the front door, walked through the porch, and opened the outer door.

"Hi. Can I help you?"

"I hope so, Mr. Russell. I can't believe I'm here, though. I understand you know somebody named *Thomas Pike*." Tim let his hand fall from the doorknob. He stood aghast, and his heart leaped at hearing the name.

"Excuse me… but I don't know you. Who are you?"

"My name is Andrew Vaughn, and I haven't slept in like… seven…eight days because of Thomas Pike." Tim looked at the young man sideways, still uncertain if this was somehow a hoax.

"What do you mean by that?"

"He's a ghost, and he visits me every night. I'm beyond caring about how that makes me sound. If you have no idea what I'm talking about, I'll leave, but I hope that you do. I think I have to help you somehow. In fact—I'm sure of it." Tim stood back, staring, then recovered and invited him in.

"Come in. Please, and tell my girlfriend exactly what you just told me." Holly hit the bottom of the stairs and walked toward Tim and the stranger. "Holly, this is…I'm sorry. What did you say your name was?"

"Andrew Vaughn."

"Andrew, this is Holly Burns. Please, Andrew, repeat what you just told me."

"I said the ghost of Thomas Pike sent me, and now I know that you know what I'm talking about because you wouldn't have even asked me to repeat it. I need this guy off of my back—I haven't slept in—what did I say, seven days? I'm so tired. What do you know about him? What do I have to do?" Tim and Holly looked at each other.

"Andrew, we do know who Thomas Pike is, and we're glad you're here…but we have a lot to go over—and forgive me, but you look terrible. Why don't you lay down in one of the guestrooms for a few hours? You're going to need your energy when you hear what we have to say."

CHAPTER 33

Tim and Holly set Andrew up in one of the bedrooms at the top of the stairs. It was in the back of the house and therefore not as sunny. Hopefully, he would sleep better.

He slept for three hours uninterrupted—until his mother's ghost suddenly appeared over the bed to stare him awake. He opened his eyes instinctively and was, of course, startled to see her glaring down at him, her disappointed gaze dictating naptime was over.

He sat up quickly to assure her he didn't need a second reminder, then stood. Temporarily satisfied, the ghost of Colleen Vaughn walked into the room's empty closet and disappeared. Now chilled and wondering what came next, he raised his arms high over his head to stretch. He was startled again when across the hall, he saw Thomas Pike watching from the fourth bedroom.

Frightened, he lowered his arms prematurely. Goosebumps rose on his forearms as he felt the aura—and the horror of the house for the first time. *Ghosts seemingly everywhere, waiting on me to do something—but what?* Bad things had happened here, and he knew there were even more to come. He was not a psychic or even a *sensitive*, yet the intuition was there—most likely injected by his mother or Thomas Pike. Wherever the thoughts came from, they painted a bleak picture and filled his heart with dread.

Andrew stepped into the hallway.

Nobody else was upstairs with him, or at least it didn't sound as if there were. He padded across the hall and pushed the door fully open—the fourth bedroom where he'd just seen Thomas—now empty. Suddenly he heard voices coming from somewhere downstairs and turned to descend. Straight ahead across the stairwell was the hall window at the front of the house, directly between the front two bedrooms. The railing in his right hand ran the length of the hallway to the master bedroom, then took a sharp left over the stairs until it met the second bedroom.

Andrew recognized the scene from the TV show—the worst scene—the one they repeated over and over in slow motion. David Bonnette had died where he now stood. For a second, his mind flashed to the TV show…and the figure of the woman standing on the balcony over the stairs. Andrew blinked twice to clear the image then bounded down them two at a time headed for the sound of human voices. He found Tim and Holly sitting blissfully unaware at the counter in the kitchen.

"…no, the van is gone! Did they give up on the story? Maybe the studio pulled the plug? I haven't seen Hoginski in days, come to think of it—Oh my God, he's up. Come in! Are you hungry? Did you rest? You look—are you alright? You still look like you're stressed out." Holly greeted Andrew excitedly. She and Tim had been bouncing wild theories about who he might be off of each other for the last three hours. Andrew decided against telling them his entire story—at least for now.

"Yeah, sorry. I had a dream, and it woke me up. I do feel a little better, though. Do you sleep here? In the house? I mean, overnight? Or do you…leave and make other arrangements?"

"We sleep here just in case my girls come back, or…hopefully we get news about them. Do you have news? Please tell me you do." Andrew dropped his head ever so slightly while preparing to respond.

"I'm sorry Tim, I don't have news about your girls, but I do think that's at least part of the reason I'm here. But…for real,

do you seriously sleep here? I saw...*the spot. The place.* Upstairs."
Neither Tim nor Holly knew of which "spot" he was talking. There
had been so many *spots,* places, and incidents—it was impossible
to single one out.

"What spot?" asked Holly.

"The spot where the TV cameraman was murdered by the
woman." Tim and Holly looked at one another. *Only If You
Dare* was trashy tabloid journalism, but the show had gotten that
segment one-hundred-percent right, and they both knew it.

"Yeah. She's our big problem. Her name is Mildred Wells.
She's killed a bunch of people, including my ex-wife. She has my
daughters right now, and I'm beside myself. I was hoping you
knew something or could help—right away."

"And you dare to sleep here every night? *Oh, God.*" Holly
listened to Andrew's words and looked at Tim, hoping the
newcomer's words would underline what she'd been saying all
along. Tim ignored her glance and remained steadfast.

"I've got to be here. It doesn't even matter where we go,
though, if we even wanted to leave. She'd find us. She's read my
papers and documents. She knew where to find Sheila and the
girls, all the way down in Amesbury. And we firmly believe—that
sometimes—*she listens to us.*" Andrew's gaze went from Tim's face
to Holly's. He swallowed hard when neither flinched.

"You mean—she gets in the house and spies on you?" Tim and
Holly nodded their heads slowly.

"Yes," Holly said.

"Why doesn't she just kill you like she killed your ex-wife
then?" Andrew was too tired to pull punches.

"She's torturing us because we helped Thomas Pike move their
son's bones. The way we understood the deal, if we helped him,
then he'd help us. But instead, he's left us high and dry—for about
a year-and-a-half now. But—back to you for a second—we've been
buzzing the entire three hours you were sleeping—He's back?!
Thomas Pike? You've seen him? What did he say to you?!"

"'*Say?*' He doesn't *say* anything! He wants me to write things down—I don't know, play a guessing game or something, and I'm not good at it. I don't know where to begin! I don't know him, and I don't know her, I don't know you—That's why I haven't slept in six days. He won't leave me alone—keeps pointing a pen in my face!"

"Then how did you find us? How do you even know who he is?"

"He woke me up last night to watch a late-night replay of that TV show. Then I—got the whole story this morning and headed over. I'm completely lost. I don't know what I'm supposed to do now that I'm here. I'm a college dropout. I run a funeral home. *I'm a total fuck up!*" Again, Tim and Holly looked at one another, just as confused as Andrew.

"Why do you think Thomas Pike sent us a person like *you* then?" Andrew's frustrations died down considerably when asked a question he could finally answer. He lowered his head and ran his hand through his hair. It was thin and stringy as if he hadn't showered in days.

"It was…my mother," he said. "My parents were killed a little more than a year ago by a drunk driver. We…*they* owned a funeral home and left it to my sister and me. I…never wanted to be part of the family business, but I messed up my life so severely that I had no other choice. Then I…hired a guy who ended up killing my sister. I hired him against her wishes, and she was pissed at me, and then he killed her when she caught him stealing embalming fluid. It wasn't just me having a bad month or a bad year, though— believe me. I was always the black sheep of the family. I've made a lifetime of bad decisions, one after another. I was kicked out of college for selling drugs—the list goes on and on.

"You're saying that your mother is dead? And that she…"

"My mother is angry for the death of my sister—the exclamation point on a lifetime of disappointments I've given her. Somehow—she found Thomas Pike and volunteered my services. Beyond that, your guess is as good as mine."

"And what happens if you disobey orders?"

"Well, I'll never get another good night's sleep, for one. That's a pretty big reason right there. That, and they can probably kill you if they want to, so there's that too. You ought to know, right? How goes *your* battle? How's your quality of life? I'm guessing it's as bad as mine, seeing as you need help from a nobody like me!" Tim smiled politely at Andrew's self-deprecation but went straight back to being serious.

"Mildred is not a ghost. She tried to kill herself years ago, and it didn't work, she ended up surviving and crawled back out of her own grave. She's a *revenant*."

"What the hell is a revenant?" asked Andrew.

"It's a French word. It means 'a person who has returned from the dead.' Kind of like a zombie, but not slow-moving and brain-dead. Revenants are, by definition, hell-bent on revenge—and we pissed her off." Tim gestured to the wall across the room. "She grabbed me right over there two nights ago, and it was like being held by a gorilla—I'm not kidding. I couldn't budge her arm with both of mine, and she wasn't even *trying*. She had me right where she wanted me—I didn't stand a chance. Then she let me go—just to torture me further—because Mildred has my daughters and she knows that's far more painful.

The most terrible thing about it is—I don't see how I can win in this scenario. I had a shred of hope for about three hours while you were sleeping, but now you tell me you're—not qualified? Tell me something I want to hear, Andrew." He pondered Tim's question for a moment.

"Well... I'm here. And I would leave if I could, but I don't believe I'm allowed that luxury. My life sucks so bad at home I don't really care, either. Can you imagine that? You're so tired, and damaged and so forth—that you don't care if you live or die?" Tim had to grin, despite Andrew's dour tone.

"Yeah, it's called getting *divorced!*" Andrew's face grimaced as if to say that Tim had missed the mark by a mile.

"What? I was just saying that…"

"Relax. I'm joking. You look too young to be married. I'm divorced, and I had a couple of months there where I felt like you do now. Just a joke, forget it." Andrew, too young to understand Tim's humor, did just that.

"So you're going to stay here for the foreseeable future then?" asked Holly. She was secretly relieved that in addition to the cameraman who Jordan Block was sending, there would now be a fourth pair of eyes to watch for Mildred.

"Well, there's no doubt in my mind that *they* want me here."

"Oh, we want you here too. We're just surprised—shocked— that you're crazy enough to take us up on the offer. Do you have any other immediate questions for us?"

"Uh—I'm still waking up, and I feel groggy, but they'll come. I guess I'd like to take a look around. Can I get a tour? I want to know everything. It could mean life or death, right?"

Suddenly, there was a knock at the door. All three heads in the kitchen turned simultaneously—nervously. "It's a big guy. He has a mustache."

"Probably the damn TV show again, but I can't let them back on the property." Tim peered out the window. The man was huge, like a bodybuilder. He held a movie camera down at his waist, clearly powered off. Maybe it wasn't *Only If You Dare*. Then Tim remembered. He walked through the dining room and into the porch to let the man in. "Hi. Are you Jordan Block's man?"

"That's me. Mark Folsom—nice to meet you. I guess I'm supposed to protect you from ghosts?" Tim eyed the young man, trying to remember what it was like to be blissfully ignorant.

"If I said yes, would you believe me?" Tim saw the man seriously considering the question, and it was clear that he did not. While disappointed, Tim appreciated his honesty.

"Probably not," he eventually replied with a smile. Mark Folsom was a hulk of a man and had most likely never been threatened by anything or anyone in his life, except maybe the other three-hundred-pound football players he used to face in the Big Ten Conference. Tim smiled back, wisely deciding to change the subject.

"Well, come on in then! With you, we're now four. Some of us don't sleep well, so the extra bodies will most likely help that. We can take shifts if need be. Come in and meet Holly and Andrew."

They spent the afternoon touring the house and property, explaining where bad things happened and where they might most likely happen again. When they got to the overgrown spruce grove, Andrew mumbled something to himself.

"What'd you say, Andrew?" asked Holly.

"Oh—no. It's just that…this is weird, being here—a kind of coincidence. My funeral home also happens to be a working apple orchard. People from Sugar Hill spend their entire lives coming every fall for apples, and then they come back to be buried when they die. The name of it is Foggy Orchard, and the apple trees are all in symmetrical rows like these spruces, except it's a little bit different. Here, you can't see the sky, and that makes it creepy. In the orchard, the trees look crazy, with limbs all twisted, jutting out in all directions. It's not creepy on a sunny summer day, but on an overcast winter day, after all their leaves are gone—it reminds me of this—I always get a tingle in my gut, like maybe someone's watching, or something. Whoops, sorry—I didn't mean to make it scary."

Mark Folsom shook his head, realizing for the first time that he was the only non-believer on the tour and kept his mouth shut. Tim noticed as did Holly, but they both knew that it would be fruitless to try and convince him.

CHAPTER 34

After the tour of the property, Tim and Holly spent the afternoon settling the two new guests into their rooms. Andrew stayed in the place he had napped, and Mark moved into the quarters on the other side of the hall. Andrew purposely neglected to mention that he'd seen Thomas Pike in Mark's room a few hours back.

Holly took some comfort in the fact that both rooms at the top of the stairs were now occupied. It added an imaginary layer of security, making her feel safer. They might awaken, see Mildred, and alert the house. Alternatively, maybe they would not awaken, and it would be their cries that provided a warning. She did her best to force the latter thought out of her mind.

There were no groceries in the house, so Tim drove into town for pizzas and a salad. On the way home, he stopped at a convenience store for a case of beer and four bottles of wine—if nothing else, it would loosen their tongues and make a nervous evening pass all the smoother. As he arrived home, the sun had set. They put all of the food on the dining room table, opened a bottle of wine, and gave a beer to Mark, who was not a wine drinker. The rest went in the fridge. Neptune sniffed the air appreciating the smell of the food and wedged his way between the chairs as he crawled under the table. Andrew broke the silence.

"So, Mark—Excuse me for saying so, but you don't believe

in ghosts, correct?" Mark seemed slightly uncomfortable with the question but entertained it anyway.

"Well, I've never seen one. Have you?" Andrew nodded and was about to explain, but Tim decided he couldn't hold his tongue.

"Sorry to interrupt, but before I forget, I need to go over a few things. I'll go on the record saying that *she's real*, and if and when we do see her—let me do the talking. That's all we want to do is *talk*. She's stronger than all of us—even you, Mark. Jordan told me you played football. Where'd you go to school?"

"Michigan."

"Very nice. I'm a Bo Schembechler fan."

"Thanks. Yeah, great man. I'll never forget him."

"Did you go any further? Did you turn pro?"

"Yeah, the Oilers and the Patriots. Hurt my knee second year with the Patriots, though."

"Ah, bummer. Well, at least you landed a job in Hollywood."

"Ha. Yeah, sort of." Mark was a man of few words, and it was hard to maintain a conversation with him. They opened the first pizza box, and the smell of pepperoni and cheese filled the room.

"I think I'm starving," said Holly, anxious to take the social pressure off of Mark. The pizza smelled so good that even Andrew, who had ordered the salad, grabbed a slice. A minute later, despite Holly's interjection, Mark continued the conversation.

"Alright, so Tim says he saw her the other night…but…did you see her too?" He gestured to Holly. She returned his gaze without blinking.

"I did. She's real. I swear on my soul." Mark shifted uncomfortably as he smirked and grabbed a second slice.

"What about you, Andrew? You saw her too?" Mark continued. It was Andrew's turn to be uncomfortable.

"No. I just got here this morning, a few hours before you did. I haven't seen anything—here, anyway."

"What does that mean?" Mark pressed.

"I see my mother all the time. She haunts me because—Well,

it's a long story, but the short version is I inadvertently got my sister killed." Andrew sat with his back to the kitchen wall, meaning he could see into part of the living room. It was dark in there, yet he thought he saw something move. He stopped talking and quietly put his pizza down. Neptune, meanwhile, began to whine.

"Neptune, stop. No pizza. Stop begging," Tim commanded in a stern voice. Mark continued.

"Oh, sorry, man—you don't have to go there, I don't want to bum you out, but, so…do you see her all the time? Is she mean to you or something? Explain it to a non-believer." Andrew didn't hear Mark's question because, at that moment, his mother's face appeared in the shadows of the living room, from an angle visible only to Andrew. *Why now?* His heart beat wildly as their eyes met. She never blinked. How long had she been lurking? Neptune's whining persisted.

"Neptune!" said Holly.

"Maybe he has to go out?" asked Tim.

"No, he came in just before you returned with the pizza."

Now that Colleen Vaughn had her son's attention, she shifted her eyes to the dark kitchen doorway over his left shoulder. He was *on deck*, but he didn't understand her clue immediately—taking too much time to follow her eyes—like the pen and flip-book debacle. *Forever embarrassing*, thought Colleen Vaughn. *Slow and selfish, stuck in his own world.* He was prone to disappointing her, but she could correct him. It would take time, but she would eventually change his ways.

"Hey, are you okay?"—asked Mark—"We don't have to go there. What are you looking at? *You're joking.* Are you trying to spook me?" Mark looked over his left shoulder, smiling nervously into the living room, even leaning back in his chair to see in further. Colleen had left because Andrew had finally gotten the message. Mark looked back at Andrew, who was now staring at the kitchen doorway, his jaw agape. Tim and Holly realized what was happening a half-second later.

Mildred was in the doorway.

"Whoa, something reeks! Do you smell that? I think the dog has to go out." Mark dropped his chair back to all four legs, still unaware—she was behind him. Neptune's whines became incessant. Mark looked back at Andrew, who was staring at a spot over his right shoulder. "Okay, okay, cut the crap. I know you're busting me. Man, the dog's out of control. Want me to take him out?" He made a move to push away from the table and caught Tim and Holly's faces. They were also transfixed at something over his shoulder. He almost turned, but Tim spoke urgently.

"Mark, don't move. And don't turn around, look at me. I'm serious." Mark looked at Tim. Both he and Holly had horrified looks as Andrew did. *Working together,* he thought. *Very convincing, however.*

The lights went out. Holly let out a brief startled scream.

"Oh, come on, stop it! What is this? Turn the damn lights back on!" Mark stood to find the wall switch and end their elaborate prank but felt a cold hard hand clamp his shoulder that sat him back down very inelegantly. The chair cracked audibly but held his sudden weight. *Too much,* he thought, temper flaring. "What the hell!" He jerked his big head a quarter turn to see who had him by the back of the neck.

Mildred stared back with her sunken eyes and rotting skin. Her corneas were dull and cloudy, and Mark knew at once it was *all real.* Nobody in the room dared move as his life hung in the balance. Neptune stopped whining. Mildred continued to stare as she adjusted her iron grip just enough to let him know she was in charge—then suddenly let him go and moved on toward Andrew.

Andrew kept still but wondered if he would pay for it later. Mother would most likely expect results. Once again, however, he was at a loss for what to do. A fly landed on his hand, and he let it sit as Mildred closed in. She looked him in the eye, studying him, perhaps wondering who he was, but did not touch him. Mark was behind her now, badly shaken, his bravery up in smoke—browbeaten. Andrew knew he was now a non-factor.

As she slowly passed behind him, he stopped breathing through his nose, praying she wouldn't grab his neck too. He kept his eyes on Tim across the table and Holly to his right, reading their faces as they stared up and over him at Mildred in horror. It seemed like forever, but finally, she appeared to his right while continuing to Holly. Holly knew she had few options and little time, so she spoke out.

"Where are the girls, Mildred? Give him his girls back, and you can have this house. We'll leave and be gone for good." It was impossible to tell whether or not Mildred had even heard the words because they did nothing to alter her course. She walked much closer to Holly than she had to Andrew, and it also took her longer to pass by. Holly closed her eyes and tried impossibly to imagine she was somewhere else, but the flies landing all over her made it virtually impossible.

Mildred paused for several seconds between Holly and Tim, and Andrew recalled the story they'd told him earlier that day. The story of how they had moved her son's grave, ground his bones up with Thomas Pike's, and dumped them in a lake. Mildred most certainly remembered their hands in her betrayal. Andrew again wondered if there wasn't something he should be doing to help. Then Mildred took three more steps and stopped directly behind Tim.

Tim felt a panic welling up. He wouldn't die this way—with his back to her, so he clamped both hands under the seat of his chair and spun quickly to face her without standing up. Mildred reacted to Tim's surprise move by grabbing his throat and violently pushing him backward over the edge of the table. The table was disrupted. Drinks spilled, and Andrew's salad fell off the table. Everyone reacted to the pounce at once by standing up suddenly and stepping back, while screaming, pleading for Tim's life in unison. Mark backed up further than everyone, hovering as close as he could to the front door. Jordan Block's movie camera was three feet away in the corner of the room, but he had no intention of picking it up.

Tim gasped for breath as the table dug into his back, and Mildred surveyed the room, waiting for the moment to settle down. Andrew, fearing his mother's reprisal, finally spoke up.

"All right, enough! Let him go! *Begone!* This is not your house anymore! You…" He took a step toward the table. Mildred called her rusty blade from Beverly Farms and spun it in her hand to hold like a dagger. Andrew, shocked to see the weapon conjured out of thin air, cut his speech short, and backed off.

Begone? Mildred hadn't heard that word since her mother had read the Bible to her. Before Gideon Walker. Before Thomas Pike. Before her life—and her *afterlife*—had been sabotaged—by some of the people in this very room.

Mildred jabbed the knife into the table inches from Tim's ear. He gasped, as did Holly. Both of his hands gripped her forearm with zero effect. Every so often, he produced a choking sound—so she softened her grip ever so slightly. Tonight was not the final piece of the puzzle, but at the same time, it was highly enjoyable to let them all think that it might be.

Ignoring the others in the room because she knew they were intimidated, she stuck her right hand in the pocket of her dress. Out she pulled a light brown object and set it on Tim's forehead. He couldn't tell what it was so close to his face, so she took two steps back toward the living room doorway arch. From here, she would wait for him to pick himself up, rise to his feet, and recognize her gift.

It was Vivian's corn doll, the one they had made together in the grove in much happier times—happier times for Tim, that is. He recognized it immediately, which gave her great pleasure—that had been the one question in her mind going in—did he know about those days? She'd hoped he would, *and indeed he did. Perfect.* Maybe he'd seen Olivia's twin-doll somewhere and put two and two together. Perhaps the girls had mentioned a *woman in the woods*. In any case, it had worked.

Tim broke down in fury and frustration. As he screamed at her, the veins bulged in his throat, but his feet dared come no closer. Holly grabbed his arm as if to ensure he would not be so foolish as to try. For Mildred, it was satisfying to watch him suffer, but sadly, the feeling had passed all-too-quickly. She stared at Tim's face wishing another look alone might rekindle her rage, but it didn't. He came off as pathetic—and a different thought crossed her mind she hadn't anticipated—*he cared for his daughters more than she had ever cared for Elmer.*

The magic of the evening burned out like a candle wick, and she began to feel a wisp of fatigue creep in—the hangover after the party. This was over, for now. She called the knife from the table, which quieted them once again, then turned and passed through the threshold into the living room. No one dared follow. She let herself out of the door at the bottom of the stairs, leaving it open for them to remember her by.

CHAPTER 35

Mildred was gone, but Andrew saw his mother staring at him from the dark corner of the dining room and sensed her dissatisfaction. At that moment, Holly found the wall switch, illuminating the horrified faces in the room—making mother's visage disappear. Fearing inevitable retribution, Andrew bolted for the open front door at the bottom of the staircase and cautiously looked outside, hoping for a miracle—something he could do to contribute.

Mildred was fifty feet away and nearly to the pond. Andrew reached for the knob and began to close the door quietly. Although he made no sound, Mildred sensed him and turned slowly around.

His heart rose in his throat as he received her full attention for the first time. They locked eyes, and Mildred seemed to study him. He wondered for a second if she knew who he was—but how could she? Had Thomas Pike said something? Unlikely. Whatever her reason, to say it was unnerving was an understatement. At this distance, she could easily change course and charge him. He might get the door closed, but he had little doubt it would protect him.

Rushing to the door so soon may have been a colossal mistake. Keeping his eyes on her, Andrew closed the door and stepped back to the bookshelf in the dark living room. Tim and the others were still in the dining room, recovering and picking up the pieces. Andrew squatted down to look out and see the pond better. Mildred was there staring at him as if marking her prey.

He felt exposed as if she had x-ray vision. She stared for two full seconds before turning and continuing on her way, taking the shortest path to the cover of the forest and disappearing in the darkness. Andrew's heart continued to beat as his brain struggled to calm it. Still crouched, he rose to rejoin the rest of the group as they nervously chattered in the dining room.

"I'm calling the police while their dogs still have a chance to follow her scent. It should be easy, right? It fucking stinks in here because of her! And what's with freaking Neptune? He was a no-show! Some guard dog!"

"He was scared, Tim, just like the rest of us. She's *dead* for crying out loud!"

"Yeah, well, I could have used some help as I was staring up at that butcher knife. I don't know Holly, what's he gonna do, warn us with his whining? Maybe he needs an adopted brother or something—And you—"—Tim turned to face Mark—"Mr. Football—where were *you*, man? Throw a drink in her face, hit her with a fucking pizza box—something! Do you get a bonus if I die or something?"

Mark, the ex-football player, kept his mouth shut because he was a beaten and broken man. He'd even forgotten that he weighed over three-hundred pounds and could throw Tim through the wall if he wanted to. He was eight-years-old again, the fat kid in school, and all he wanted to be was *out*, even if it cost him his job.

"Hey, fuck this man. I quit," he said under his breath as he turned to the door, opened it, and left, just like that. Holly turned her head to Tim, mouth aghast. Both of them turned to look at Andrew in the living room archway, who appeared as pale and afraid as they were.

"What is she, a witch *and* a revenant?" he asked. Nobody had an answer, and his question provoked them.

"That's an excellent question, Andrew"—Holly interjected—"I don't think we know the answer. The way she flashes that knife— it's like from out of thin air, right? Did you see the same thing? Did she pull it out of her sleeve or her dress?"

"No, definitely not,"—Andrew replied—"It was like a magic trick. Scary as hell. That's a very dangerous talent." Tim absorbed the revelations as if it was all too much to take. He had no time to entertain these overwhelming observations.

"I—I've got to make some phone calls."

CHAPTER 36

Tim's first phone call was to Chief Galluzzo, who didn't appreciate being called to duty after his dinner. The sleepy small town he had chosen to work in had changed recently from a cushy job to a real grind, mostly because of the man on the other end of the line. He bristled at Tim's *tone*.

"Bring the dogs, Chief. She just left—and she'll be easy to track if you hurry. She'll lead them right to my daughters. How long will it take you to get them?"

"Tim, the dogs belong to the *State Police*. I've got to get a hold of them, and then we have to hope that we have some canines in the area. They move them around according to demand. I'm guessing Concord might have…"

"Call them quick. We're going to have to—"

"…office hours, and—"

"Just fucking call them!" He slammed the phone down. It was probably unwise to hang up on the Chief of Police, but in this case, Tim knew he was right. He'd been right all along about Galluzzo who'd had no problem employing Bob-fucking-Simmons as half of his police force. He was incompetent.

Two seconds later, he picked up the phone again as he pulled out Jordan Block's business card from his wallet.

"Jordan, it's Tim Russell in Sanborn. Your bodyguard just walked out after seeing our Lady face-to-face."

"Wait, wait—slow down—he's gone? Where'd he go? And you saw her?"

"Yeah, that's right. *Andre the Giant* was a coward in the end. He left your camera here too."

"Did you film anything?"

"Hell no. I was too busy staring at the business end of a butcher knife as he cowered in the corner. I don't know what you want to do about it, but you're down one cameraman, and we're down a pair of eyes and ears."

"She pulled a knife on you? How close was she? Did you get a good look at her?"

"She had me by the throat, how's that for close? She blew up our dinner table—just showed up—snuck in, quiet—*like a ghost*. Stunk up the place too. She's rotten, man." Jordan couldn't believe his ears.

"I, uh… I don't know what to—Uh, did anyone else see her?"

"Yeah, four of us, including your boy. Ask him if you don't believe me—if you ever see his ass again. Listen, I've got to go. I'm going to try to follow her with my dog until the State Police get here with theirs. Send us another bodyguard—and tell the next guy the truth before he takes the job."

Jordan Block hung up the phone in disbelief. *She had him by the throat. Mark, his supposed prize bodyguard had seen her—and quit on the spot. The State Police were on their way.* This would make the news tomorrow.

Hot damn. Time to make some phone calls and keep things as quiet as possible.

CHAPTER 37

Mildred entered the woods and began dropping every bird
and squirrel she came into contact with. She was in no real
hurry, except that she didn't want Tim or Holly to come running
out after her so quickly that she would have to kill them too early.
She knew all about the sawed-off shotgun in the kitchen drawer
and had deemed it dangerous. A gun like that was capable of
obliterating her revenant heart if fired close enough.

She'd killed every living thing in the four acres closest to the
house before Tim came bounding out of the house with the dog.
By then, she was almost finished in the grove and about to sprint
to Belmont for a large pond where she would lose them before
doubling back to Northfield and the coyote den. Tim's dog—
Neptune—got hung up immediately with the first dead squirrel.
Mildred was as good as gone.

CHAPTER 38

The police dogs arrived late, which came as no surprise. Once started, they lasted less than an hour in the pitch-black woods before calling it a night—there were just too many dead birds and squirrels to keep the dogs focused on Mildred. Tim was more than upset as nothing seemed to work—and Mildred's threat remained. Andrew found himself checking over his shoulder—he was very shaken by Mildred's appearance, much more than by Thomas Pike's. Mildred was angry and dangerous, even wielding weapons. Mother or no mother, how long could he last against a being like that?

Holly struggled to keep everyone on the same page and keep them calm under pressure. It would be a long night ahead for sure, especially with Mark the bodyguard gone, but at least they had Neptune, didn't they? Even if the dog's only warning was a whine rather than an intimidating bark? It was better than nothing, and leaving was a false hope of Holly's. Neither Tim nor Andrew would want to go. Besides that, Tim was right. If Mildred wanted them, she would find them at Holly's house just as quickly. The only real way to get through this was by facing the problem head-on, for better or for worse—life or death.

It was very late when the police finally left, and there was nothing to do but go to bed—the last thing anyone wanted. Tim,

Holly, and Andrew were exhausted and dragged their feet, but sooner or later, they were all upstairs, in pajamas, brushing teeth. The clock said 2:42 am. Andrew looked into the bedroom across the hall and wished Mark the bodyguard had remained, but now, the room was dark and vacant—a haven for nightmares. Only Mark's bag remained. To have an empty room across the hall was unsettling, to say the least.

Tim and Holly had showered and brushed and were in their bedroom at the front of the house talking amongst themselves, muffled through their common wall, the door still ajar. Andrew wondered for a moment if he should or should not leave his door open. To keep the door open would be more helpful and more connected to Tim and Holly, but to close the door would make him feel safer against whatever—*whoever*—might come up the stairs. He was alone in the back of the house—and would be first to be attacked most likely. *Fuck that.* He closed the door.

Andrew checked the closet, knowing full-well that it gave him no insurance against his mother, but it gave him a small sliver of peace-of-mind. He crawled into bed, leaving the shades up because he didn't want the night lasting any longer than it had to. Luckily, despite the long day and the grueling evening, he fell asleep in less than half an hour.

CHAPTER 39

The dreams began almost immediately. Thomas Pike invaded his mind, educating Andrew on *all-things-Mildred*. Andrew knew it was Thomas, too—like a grim tour guide escorting him through a nightmare. The first thing he was forced to watch was little Elmer's drowning down at the pond, not one-hundred yards away from where he now slept. The death was slow and grueling, and Andrew saw everything from the push of the oar to the underwater stare-down—son vs. mother—Elmer's last act of defiance—relaxing entirely in the end, allowing her to finish him, all while staring directly into her eyes.

Andrew attempted to awaken but wasn't allowed to. Unbeknownst to him, his mother stood over the bed, her hand pressed on his forehead, keeping him under. Elmer's murder ended but dissolved into another dream—Mildred visiting Thomas' grave on Tower Hill. Andrew witnessed her confession to the killing, reciting her intentions to bury herself next to Elmer, leaving Thomas alone across town. After her monologue, she even spit on his grave.

The dreams continued with David Bonnette sneaking into the house to film the property for *Only If You Dare*. From Andrew's perspective, he could see Bonnette nervously making his way through the house, but could also watch as Mildred waited above. It was painful, like a cat stalking a mouse, and Andrew's heart went out to the defenseless Bonnette. It ended with all of the violence the found-footage suggested and more—which was more than painful to watch.

Andrew sat bolt-upright in bed, sweat beading on his forehead. He searched the room with his eyes, but there was no sign of Mildred Wells—or his mother, or Thomas Pike. The place was quiet, as was the house as far as he could tell through the closed bedroom door. Sitting up unsettled, he considered his options. He could "take a break" and go to the bathroom, but he might wake the dog, or Tim or Holly, who had their bedroom door open down the hall.

He laid back down feeling boxed in, but it didn't last long. Fatigue set in heavily once again, akin to a sugar crash. He was tired, but he couldn't settle, and his mind began to wander. *He should go. He should—leave. Quit.* Mildred Wells was bad-ass, even worse than his mother. Better the devil you *know*—than the devil you don't know.

Ten minutes later, he made up his mind and began packing his things. Very quietly, he opened the bedroom door and peered out. It bothered him immensely that he would have to walk *toward* the dark room across the hall to take the stairs, but he made it—and then he felt even worse descending backward, painfully slowly as to reduce the creaking of the stairs. Very carefully, he planted his feet as close to the wall as possible, testing each stair for noise before fully committing to it, head on a swivel, watching for anyone coming out of the dark bedroom above or the living room below.

Soon he was downstairs, making his way through the dark house toward the side door, the furthest exit from the bedrooms. He used his nose more than anything—he'd most certainly smell her before he saw her. Before long, he reached his car, thankful that he'd parked behind the other vehicles. The engine started somewhat noisily but calmed itself to a low idle as he put it in reverse and backed into the corner of the driveway, lights off.

Without even stepping on the gas, he let the car drift by the front of the house, under the bedroom windows and down the last incline of the driveway, out onto Lancaster Hill Road. He had to hit the brakes momentarily, and he saw the white building behind him turn pink for a quick second, but after that, it was smooth sailing. One hundred yards later, when the house was lost in the trees, he pulled the lights on and stepped on the accelerator, breathing a sigh of relief. *Sorry to disappoint you again, mom, but that one had a knife. If I have to live with ghosts, I'll take Thomas Pike all day long.*

Lancaster Hill Road was made of dirt, and there were many 'permanent' potholes for the first half-mile or so. After that, it smoothed out some, and he was able to drive a bit faster, reaching nearly twenty-five miles per hour. He was exhausted and shaken. Sugar Hill was an hour's drive—perhaps he'd find a motel along the way and get some real sleep. Maybe nobody would find him there, and he could have one solid night's sleep to recover.

The dashboard lit the interior of the car just enough to read the instruments. The radio was off, and dark, and he decided a little music might help lighten the mood. He turned the knob and spun the dial looking for any radio station even halfway listenable—this was, after all, rural New Hampshire. Soon he came upon a station in the middle of playing the song "Thin Line Between Love and Hate," and left it there.

> *The sweetest woman in the world*
> *Can be the meanest woman in the world*
> *If you make her that way, you keep on hurting her*
> *She keeps being quiet*
> *She might be holding something inside*
> *That really really hurt you one day...*

Andrew couldn't help but hear the lyrics and begin to analyze them, break them down, and apply them to his new life and where it was headed. Who was the woman in the song—*Mildred?* She certainly didn't appear to be sweet, at least according to the dreams that had been planted in his head—but then again, that's just one side of the story, isn't it? Thomas, however, had his mother's ear, and his mother's endorsement might back Thomas' opinion up.

Then it dawned on him: Maybe the "sweetest woman" of the song *was* his mother—and Andrew had hurt her so badly, so many times, that he'd turned her into the banshee she was today… It was a profound thought—perhaps too deep—he might be overanalyzing. The song began to bother him, and he considered changing the station, but just then, the signal cut off.

Was it a dead spot? *Must be the trees.* He looked down at the dash. It was not a drop in the signal because the radio was dark—switched off. He reached down and turned the knob again. He felt the click, but no music played. The dial lit back up, however, illuminating the front seat ever so slightly—just enough to see his mother in the passenger seat staring at him in disgust.

Before Andrew could even react, the ghost of Colleen Vaughn reached for the steering wheel and yanked it hard to the right. Andrew's car veered violently on two wheels, off the road, and over the gulley. Andrew had zero time to react. His last moment of consciousness was a split-second realization that he'd failed his mother again, and he had severely misjudged the lengths to which she'd go to fix him. *'The devil you know' can still kick your ass.*

Andrew's car flew over the gully and smacked into a giant sugar maple head-on. The front end accordioned, and the vehicle was immediately totaled. Andrew had always considered seat belts optional. He hit the dashboard hard, breaking both legs before continuing through the windshield. On his way, his mind replayed his sister's death. Instead of seeing *his* whole life pass before his eyes, he saw Rebecca's. The guilt weighed heavily even in the short time he remained conscious.

He hit the tree full-on—loud and ugly. More bones broke, and bark removed skin. The car stalled out immediately, and all went dark except for the one remaining headlight, which slowly dimmed and died three hours later.

CHAPTER 40

Holly woke just before 6 am needing to pee, which was a ritual she hated. At least today, however, the upstairs was not empty. It was good to know someone was staying down the hall just outside the bathroom. At least she would know that particular quadrant of the upstairs was safe—as long as Andrew had survived the night. Neptune was awake but chose to stay with Tim, already used to Holly's routine. She would be back in a moment.

On her way to the bathroom, Holly noticed that Andrew's bedroom door was open, and she silently commended him for his bravery. *Or was he already up?* As she passed, she couldn't help but look in and see the disheveled covers on his empty bed—Andrew was up. *Was he downstairs alone?* Another thing she was reluctant to do—be the first one downstairs. Very brave indeed. Holly peed and returned to the bedroom. Tim was just waking up.

"Andrew is not in his room," she notified.

"Is he downstairs?"

"I don't know, and I'm waiting for you before I go down there." Tim knew the drill and got dressed. Before they left the room, he grabbed the sawed-off shotgun that he kept by the bed and said a small prayer that he would never have to use it. Their first stop was the front door at the bottom of the stairs to let Neptune out. Holly had gotten in the habit of bringing a jacket upstairs with her to bed because it wasn't safe practice rushing into the kitchen haphazardly. Tim looked down the length of the house however, hoping to see Andrew wave to him from the kitchen with a cup of coffee in his hand, but it didn't happen.

As soon as Neptune was finished doing his business, they went back inside and slowly checked each room one-by-one on the way to the kitchen. Holly trusted her nose primarily. If one day a room didn't pass the smell test, they could always—*always what? What could they "always" do if one morning the living room smelled as though something had died in it? Run to the road? Shoot Mildred and run?*

When they got to the kitchen, there was no scent of brewing coffee and, of course, no Andrew. Tim continued through the breakfast area and looked out the side door into the driveway— Andrew's car was gone.

"You've got to be fucking kidding me," Tim complained.

"No. Don't tell me..."

"He's gone! Well, let's just hope he went to pick up some donuts. I didn't hear a car, did you? What time did you wake up?"

"Ten minutes of six. He was exhausted too—but maybe he couldn't sleep. Last night's dinner was—stressful, to say the least."

"Well, at least we know Mildred didn't take him unless they drove off together. I think he quit on us—for the exact reason you just said. Last night's dinner would scare the shit out of anyone. Hell, we lost Mark immediately." Holly shook her head in disbelief.

"I didn't think to check and see if he took his bag with him." Five minutes later, they knew for sure he had quit.

CHAPTER 41

The first thing Andrew saw was the sunlight burning through his closed eyelids. He hurt all over—*bone-deep pain*—and before he could move, he had to test parts of his body with tiny motions. Where was he? Was that all a dream? He didn't dare open his eyes for fear he would not be safe in bed. The cool breeze on his face and his chilled body temperature told him the awful truth before he was ready to acknowledge it.

His back felt frozen, and it was—but it responded to his test, and then he did the same thing to his right shoulder. His right arm was over his head and had settled awkwardly on the uneven ground, but it too woke up with time and responded. Slowly he rolled a half turn, wincing as he did, a clump of dead leaves stuck to the side of his head.

He reached up and pulled them off, realizing they were covered in congealed blood. His hand was bloody too, as was his shirt. Both legs were in great pain, and his car looked as if it had tried to climb the tree and died halfway up. The steering wheel, while still in its original position, was only three feet from the tree itself. The hood was truncated so much he couldn't even imagine an engine fitting in the short space. Safety glass littered the road as did plastic parts and lenses. Blood was everywhere—his blood. It looked as if a deer had been hit by an eighteen-wheeler. He couldn't remember a thing.

CHAPTER 42

As Holly and Tim finished their coffee and their frustrated conversation, someone knocked on the porch door, and Tim ran to the window.

"Oh my God—it's Andrew." They barreled through the porch to let Andrew in, but before they got there, Holly screamed. Andrew's clothing was soaked in dark maroon blood—some still glistening, other patches dry and beginning to flake. Nothing dripped, however, as it had hours ago. "What happened?! Did Mildred do this?" Andrew tried to speak, but the words came out slowly. Holly interrupted while staring at his forehead.

"Andrew—you're all stitched up. Where were you?!" Andrew brought his hand up and felt. Holly was right—there they were. Suddenly his memory flashed, and he saw his mother staring at him in the glow of the dashboard. His legs wobbled, and suddenly he needed to sit down, so he spun quickly and landed hard on the front step. Holly and Tim tumbled out of the porch and onto the lawn. Both knelt to assist him as if he had fainted.

"You're covered in blood, Andrew. We've got to get you to the hospital, but…it kind of looks like you already went. Did you walk out or something? You must have a concussion. Can you tell us what happened?"

"M…mother…don't remember much, but I just did—just

138

now—she was next to me in my car. Crashed it on purpose." Tim and Holly looked at each other, dumbfounded. His story was coming out too slowly, and they weren't fully understanding.

"Were you in the hospital? Did you get up and leave?" Andrew caressed his stitches—thirty-one of them on his forehead—once again.

"No hospital. She was a doctor—long time ago. Knows what to do."

"I thought you said your parents ran a funeral home?" asked Tim.

"Before. Before that. She was a doctor."

"Where did you crash?" Andrew pointed to the road.

"Tim, why don't you take him inside and get him cleaned up. I don't think I'll be able to support his weight if he falls. He seems like he has a concussion on top of everything else. I'll go and see if I can find his car." Andrew sat on the step, staring off into space. He was in a daze and a great deal of pain. It was inexplicable, really—so much blood—too much blood.

All of a sudden, he saw his mother break through the trees lining Lancaster Hill Road and cross the field behind the pond. Her eyes were locked on him as she shook her head, "No."

"Uh, wait, I'm okay. I don't have a concussion. She wants me here. I just froze for a second because—I couldn't remember, and—then I did all at once. It was all a blank until a second ago. Now she's out there in the field looking at me. Looking at us, I mean. Can you see her?" Tim and Holly spun their heads in horror, reminiscent of the days when Elmer Pike used to fly his kite. They saw nothing.

"Where? I don't see her."

"No?" Andrew seemed disappointed yet unsurprised. "Ah, well… I might have guessed. She doesn't haunt you guys—only me. She's right there, to the right of the willow beyond the pond. You can't miss her—unless she wants you to, I guess." Holly turned her head back to Andrew, stressed but somewhat relieved that she couldn't see the ghost.

"What's she doing out there? What does she want?"

"She wants me to help you. Same thing as yesterday, but she knows I cut and ran last night and pissed her off—for the millionth time."

"So, you *did* leave! I knew it. Hey, look, Andrew; you don't have to stay. It's *not* safe here, as you've already seen. I don't want that on my conscience…" Andrew began to laugh softly at Tim's naivete. Then he winced in pain.

"Look at me, Tim. I'm not going anywhere. My mom will see to that. *Ouch.*" Andrew lifted his shirt as if to search for where a shooting pain came from, and in doing so, revealed another run of stitches that traveled halfway across his abdomen. Holly gasped.

"Andrew, you've got to get those looked at! The bruising, the inflammation…there could be an infection!"

"I don't think it's nec…"

"You're going! Get in the car. Tim, come with us." After a minute of arguing, Andrew begrudgingly agreed and got into Holly's VW, bloodying the seats. Tim followed in his truck in case one of them was called back to the house.

Two minutes later, they came upon Andrew's wreck, and it was so shocking—it was as if they had seen a corpse on the side of the road. The car was indeed *dead*—wedged against the tree at a near forty-five-degree angle. The windshield was completely blown out, and there were particles of glass a full twenty feet to the right and left of the vehicle. A small branch of the tree was broken off precisely opposite where the windshield used to be and lay next to the car, covered in blood.

Holly was so astounded, she pulled over shaking just after the wreck, and Tim followed suit. They got out and approached the car. Tim, shocked at the amount of blood on the ground, felt as if he were visiting a grave. Nausea struck, and he threw up in the ditch. Blood was everywhere, especially the hood of the car, where it ran off what remained of the hood in all directions, pooling on the ground below.

"I don't feel good either," said Holly. Andrew stood there in a daze as if the accident had happened to someone else. "Andrew... how did you survive this? How did you walk away? How did you make it the mile or so back to the house? The blood—*your bones...?*"

"I don't know. I don't remember. All I remember is seeing my mother in the passenger seat, and then reliving my sister's murder in a dream, and then knocking on the front door. I'm in a lot of pain, but I think she wants it that way. Other than that, I'm okay." He lifted his shirt again to look at his abdomen, and Holly had to look away.

"Tim, we need to do something. We either go public, or we go private, and we'd better make up our minds soon; otherwise, the crowds come back, the TV show comes back, and it all gets in the way of getting the girls. Andrew, your mother said you're good to go, right?" Andrew nodded. "This must be Thomas Pike's plan. He knows Mildred better than anyone."

"We can't take him to the hospital if we're keeping this quiet, and we'd better move this car before someone drives by. We're lucky no one has already." Holly was right. The hospital would want to know how Andrew had managed God-only-knew how many homemade stitches. The police would get involved—and there was simply too much to explain, none of it having anything to do with Mildred.

Tim didn't say anything but went to the lockbox in the bed of his pickup and pulled out a chain. Sixteen minutes later, he pulled the crumbled wreck of Andrew's car up the driveway and around the side of the house where he left it on the lawn, invisible from the road.

CHAPTER 43

Holly kept a close eye on Andrew's state of consciousness as she cleaned his wounds and examined him closer. There was no abnormal swelling—he looked like someone who just had day surgery. As Andrew showered, Tim and Holly waited, listening from the hallway in case he fell in the tub. When he came out of the bathroom, he looked ten times better—the incredible amount of blood on his clothing had exaggerated his condition, but still— what he had been through was beyond explanation.

Tim picked up dinner while Holly continued to monitor Andrew. He was doing well, and with food in his belly, he would be even better. Tonight was Chinese food, and they were all on their second beer as the phone rang. It was Jordan Block.

"I'm working on getting you another cameraman, uh— *bodyguard*. Is everything okay over there?"

"Sort of, Jordan. You'd better hurry up—it's never a dull moment over here."

"What do you mean?"

"It's a long story, but we have a visitor—and—I can't even explain it. You wouldn't believe me. Are you in Wolfeboro?" said Tim.

"No, I'm not. Tell me. What the hell's going on over there?"

"Well, we have a visitor. He came out of nowhere. You won't

believe this because I'm having a hard time myself. His mother haunts him—and—he tried to leave us in the middle of the night last night. The woman yanked the steering wheel and crashed his car, and he's sitting here covered in stitches that *she* gave him." The line was silent for several seconds.

"Wait, I don't get it. Is his mother Mildred Wells? Who is this guy?"

"No. Andrew's a new guy—with a new mother. That's why I wanted you to come over. It's getting weird over here, like, *you can't write this shit.*"

"Why's he there? What's he supposed to do for you, according to his mother? Is he a tough-guy? Does he have some special talent?" *Good question, Jordan.* Come to think of it, Tim couldn't help but wonder that same thing.

"Hey, Andrew."

A nearly inaudible "What?" was heard in the background.

"What do you suppose you're going to do to help us get rid of Mildred?"

"I have no idea," was the answer.

"Did you hear that?" asked Tim, who was laughing at the lunacy—that, and he had a two-beer buzz-on.

"Yeah, I did. So you have another ghost over there? Are you shitting me? Tim…tell me straight. What have I gotten myself into here? Are you all off your meds?"

"I'm not on meds, Jordan. You're invited to look at his fresh stitches any time you like. I towed his wreck, and it's sitting right next to the barn. Come and see all the *blood*. It looks like he was murdered on the hood. I towed it before the TV show could drive by. No police either, so that might be a problem later on. I might need your help with that one."

"Good work—and don't worry about the TV show. I got rid of them for you." Jordan Block leaned back in his chair, deep in thought, at a momentary loss for what to do next. He bounced the end of a pen off of his nose as he pondered. He was only $100,000 invested in this project so far, and he'd get a good chunk of that back sooner or later if all else failed, and he had to sell the house. If Tim turned out to be wholly unreliable and this whole thing was a sham, he hadn't wasted much money.

"I can't be there right now, but let me go, and I'll work on getting you another bodyguard. In the meantime, try to film some of this stuff. Take pictures of the stitches and the truck too. Mail them to me. I'll make it worth your while." He emphasized these last words.

"I can't promise you much in terms of filming Jordan. We've got our hands full. No shit." Block squeezed the pencil in his hand and snapped it.

"Yeah, well—*do your best.*"

"Right," said Tim. They hung up. Andrew spoke as if he'd been waiting for an hour.

"Tim, we've got to fortify this place. She walked in here like she owned the place, and we had no answer."

"Yeah, I know, but we can't. I don't want to mess with Mildred while she's got the girls, Andrew. I can't take that chance." Andrew was prepared for Tim's answer.

"That's one scenario. But what if things change? What if one day instead of corn dolls she drops…something else on your dining room table? Something that makes you wonder how well the girls are doing?" Tim frowned. Andrew spoke plainly, pulling no punches. It was uncomfortable, and Tim didn't like it—but he didn't dismiss it, because Andrew, in the end, was right.

"I've already done some things,"—said Tim—"let me show you something." He stood up and went to the kitchen. When he got there, he opened the drawer that usually held the sawed-off shotgun and froze. *It was gone.*

"What's the matter? Asked Andrew—and then Tim remembered. It was still upstairs in the bedroom. *Careless.*

"Nothing. Stay right here; I'll be right back." A minute-and-a-half later, he returned with the weapon. "So that you know, we've got this. I'm guessing it could obliterate her heart if we get close enough. I keep it downstairs in that drawer during the day and next to my bed at night. I guess I forgot to bring it down this morning."

"That's not a bad start—but this house is still a sieve, Tim. She walked right up to our dinner table yesterday undetected—*and you own a dog*. And she listens in on your conversations. That's how she knew where your ex-wife lived, and that's why Sheila's now dead—and your girls are in her possession." The words stung, and Tim turned to look out the front window.

"I guess a bell on a string in the turret isn't cutting it, huh?" Tim was quiet for a moment after that. "I wanted to try and negotiate with her, but it hasn't happened. Holly kind of interrupted the first time, and you all were at the table the second time. There hasn't been time for negotiations—it's always a threatening situation. We haven't had time to talk about the girls; it's all about staying alive. She probably doesn't want to talk anyway. She just wants vengeance, slow, and painful."

"Well, in the meantime, let's stop her from coming and going as she pleases since the plan's not working anyway. Make her knock at the door or break a window or something. At least we'll know when and where she's coming in. Let's nail the windows and unnecessary doors shut for starters."

Tim had to admit that it was a good idea—one he should have thought of. He and Holly had been bone-tired for a year-and-a-half. A fresh perspective was more than welcome. They spent the rest of the day nailing windows shut and even the side door and the front door at the bottom of the bedroom stairs. Now the only legitimate entrance/exit from the house was through the front porch. Mildred would not be able to enter any other way without breaking glass or splintering wood.

CHAPTER 44

Mildred pulled the Book of Shadows into her lap as the girls slept. She kept them down more than twenty-hours per day as part of the acclimation—they simply weren't ready for more as yet. In the meantime, it had been many years since she'd spent any time with the Book—hefted it, smelled its pages. The last time she had truly opened and explored it, was back in Gideon Walker's shed. She was but a girl then, so inexperienced, so naïve.

The Book wasn't even complete at that point—since then, it had filled out and matured nicely, most likely a reflection of Walker's advancement. Her reading had paralleled his up to a point. They'd learned together, more or less. Together, yet separately—until her escape. The pages had been revealed slowly, over time, because neither was ready for the whole thing all at once.

Thumbing through parts of the Book was nostalgic. She remembered creating her first *runes*. Back then, she didn't even know what they were or what they did. And nowadays they were obsolete little blocks of wood because she'd killed all of the others of her kind, and there was no need to monitor how many revenants were awake or asleep.

She also had little need for *ether* or the ability to knock out her opponents with the liquid—but she remembered seeing the page for the first time so many years ago. The ability to change her clothes had come in handy on a few occasions. Also, the spell to dumb-down the girls—while they—*grieved*, for lack of a better word. *Flip, flip, flip.*

Finally, she came to a page she had never seen but recognized nonetheless. Now that she was dead, she remembered Lyman Helms sneaking up behind her as she was escaping Gideon's cult. He whispered some words in her ear, and as soon as he was finished, she forgot he was ever there. She'd heard the words only once in her life, yet reading them brought everything back. She could even recall them:

"Be quiet, or Walker will hear you, and you'll be right back upstairs. Listen carefully:

Et ultimum carmen brevis est, sed est maxime momenti. Ut pars fiet ex mortuis vivos, unum oportet esse current sponsored per socius. Et plangent membrum est: We welcome tibi. Nos receperint vos. Nos receperint vos."

She would not learn the purpose of those words for years to come—which was mere moments after digging herself out of her own grave. She hadn't expected to be alive, or better put—*undead.* They had robbed her of a decent death—not only Helms but Walker and the whole revenant way of—death. How many times had this happened to souls unknowing?

The words stared her in the face, and just over the top of the book, in the darkness of the den—the girls slept—albeit artificially. It was impossible not to look at the words and then raise her eyes a matter of a few degrees to dream, and to focus as the temptation beckoned. Was it her thought, *or the Book's? It's too early,* she thought. Better to let the girls decide, when the time came. Much, much, better for the long term. *For all of them.* Honesty was the best policy, or at least she'd heard as much.

But it would be so easy to just get it over with…

Et ultimum carmen brevis est, sed est maxime…

(You could say you didn't know…)
Ut pars fiet ex mortuis vivos…
Daughters…forever. A second chance.

Mildred hovered over the page for another moment, then closed the book.

CHAPTER 45

Andrew Vaughn got ready for bed, feeling slightly better about what they had done to the house. All the windows and doors (except the front porch) were now nailed shut, and they had moved the dining room table against the porch door so that it would make tremendous noise if it were pushed against the wide pine floorboards. Tim did a test run but had to stop because one of the table legs didn't slide well and started a long scratch in Tim's beautiful renovation.

"Whoa, whoa, whoa!" He yelled to Andrew, who was playing the role of an intruding Mildred coming in through the porch. "Shit. Look at that. Well, at least we know it works. Makes a hell of a noise. And screw it, it's not my floor anymore anyway."

There was a better sense of security. At least they would know when Mildred was coming and from where. Andrew also switched his bedroom to the front guest room away from the stairs. Holly seemed momentarily upset but couldn't argue against Andrew's safety. They stayed up too late as they seemed to do every night, drinking nervously and trying to laugh, unconsciously shortening the time between that moment and sunrise. The lights eventually went out at 12:15 am.

When Tim heard the noise, he thought it was part of his dream at first—but he'd been on-edge for nearly a year-and-a-half, and his subconscious knew better. *What was that?* He looked over to Holly, who was already staring at him, speechless, proving it wasn't something from a dream. Then he looked at the dog. Neptune's ears were perked as he waited for the distant sound to repeat itself to be sure. It did not. Then he began to whine, gently.

Tim's heart picked up the pace, racing at twice its average speed as fear ran down his body. This was nothing like a dream, where you might either confront your attacker or just run away. He'd faced this particular "nightmare" before and lost both times badly—not even a contest. He reached down on the floor by the bed and grabbed the shotgun realizing for the first time that he might have to use it this time, regardless of whatever had happened to the girls. Perhaps he could conceal it somehow…

He would have to protect the three of them—Andrew was right—there was no guarantee that the girls were…safe. He couldn't bear to finish the thought, nor was there time. As quietly as possible, he swung his feet out of bed and stood, listening to the house but hearing only silence. *Was Mildred making her way through the downstairs? Or worse—finding a place to hide?*

He peered around the doorjamb into the hallway toward the top of the stairs—still nothing. There was no sound or movement from Andrew's room across the hall, either. *Was he still asleep?* Choosing his footsteps carefully, Tim crossed the hall. Despite his best efforts, the boards did creak, and he knew that if Mildred were down there stalking, she would hear him.

Tim peered into Andrew's room and saw he was indeed still sleeping. For a moment, he considered letting him continue, then thought better of it. Guest or no guest, this could mean life or death. An extra set of eyes and ears, and another brain to process it all might help. Tim tapped Andrew's foot with the business end of the shotgun, and he sat up in bed, startled. Tim held his finger to his lips. *Shhhh.*

Andrew's eyes went wide. In seconds he was just as awake and scared as Tim and Holly. He'd been here less than forty-eight hours, and already he knew the whole deal of what it meant to be haunted by Mildred Wells. Very quietly, he put his shoes on and grabbed the baseball bat he slept beside. Despite the odd squeaks and creaks of the floorboards, the four of them made their way down the hallway as best they could, keeping the noise to a minimum.

The stairs were a completely different story. They were so noisy as a group that Tim gave up and walked down the last six normally, albeit cautiously. Neptune seemed oblivious as if it might be an opportunity for a snack in the kitchen. The sense of danger or whatever it was that had made him whine was forgotten.

Tim pointed the shotgun around the corner and looked down the length of the house. The kitchen light was on—just as they'd left it. Nothing moved, and shadows remained fixed. The entire downstairs checked out, with no sign of a break-in—still, nobody dared speak. Tim put his finger to his lips once more, reminding everyone that there was one more room. He pointed to the ceiling.

After directing them all to stand back, he threw the door open and pointed the shotgun up the turret's stairwell. A cool breeze hit him in the face, and any hopes that the noise they'd heard was a false alarm went up in smoke. He flicked the light on just inside the door, and the room above lit up. Again he studied the shadows for movement, and there was some—but he realized it must be the curtain. The contents of the room were not within their line of sight from this awkward vantage point. Tim whispered to Andrew and Holly:

"Don't follow me—I might have to jump down." He then counted slowly with his fingers. 1…2…3…and bolted up into the turret. Andrew ran to the area of the kitchen floor just outside the turret door and squatted down to see better up the staircase. Tim let his eyes get just above the floorboards as he scanned the room quickly and defensively. He would not be jumping down. She wasn't there.

"Nobody?" Andrew asked out loud. It was the first word any of them had spoken since they'd gone to bed.

"No. But she was here." Holly felt a wave of gooseflesh crawl her back. Mildred was in the house not ten minutes ago, but where was she now? Was she watching them from somewhere outside as they stood in their illuminated fishbowl? Or was she at the other end of the house right now, *quietly breaking in?*

"Oh shit, Tim. She might be watching us. I don't feel safe down here." Holly pushed past Andrew with Neptune and headed up the stairs. Andrew followed and sat on the top step, standing guard in case Mildred appeared below in the doorway.

There it was—an unbroken open window. The four nails Andrew had used to seal it were gone. It was if they'd been pulled straight out of the wood and discarded. Four neat little holes with no surrounding damage, as if they'd been pried. The rest of the windows were still nailed shut.

On the desk was tonight's horror—two locks of blond hair bundled individually in strips of black fabric—strips of Mildred's dress. Tim nearly threw up. Frustrated, he burst into angry tears and put the girls' locks up to his nostrils in an attempt to catch their scent, or their shampoo, or something…something… anything. Instead, he caught only rot and the stench of death. *The dress.* His emotions bloomed all at once, and he grew frantic, spiking the locks to the floor as he screamed aloud:

"No! No, God, No! Why? Where is she? Where are my girls?" Andrew wisely reached over to the desk and silently secured the shotgun. "Where the fuck is she?! She must be looking! She wants to see me like this, right?!" Tim stuck his head out of the open window and screamed again. "'Where are you, Mildred? Where the fuck a—" He stopped, mid-sentence.

Not forty feet away, standing on the crest of the barn, stood Mildred Wells.

Mildred's facial features had long since been compromised by time and biology, but inside she was smiling. A surge of dark anger pulsed through her body, and it felt good. Tim's pain was satisfying—a temporary balm for her own and her broken heart. The pleasure wouldn't last; she knew that much.

Her own family was wrongfully taken, broken, and chewed. Well—except for one. She wasn't perfect after all, just like anyone else. But no one would ever take from her again. She stared at Tim Russell and Holly Burns across the roof, enjoying their anguish.

The dog was with them.

The other person—the newcomer—was in there too. The young man. She did not trust him. Surely he knew her whole story by now—and he'd even seen and smelled her up close and personal. *Who would stay after that? He might be there for a reason. Perhaps to try and get her. Who on Earth?—Thomas?*

Holly and Andrew struggled to see what Tim was looking at, but the glare on the inside of the windows made everything outside nearly invisible. They never got to see her standing on the peak of the roof, or her broken smile. As Andrew craned his neck and cupped his hand, trying to catch a glimpse, he felt the shotgun ripped from his hands. Aghast, he stepped back. Tim had it again, and as soon as he had it, he stuck his head back out the window and let both barrels go.

Mildred saw the weapon at the last second, and then felt the sting of hundreds of little BB's on her dead chest and face. Many embedded themselves to remain there—but many missed entirely because the spread of buckshot was too great. What might have been a deadly blast from three feet was only minorly disfiguring from forty.

She hadn't moved since he'd spotted her, and because the gun was out of ammunition, she remained calm, staring directly into his eyes for another moment. Her "smile" was gone now, replaced by requisite anger. The pleasure of this night was over, and the disappointment of her reality began to seep slowly back.

Both Holly and Andrew screamed. Neptune cowered immediately, acting as if the world might come to an end. Tim realized he'd lost his cool and made a big mistake, but he couldn't back down just yet.

"Tim! Oh my God, what are you doing—! Stop, stop!" Holly shouted, and Andrew grabbed the shotgun.

"Your daughters, man. Don't do it!" Tim kept his eyes locked on the wraith across the roof, praying for their collective safety. He would listen to Holly and Andrew later...take his lumps then— but for now, she remained. *Too far. It was too damn far for this gun—but maybe that's good. I shouldn't have done that. I lost my shit. It didn't even faze her. Don't come for me now. Oh, God, please, no. Don't come.*

"Give me that gun."

"You're gonna regret it man, don't—"

"Give that fucking gun right now before she comes. Hurry." Andrew obeyed. Tim reached into his front pocket and pulled out two more shells. He'd have to wait until she got close this time. Very close.

Fatigue washed over Mildred's body, and it wasn't because of the shotgun wounds or her fading pleasure. She hated the man across the roof from her, but at this very moment, she was too tired to care about him or his level of discontent. She was long overdue for an extended healing sleep—*perhaps that was it*. But there was no time for that now because the girls needed her. The debilitating hum of anger had returned, buzzing behind her eyes. Fading fast, she turned away from the turret, walked down the backside of the roof, and disappeared.

Tim saw her turn in the opposite direction and breathed an enormous sigh of relief. *Thank you, God.* He dropped to one knee and let his body slump. Andrew and Holly noticed his body language but needed confirmation.

"Is she gone? Is she gone?!" asked Holly frantically. She and Andrew cupped their hands around their eyes and pressed their faces to the window, and neither saw more than a flash of gray apron. Tim gave a thumbs-up signal but did not speak as he slowly pulled his head and shoulders back inside, his shirt soaked with sweat, his breathing hurried.

"I lost it. I'm sorry. I lost my cool. That was dumb." No one said a word. Holly picked up the locks of hair off the floor and placed them on the desk. They spent the next two hours checking the other windows and doors as a group. Despite Tim's regrets, he never put the shotgun down. After tying Neptune out in the hallway, they eventually went to bed at a quarter past four. Only the dog slept.

CHAPTER 46

Ed Bodwell, the former vigil-leader turned trespasser, heard the shotgun blast from his tent in the fifth row of the grove. This time he wasn't so drunk that he slept through it like he had the car crash. The sound of the gun ripped the quiet New Hampshire night in two and sat him upright awkwardly, wrenching his back. He felt his hip for the clasp on the holster, then slid the long gray barrel of his 1911 out into the night. He knew he wasn't supposed to have any guns on Tim Russell's property, but then again, he wasn't even supposed to *be* on Tim Russell's property anymore—why not bring along some protection?

Ed unzipped the tent flap and climbed out, leaving his flashlight off for the time being. If Tim and his girlfriend were awake at this hour, he sure as hell didn't want them to look out into the field and catch him trespassing. The grove was, of course, dark, and it made getting to the meadow noisy and tricky. He ran into several branches and stepped on many more, taking one across the face, drawing a thin bloody scratch.

Just before the treeline, he heard something behind him as it methodically passed through in the night. Startled, he turned to the direction of the sound and ran the possibilities through his mind. New Hampshire did have black bears, but rarely this far south. Folks up north had to pay special attention to how they disposed of their garbage, but this was seldom the case in Sanborn. It didn't sound like a deer, but he was no expert, especially without the benefit of sight.

Bodwell took a knee and raised the .45 in the direction of the footsteps. They stopped, which frightened him. *Did it see him? Was it—whatever it was—watching?* Five seconds passed, and he flicked on his flashlight. The row of overgrown spruce before him lit up loud and bright, shrinking his pupils to pinpoints. Beyond the first row of spruce was a very shadowy hallway followed by an even darker second row of spruce. Beyond that, he could see nothing at all.

He realized that if he hadn't done so already with his abundance of twig-snapping that the flashlight had *for sure* given away his position—and since Ed had no idea where "it" was, he began to sweat. The grove was still, and although he wanted to explore the reason for the gunfire at the house, his instincts told him he'd better watch his back.

Finally, he heard the crunching of footsteps again, and it was most certainly only two feet making the noise—eliminating deer and bear. *Could it be Russell?* He scrambled to find a gap in the trees so the flashlight could penetrate three rows deep, but it was difficult, and something told him he didn't *want* to know anyway.

Sure, he'd told Tim that he believed there was a Mildred, but it was a half-truth. He'd come for the company and the barbeque. The opportunity to hang out with some real people for the first time in six months—since his wife Alice had died. Now, here in the woods, the man who'd stayed on-property looking for a sense of purpose—wanting to feel as though he was helping—but in reality just being nosy—might get a deadly dose of *mind-your-own-business*. His mind began to explore uncomfortable possibilities it never really had before.

Within thirty seconds, he could tell that the footsteps were headed in the opposite direction, and he made the sign of the cross. *It left.* Now he could explore what the ruckus was about at the house.

CHAPTER 47

Tim physically shook for more than an hour after firing the shotgun, as if he'd drunk four cups of coffee. He realized how lost he was, how badly Mildred affected his family and his everyday life, and how disappointed he was in himself. Holly was even more shaken than Tim was. He admitted that he'd lost his cool, and in doing so, had shown Holly how frightened he was, scaring her further. Indeed not a good thing, but nothing he couldn't make sure never happened again.

Because the nailed windows and doors had not worked out to be as secure as they'd hoped, they kept Neptune's bed in the hallway, leashing him to the railing. Holly was initially against this, and Neptune didn't understand what was going on, so Tim added a length of rope so the dog could easily back his way up to just outside the bedroom door where they could see him. He protested the new location for less than a minute before giving up and collapsing on his bed.

CHAPTER 48

Ed Bodwell stepped into the meadow and looked toward the house just in time to see the light in the turret go out. The kitchen light below was still on, however, and he could see three adults milling about the room in jerky, hectic fashion. Whatever the commotion had been, it was over now—he'd missed it.

Still, he had nothing better to do and wasn't yet ready to go back to his tent. Perhaps it was best to give whatever had wandered past him in the dark (hopefully not the "legendary" Mildred Wells)...time to walk a bit further away before zipping himself into what might amount to a canvas body bag if she were the real deal. *A tent would be a terrible place to be if something wanted to hunt you, come to think of it.*

He'd be a sitting duck in there with someone or something roaming the area. Sure, tents were fun in the confines of a campground or with a family, but those footsteps had spooked him, and all he could do now was think about everything he saw on that damned TV show. He was familiar with the "Legend of Mildred Wells" that *Only If You Dare* had taken so much time and energy to hype. He knew that Mildred and her son had at one time been buried less than a hundred yards from where he now stood. Only thirty or so rows back—the last row of the grove.

He'd walked the whole grove and had seen the very spot,

which was now just an abandoned garden of some sort. There were even some garden markers still stuck in the soil—spinach and lettuce if he remembered correctly. *Disgusting.* Why someone would plant vegetables in the middle of a forest where people used to be buried seemed odd.

Suddenly the kitchen light went out, leaving the entire house dark for a moment. Then the living room light went on, and he saw the three adults passing through on their way to the bedroom staircase. *That's all she wrote*, Ed thought. They were going to bed, meaning he should too. *The show's over—dammit.*

Surprised at himself, he full-on hesitated when it came time to walk back to the tent. A mild wind had picked up, and the noise it made through the trees gave him added pause. He even wondered for a moment if he should just go *home*—but the thought of the empty house—without Alice—was unbearable. He'd done that for the last six months and had slipped into a cauldron of depression—the worst days of his life by far.

The drinking he did tonight paled in comparison to the harm he'd inflicted on his liver those first lonely months. Retirement and everyday life—something he had dreamed of as a working man—was nothing but a slow-drip nightmare of boredom and loneliness. At least being here on Tim Russell's property gave him a sense of purpose. It was something to do. Maybe he could help—*he and his guns.* There just wasn't anything to go home to.

Ed Bodwell finally gathered enough courage to walk toward the dark woods. He could not snap on his light for fear of attracting attention from the house. They'd seen him arrive—his first night here—and the flashlight wasn't even lit. Suddenly, a branch brushed his ear as he ducked through the wild part of the forest on the way to the grove.

When he reached the first row, he clicked on the flashlight and quickly scanned both ends of the corridor. He did so for the second row as well. When he broke through to the third row, he found his tent, about twenty yards to the south.

Climbing into the tent was the equivalent of putting on a blindfold. He heard the night-breeze outside perfectly but could not see through the canvas. The muscles around his ears eventually grew tired as he listened for footsteps. He took a long bubbling pull off of the whiskey bottle and waited for the alcohol to numb things up for him. Finally, he fell asleep, but only about an hour before dawn.

CHAPTER 49

Holly and Andrew sat bleary-eyed at the counter in the kitchen while Tim fried some eggs. Thankfully, the house had not suffered a second visit from Mildred during the night. That was the good news. The bad news was that none of them had slept at all. Andrew broke the silence.

"I never told you about the dreams Thomas Pike put in my head, did I?"

"What?!" said Holly. Tim turned his head, wide-eyed.

"Yeah. I forgot to tell you because that was the night I...left you. The night of the car crash."

"What dreams? How do you know Thomas Pike made you dream them?" Holly asked.

"Because he was like a tour guide or something. Like the freaking *Ghost of Christmas Past* from "A Christmas Carol". I saw Mildred visit Thomas' grave and spit on it after giving him a piece of her mind. Then I saw her kill the cameraman at the top of your stairs."

"We saw that too! The one in the graveyard on Tower Hill! Did you see little Elmer come out of the woods after she left?" asked Holly.

"No. I didn't see that part. It went right into the 'cameraman dream.' Did you see that one? Horrifying. She didn't waste any time on him. It was like watching a panther stalk a calf. Just *ugly*. And I was in some weird point of view where I could see both of them even as he was coming through the house. I knew it was going to happen, but I couldn't wake up."

"Oh my God, no, we didn't see that one, and I'm glad I didn't. We saw her kill Annette and Henry Smith, though. That was *terrible*. Poor Annette. I still have nightmares because, well, because of nearly everything that's happened since I sold Tim this house, but more so because of those dreams."

"You sold him this house?" Andrew asked. Both Tim and Holly nodded.

"That's right, Andrew. You might say she didn't do her homework and threw me under the bus." Despite Tim's fatigue, he managed a smirk.

"That was because I told you, people die in these houses all the time! Many people were also *born* in these houses. I'd be in the library all the damn time looking up...ah—I'm not going to get into it again." She looked at Tim and saw he was teasing her. "You're a terrible person, Tim Russell!" Holly managed a smile, recognizing that she'd been drawn into a teasing trap and had fallen for it. Andrew saw the humor and broke into a smile of his own. He couldn't remember his last laugh.

"Did Thomas "tour guide" your dreams as well?" Andrew asked Tim.

"Uh...I don't remember him escorting us like the *Ghost of Christmas Past*, but I...we knew he was there, didn't we, hon?"

"Yeah, I don't remember for sure either, but I knew it was HIS account of everything." They ate in silence for a moment.

"Another thing I remember as being—just weird. Inexplicable, in a way—" Andrew continued.

"What's that?"

"After she killed the cameraman...what was his name—*Bonnette?*"

"Right. David Bonnette."

"Okay. After Mildred killed him, she sat down on the stairs for—I'm not sure how long, but it was a good chunk of time, like maybe three full minutes. It was like watching an unedited store security tape or something, where nothing happens. All she did was sit down for like—a long time, thinking with her head down."

"Three full minutes? What, like she was sad? Or tired or something?"

"I don't know! I mean, obviously, Thomas wanted me to see it, right? That's my point—it looked like an unedited tape, but yet you'd think Thomas would have 'edited' the unnecessary parts… Does that make sense?"

"That is weird. I agree. I want to see exactly what you saw. Come show me." Tim put down his fork, and the three of them made their way through the house and up the stairs to the spot where David Bonnette died. Andrew ran them through what he saw in the dream. Tim stood in the doorway of one of the back bedrooms and Holly in the other.

"Okay, so he was right here where I'm standing in front of the bathroom, and she was…over there." Andrew, realizing the morbid act that had happened precisely where he stood, swallowed hard. Playing the part of David Bonnette was more than eerie. He looked out over the stairwell across to the little balcony between the two front bedrooms—only about ten or twelve feet away. To have been David Bonnette staring across the dark staircase at an angry dead woman swarming with flies would have been, well, the worst nightmare imaginable. And to have her round the banister and come at him down the short hallway as quick as a cat—Andrew was happy that at least Bonnette didn't have to feel that way for very long.

"So he dropped the camera and fell backward, then she was on him instantly. Like, snap your fingers, it was over…and then all of a sudden she's got the knife out of nowhere and—she sticks him in the chest. I'll never forget seeing that—not as long as I live. I've seen stuff like that in some movies, but it's not the same. Not *at all* the same…" Andrew trailed off, reliving the nightmare privately. Holly and Tim were speechless. Andrew's body language said it all. Mildred was fast—*as quick as a cat*—on top of everything else she could do—something they had not witnessed as yet. Horrifying. Holly broke the silence.

"Uh, so…what happened next?"

"As I said, she stepped over his body and took a seat on the top step. Like this. Then she just sat there."

"Okay, give us the first minute then. Head movements, hand movements, the whole thing. I want to read her body language. Why does a revenant need to take a break? Is it physical? Is it emotional?" Andrew sat like a statue for about twenty seconds, then shifted his hands to his face, as if he were exhausted. He remained that way for ten seconds, then removed his hands from his face and placed them on the top step, his head still looking down at his feet.

"It looks to me like you're—*she's*—tired," said Holly.

"Yeah. Or sad? Or both? That's what I thought, although I might have leaned toward 'troubled.' I didn't even consider that she might be weak," said Andrew.

"Oh, she's plenty powerful, don't forget that. Please don't get sloppy and underestimate her," replied Tim. "She'll kick your ass, just like she kicked mine and David Bonnette's."

"You know what? I do think she's tired," said Holly.

"She didn't feel tired when she nearly took my head off the other day," said Tim.

"Yeah, well… Thomas Pike showed Andrew this 'unedited' dream for a reason…I think. It reminds me of something a friend of mine told me once—we went to college together. He got married too early, and they had a kid before they graduated. I can't recall if it was a boy or a girl, but that's beside the point. It was a messy divorce." Tim's ears perked up.

"I'm listening."

"Well, they did all the stupid things to each other that they do on soap operas and romance novels. Screaming arguments. Dramatic exits. Throwing things at each other—all the wrong stuff. It was like they learned how to be married by watching television. Obviously, they broke up, and the child was used as a chess piece and a weapon. One year he went to pick the kid up for Christmas, and the mother pulled the football away at the last second, claiming it was her year."

"Deja vu," said Tim.

"I knew you'd say that. I didn't tell you this when Sheila took your New Year's because I knew it would only fuel your fire. Anyway, she tells him last minute that it's not his year and he challenges her—says he's coming anyway and *to 'have the kids ready.'* When he arrives, the house is dark, and her car is hidden in the garage—she wanted to make it look like they weren't home. So he parks in the driveway and waits, and waits, and waits. Hours go by, and he even gets hungry, and orders a pizza—had it delivered right to his car.

Meanwhile, he's just sitting there marinating in misery, seething. It started to rain. He was alone with his thoughts, trying to prove a point—tired of her bullshit—and very angry. He told me he was so angry for so long that he began to wish it away. It was taking a toll on his body physically—not just from that day, but the whole slow burn built up over a year or more, capped off by a multi-hour waste of time just before the holidays. It got dark. Finally, he began to pray. Guess what he prayed for."

Tim, who looked worked up over the kindred spirit's plight, spoke first. "He prayed for his kids. He just wanted to see his kids, with no bullshit—for once."

"No. He prayed for his anger to end because he couldn't shake it. It wouldn't leave him even though he was exhausted. It was eating him up and ruining his life. He'd been too angry for too long—and in the end, he believed the stress would kill him. He was bone-tired, going to bed angry and waking up angry. It's a horrible feeling."

"So…you think she's just going to self-destruct?"

"No, I'm not saying that. I don't know how this all plays out. I just think she's rotting from the inside as well as the outside." The room was quiet for a moment as they pondered Mildred's odd behavior, but no definitive conclusions were drawn.

"It's weird, and I don't know what to make of it. Here we go again with Thomas' guessing games. I wish that motherfucker would just write it down or *tell us*—, but he likes to do it the hard way," Tim said.

"Amen! Tell me about it," added Andrew. "I'm probably worse at it than you are. He can't write. I saw him try. It doesn't work. He can hold the pen, but that's about it. He's the reason I was so exhausted when I first arrived here. I think what he showed me in the dream was a clue, but beyond it being a sign of Mildred's weakness, there just isn't enough information given to figure anything else out, like how to kill her or make her leave or whatever. If there were more to it, I'd be seeing him nightly as I did up in Sugar Hill."

"Maybe she's self-destructing. That's all I can think," said Holly. "The longer we stay alive, the weaker she gets."

"Oh, it's got nothing to do with how long we stay alive. She could kill us all ten times over if she wanted to. We're 'lucky' she wants to drag this out. Maybe she'll just tire herself out before she kills us."

CHAPTER 50

Olivia rolled her wrist, and the acorn appeared in her hand. She might have been more surprised if not for the protective sedation. It was still too early to lift that spell—it might even be years before it was safe to do so completely. Their mother's death was still unknown to them, and the news would have to be broken at some point—minus the real truth, of course. And they would ask other questions too—especially when the smell hit them. It was simply too early.

For now, playing games was a good start. Mildred saw the faint smiles of satisfaction with every successful "call." The acorn was only across the den, but it was a fun game for young minds, and brand new to them. She knew that soon they would grow bored of it and ask for bigger challenges. Olivia invented a game where they called multiple acorns back and forth from each other's hands for hours at a time. Were they lucid, they might have giggled more and taken it outside for greater distance calls, but as soon as they showed signs of being fidgety, Mildred put them under again.

It was work, but a welcome distraction. It took less out of her than the revenge game had recently, and there was obviously no time for a much needed long-term rest. And of course, they would never be free—not as long as the girls were missing. The three of them would be hunted for a long while, and it would take discipline and stamina to make it as a family. Mildred's emotions were unsettled and ran the gamut. She still lusted for payback, but also enjoyed her time with the girls. It was too early to give either one up.

Just then, Olivia awoke and roused Vivian. Mildred allowed it as they'd been under for nearly two days. Vivian opened her eyes, but her motions were listless as if she might want to sleep more. Olivia was quite the opposite and attempted to start another game of pass the acorn, but Vivian wouldn't have it. Curious, Mildred watched the scene play out.

Olivia set the acorn on Vivian's leg, but Vivian brushed it off and let it fall to the ground. Olivia called it to her hand anyway and threw it back, hitting Vivian in the forehead.

"Stop it!" said Vivian, but Olivia called it back again and repeated the cycle.

"Stopppp!" repeated Vivian. Mildred let it continue. This was the liveliest she'd seen either girl since the—*adoption*. Was Vivian fighting the spell? Was she growing and gaining strength? Olivia repeated the action.

"Stop, or I'll tell mom!" Mildred's ears perked, and she straightened, hoping for a moment that Vivian might turn to her, looking for relief from her bullying sister. But Vivian's eyes remained fixed. Olivia threw the acorn one more time.

"Mom! Mommmm! Where's mom?" Mildred rose from the shadows to better reveal her presence—as if to say *I'm here, Vivian.* Vivian looked directly at Mildred and spoke once more:

"Where's my mom? Why haven't we seen my mom? When can we go home?" Mildred waved her hand in disappointment, and both girls dropped heavily to the floor. If Mildred still had blood, it would have boiled. Instead, she felt a bitter fire explode in her chest, coursing through her brain and every one of her dead muscles.

Vivian had known. She'd known all along. Somewhere beneath the haze and confusion of Mildred's spell, Vivian knew her mother was missing from her life—and that ran contrary to all that Mildred had believed to this point. *Did Olivia know too? Did Vivian's cries sink in before Mildred's spell had a chance to pause their thinking? Was this all for nothing? A fool's errand?* The frustration bubbled up and into the forefront of her mind.

With the girls out cold and on the ground, Mildred called the Book of Shadows into her hand, opened it, and began to read aloud. The girls would not be waking anytime soon. Furious, she left the den for a reflective walk through the woods. Hours passed with no sign of the searchers. *Had they given up so soon?*

Just to be sure, she walked to within a mile of the house and began dropping bird and squirrel bodies again in case the dogs came back. Not Tim and Holly's dog, but the trained ones—the police dogs. The house dog was barely a dog at all. Not a working dog by any means. More of a helpless pet, and a hurdle to her intents and purposes.

Somehow, somewhere in her revenant heart, she felt something for the whiny beast. He hadn't shown his teeth, growled, or run away when they'd met that first night in the woods. Nor had he done a thing as Mildred had his master pinned to the dining room table. The dog was the first being in over a century to show her even a trace of affection.

On her way back to the coyote den, she killed six more squirrels but picked them up this time and carried them back with her. She also gathered some odd leaves, flowers, and bark. She needed something to go right—some sort of satisfaction to erase the pain of Vivian's words. Today had been extremely disappointing, and she needed a lift. When she arrived back home, she began skinning.

CHAPTER 51

Ed Bodwell decided to spend his days getting to know the surrounding woods better because the nights had become too spooky—if he messed up and didn't drink enough to knock himself out, he'd spent hours in the dark listening—incessantly. It was all due to fear. Fear because he didn't know these woods like the back of his hand yet. He also hadn't set up a proper warning system so he could distinguish between noises and approaching intruders.

Yesterday he'd snuck out of the woods to his truck and driven to the hardware store for nearly three hundred yards of fishing line and to several pet stores to purchase nearly thirty cat-bells. Now he marched the grove stringing the line in concentric circles, knee-high around his tent hanging bells on each length. The bells were high enough to avoid wandering squirrels and rabbits and low enough to remain still in a stiff breeze.

He ran out of fishing line not three rows deep, which seemed reasonable enough, and when he was done, he kept walking for lack of anything better to do. Sundown was still more than three hours away, and there was nothing but this walk, dinner, and the bottle between him and bedtime. As he approached the end of the grove, he began to notice a slew of dead animals—three squirrels and a crow. *What's going on here?*

CHAPTER 52

Tim, Holly, and Andrew all went outside together with Neptune for his last urination before the morning. They went along because it was too damn scary to go alone, and it was also too damn frightening to stay in the house alone while the others walked the dog. Each carried a weapon of some sort, praying that Mildred Wells had given them the night off.

"I like putting him in the hallway as the stairs come up. Even if he only whines at her, it's better than nothing," said Andrew. Holly frowned but agreed.

"It's necessary," Tim added when he saw Holly's reaction. "So. Anyone want to place any bets on what goes down tonight?" Their heads collectively sagged at the prospect of another sleepless night.

"I'm going to go with my gut and say that Mildred leaves us alone and that it's Thomas Pike that shows up—this time with another one of his golden clues. I mean, let's be optimistic. We were talking about it today at breakfast. It just feels like a Thomas Pike night. Plus, he's due. I kind of feel like he wouldn't leave us high and dry for very long. We continue to go toe-to-toe with her every night, without his guidance, right?" Both Tim and Holly reacted passionately yet differently.

"Hahahahaaa—You don't know Tommy *like we know*

Tommy!" was Tim's reply. Holly's was much more severe and scolding.

"He left us for more than a year—betraying us—and put us through hell. Don't believe for a second you can count on him."

"Yeah, but he sent *me*, didn't he?" added Andrew.

"But how's that working out for us?" asked Tim. He was jesting, but he was also speaking the ugly truth."Why'd he send you? Of all people? Because your mom told him to?" Andrew didn't smile back. "Hey, sorry, man, I'm just kidding. But seriously—why do you think they chose you?"

"I have no idea, and you know that—but you understand what I'm saying. Thomas came back. He didn't betray you. What's your prediction for the night, Holly?"

"I…I'm just going to say that Mildred leaves us alone and we all get some sleep. I don't care if it's naive to think so. I don't want to jinx us. Your turn, Tim."

"I'm going to say that…*HEY! Neptune! No!* What are you eating? Holly, shine the light over there, what did he just eat?" Tim ran over and did his best to open Neptune's jaws, but it was too late. Whatever it had been was gone.

"Neptune!" said Holly frustratedly. "Sometimes he goes for the rabbit turds. They make him sick, though if he eats enough of them. Disgusting. Come on, Neptune. Pee already! I want to go back in." After several minutes of close supervision, Neptune finally peed, and they all begrudgingly prepared for bed. Tim never got his turn to make a prediction.

CHAPTER 53

Holly got her wish—and it lasted three hours. The three adults, all exhausted, fell asleep almost immediately and caught up on some of the sleep they badly needed. Neptune fell asleep as well because he'd been drugged by Mildred's squirrel meat. As a result, he would get far more rest than anyone that night.

At 3:15 am, Mildred let herself in, listening carefully to the house and all the snoring coming from upstairs. By 3:19, she was halfway up the stairs, and by 3:27, she had stepped over Neptune's sleeping carcass. There was only one person who might be awake, and that was Holly. Mildred paused and listened once more for more feminine tones of deep sleep breathing—and there they were. *Good.*

Tonight was all about Plan "A"—*revenge*. Plan "B" might not even exist anymore—Vivian had cast severe doubts on the motherhood idea, and Mildred needed to put it aside at least for the time being. With Neptune behind her snoring heavily, the three adults of the house were now within striking distance.

She crept forward five more feet very slowly—and at 3:32 peered in at Tim and Holly. Then she turned and crept seven more feet toward the guest bedroom.

At 3:41, she stood in Andrew's doorway, stepped inside, and shut the door quietly.

At 3:46, she placed the extra pillow over his face and pressed him deep into the mattress. A small amount of sound escaped, so she added her chest and bodyweight to the effort. Andrew's kicks and struggles bounced off the bed but were not enough to be heard. Finally, he lay still.

At 3:52, she stood up slowly and removed the pillow. Andrew's face appeared blue in the filtered moonlight. The discovery of his body would be devastating for them, yet satisfying for her. The slow grind was playing out rather well. She was almost done toying. There wasn't much left to Plan "A," and soon it would be time to close the book on Tim Russell and Holly Burns—but there *was* time for one more bit of fun tonight.

With no more need for stealth, Mildred strode across the hallway, creaking as she went, not caring as much if they woke up—in fact, they were expected to. The first thing she did was call the shotgun from Tim's side of the bed and place it gently in the hallway. They were still asleep. Why not see how dramatic she could make this?

Mildred walked casually to the edge of the bed and peered down at Tim, inches from his face. They began to share her flies. Finally, Tim opened his eyes and shrank back into the bed, screaming. Holly did the same, except she didn't yet realize what was happening. When she finally did lay eyes on the shadow standing over Tim, she fell out of bed and backed herself into the far corner. She screamed for help. *Why wasn't Andrew coming?*

Tim thought about going for the shotgun, but Mildred had taken up all of his personal space. Here they were, nearly face-to-face once again in the span of but a few days, and he knew better than to lash out. This was her show, and she could do anything she wanted, no doubt in his mind.

Mildred stood over Tim, practically begging for him to try something, but it seemed he'd learned from their last encounter. She wouldn't mind giving him another beating, but it would not be as satisfying if he didn't throw the first punch. Holly wouldn't stop screaming—perhaps it was time to prune that branch. There wasn't anything left to do, after the corn dolls, the locks of hair, and the soon-to-be discovery of Andrew's body.

Perhaps kill Holly now and leave him with nothing—then hunt him down in a year or so—after he'd moved and began to put his life back together.

But surprisingly, she heard a click behind her. Andrew stood in the doorway.

"Back off, or I'll blow your heart out of your chest."

How?! She'd smothered him for at least six minutes. Truly astonished, she turned slowly to face Andrew and size him up. *Something felt wrong about him.* Again—why was he here? Or a better question: *Who put him here? Was he sent by an unknown revenant? Was he a revenant himself?* He certainly was not like her. He was weak, and—

"Where are his girls? You're going to take us to his girls right now. Take us there, and I'll let you go." Andrew obviously had no real idea of who she was or what her goals were, which only added to his mystery. *He had no clue.* It didn't make any sense, and it made her feel strangely uneasy. It was time to go.

With a wave of her wrist, she pulled the shotgun out of his hands and turned it on him. She could give him both barrels here and now just to see what happened but in a way *she already knew.* Somehow he would live, and after that—Well, what had happened so far was a sign that he most likely had more energy than she did. It was best to get away now and figure a better way around him.

Holly stopped screaming, just as surprised as everyone else. Tim lay on the bed two feet behind Mildred, blown away by Andrew's courage. Andrew shivered, terrified that his weapon was now in her hands as he knew it would be, but what other move did he have? By now, he realized what his mother had put him up to—he would live—or maybe be brought back from the dead—but the *pain*… The pain of a car crash had been nearly limitless. Whatever had just happened to him in the bedroom left him feeling nauseous—but he knew a double-barreled shotgun blast might very well cut him in half. What could be worse, aside from perhaps being burned alive?

Mildred began to walk toward Andrew, pointing the shotgun, backing him up into the hallway. Before she took a left toward the stairs, she swung the gun like a bat, connecting with his jaw. Andrew fell to the floor unconscious. Mildred stepped over the sleeping dog and walked down the stairs pulling the nails from the sealed door and leaving it open as she headed left for the woods.

CHAPTER 54

"Oh my God, Andrew!" Holly rushed to his side and examined his head as best she could. He was already starting to come to. "Can you hear me?" she said. He blinked.

"Yeah, I can hear you. Oh, shit, that hurts." Andrew sat up as the clouds in his head slowly parted. "Well, we were all wrong with our predictions except for Tim, maybe, because he never made one." Holly had to think for a minute what he was talking about and then remembered—the predictions they had made about what would happen that night. Holly had said that they would get a good night's sleep. Andrew noted that Thomas Pike would visit someone and give them more information on Mildred. Tim had been cut-off before making his.

"Oh, I made one, Andrew. I just didn't want to share it. It was something like what just went down. I was right about that, and about one other thing though—we all survived."

"Sort of," Andrew semi-agreed. Just then, Holly noticed that Neptune had remained unnaturally silent.

"Neptune!" She abandoned the recovering Andrew and ran to the dog's side. Thankfully he was warm and breathing, but still unconscious. "She…drugged him. Or put him to sleep. That thing on the lawn that he ate last night! Tim, do you think…" Tim nodded.

"Yeah, I bet that was it. She laced something and left it out in the grass—which is creepy as hell because it means she's watched us take him out to pee. I'm surprised she didn't just kill him. Maybe that would have made too much noise? Tim's words left them all speechless. Andrew changed the subject.

"Did you see what she did? The same thing she did with the knife in the dining room, except it was the shotgun—right out of my hands." Holly, whose mind had not stopped racing for ten full minutes, interjected, near panic.

"Tim, listen. It's time to go. We need a break. You wanted to stay here because you wanted to negotiate with her—but it's not working. She comes here almost nightly, and we're not getting anywhere! We're all bone-tired, and at the very least, it wouldn't be a bad idea not to be so available until we can at least regroup and recover!" Tim grimaced and lowered his head, knowing he had to disappoint her one more time.

"You've got a point, Holly, and I think about this very thing every day. But I think maybe you should go, and I'm not saying that to be dismissive, I just—I know this is killing you. I know it's no good. *I* have to stay—not to be a hero but because my girls can't afford for me to take a personal day. Besides that, I'm not sure Andrew even has the option to leave—*do you?* What happened to you tonight anyway, Andrew? How did you end up with my shotgun in the hallway?'"

"It… It's all cloudy now. She hit me in the head pretty hard and I have a huge headache, but I'm pretty sure I just picked it up off the floor in the hallway." Tim looked at him, momentarily puzzled.

"Well, that's weird. Did she put it there? But then, why would she leave it there for you to pick up?"

"I…I don't remember. I'm not even sure I picked the gun up in the hallway. I just remember pointing it at her and telling her to back off. It's almost as if I sleepwalked."

"Sleepwalked? Did you have a Thomas Pike dream?" Andrew

shook his head no as Tim tried to make the pieces fit. "Hmmm. But—you didn't remember your car crash right away either, did you?"

"Uh, all I could remember that time was seeing my sister get murdered again—in a dream. Then some bits and pieces came to me later, like part of being sewn up."

"Okay, well, hopefully, this will come to you. But, Holly—honey—you can't stay here. At least take a break. Visit your mom, or your friend Amy. Come back later if you feel up to it, but this is going to be a Mildred Wells/Thomas Pike/Andrew's mom 'extravaganza' until the end, and we're going to see it through. Andrew will stay with me."

Holly said nothing but only stared at Tim blankly with frustration. She was exhausted and couldn't think straight. *Why couldn't he see it her way, at least for a day or two—enough to gather their strength, think outside the box and come back with a new plan?* They'd reached an impasse as a couple, and even though they weren't "breaking up," it felt as though they might be. It was also possible she might not see him alive again. Still, Holly could stay no longer. She wasn't herself, wasn't helping the way she knew she could if not so strung-out. She also couldn't support a plan she didn't believe in.

"Alright, I'll go to my mom's. But try to be near the phone as much as possible. I'll buy you some more phones. Put one in every available jack. I'm going to check in early and often. But I don't want to leave this minute. I'll leave when the sun comes up." She might have left immediately if it weren't for the thought of driving down Lancaster Hill Road in the dark. For this reason, she decided to wait.

At dawn, Neptune was back up and around, as though nothing had happened. At least now, he wouldn't have to go to the vet—although in a way, she longed for a reason to take him with her. Mildred's shocking show of humanity surprised her, however, and Holly's worries for Neptune's well-being faded to the background.

Neptune, as much as it pained her, should stay with Tim. He was another set of eyes and ears and a passive warning system. *Just check the lawn before those late-night walks, Tim.* There were hugs and tears as she packed her things into the Volkswagen and drove out, and she even wondered if being away would prove to be any more restful. It would certainly be safer, but *restful?* Maybe not.

CHAPTER 55

Tim and Andrew had breakfast and coffee after Holly left.

"Well, I feel a little better that she's gone," said Tim. "I hated seeing her so upset. I'll bet you dollars to donuts, however, that she'll be back as soon as she clears her head."

"Yeah, you can't blame her. I mean, she's right. We aren't getting anywhere with Mildred. She's walking all over us. I just wish we'd been given some more help—from Thomas. That guy is a real downer. This has been the most painful week of my life." Andrew's scars from the car crash were still fresh, although healing.

"Do those wounds still hurt?" said Tim.

"No, not really. The one on my stomach does, but this morning it's all about this damn headache!" He raised his hands and massaged his temples.

"The same one you had right after Mildred left?"

"Yeah."

"Do you remember anything else, besides picking up the shotgun in the hallway?" Andrew had taken a bite of toast and was chewing it as he stared at the wall, deep in thought. He was in the middle of remembering something.

"'Just as you said that—*YES*. Yes, I do remember. Wow. I remember it all. *She smothered me* with a pillow. My God, you're right. She's strong. She pinned me to the bed—I couldn't see, I couldn't breathe, and I couldn't move. I'm not sure she didn't kill me." Tim took a nervous step back.

"Whoa—*you*—you're not a ghost now, are you?" Tim stepped forward again and poked Andrew's arm. It was solid—not ghostly.

"No, I don't think so. But isn't it strange that I could have easily died two times now since I got here?" Tim put his coffee down, wide-eyed.

"Your mother," said Tim. Andrew nodded. "It never occurred to me that you might have died in that car crash, but it makes sense now that you know you were smothered." Andrew kept on nodding. "And—*my God...* If she killed you last night, that means she might have been coming to kill us too."

"Meaning Holly was right to leave, and maybe we should too," Andrew finished Tim's thought. Tim kept quiet as he thought it all through. There was a distinct frown on his face. Fifteen seconds later, he spoke again.

"Where the hell is Jordan Block and his new bodyguard?" Andrew could tell that Tim was not ready to leave. "And Andrew, if Holly calls and you answer the phone, don't tell her you might have died last night."

"Okay, well, I hope you have a ton of aspirin here, and if you don't, I should go out and get some because I have a feeling I'm going to be in a lot of pain until this is all over." While Andrew went to the Franklin Pharmacy, Tim got on the phone.

CHAPTER 56

"**P**ut me through to Jordan Block, please. Tell him it's Tim Russell, and tell him I caught the woman on camera." Tim was tired of waiting and didn't wish to be held up any longer. Block himself picked up less than a minute later.

"*You got her?* What was she doing? When can I see it?!" Jordan Block was elated.

"You can see the footage as soon as you send us the fucking bodyguard, Jordan. You're missing out big time. Lots of sightings—almost nightly actually, and we don't even have time for the perfect close-ups if you know what I'm talking about." Block was temporarily confused.

"Wait, so you didn't get her on camera, but you've seen her? Why'd you tell my secretary..."

"Because our lives are being threatened nearly every night, Jordan, we need help here, especially if you want somebody to film it. You should probably be sending *two*, one for protection and the other for filming. Why's it taking so long? The camera is still downstairs in the corner where your last guy left it.

Listen to this Jordan—you'll finally understand after I tell you—she was standing over my bed last night. I woke up to flies landing on my fucking face. You'll forgive me if I didn't have time to hoist that thing on my shoulder and ask her to strike a pose."

The other end of the line was silent for a moment, then Tim heard a silent curse under Block's breath. He was pissed.

"Look, don't ever lie to me again to get me to come to the phone. *Ever*. I'm no dummy Tim, and even though I bought your house, I could probably sue you for many things—even if they're frivolous— to make your life shit again, at least financially. So don't yank my chain. You want me, you call—and if I'm busy, you leave a message. I will call you back. Let's just start there, alright?" Block continued:

"Second, I'm trying to find you a bodyguard who will not only uproot his life and fly across the country but who will accept the fact that this is a dangerous job. That other asshole blabbed to all his buddies. He told them what happened, and half of them believed him. He was my best guy. They all looked up to him. Some of them think he's crazy now, but they don't dare say it to his face. I'm suing his ass too so that he keeps his mouth shut from now on."

"Third, I'll give you fifty grand if you pick up that goddamn camera and get a decent shot of her coming at you. Drop the thing when she gets to within twenty feet if you have to, but there it is, on the table. *Fifty grand*."

"That's not happening, Jordan. It's not like she comes at us in broad daylight from the middle of the field. You turn, and she's in your face. Holly left us last night. She needs a break. Can't take the sightings. Hell, I can't take them either, I'm just more desperate than she is."

"'Us'?" said Jordan. "Who's 'us'?"

"Excuse me?"

"You said, 'It's not like she comes at *us* from the middle of the field.' Who else is with you?"

"I told you already. The kid who was in the car crash and his mother stitched him up. Come on, Jordan, tell me you're paying attention. There's a hell of a movie writing itself over here. Sue if you want, but gimme a fucking break and do your job."

"Why can't this douchebag pick up the damn camera and point it at her? Tell *him* I'll give him the fifty grand."

"Because it's not about the camera. It's about survival."

"This smells like bullshit, Tim. You'd better not be bullshitting me."

"I'm not bullshitting you, and neither is your ex-bodyguard."

"I've got to go. Let me work on this. I'm going to have to open my wallet a little wider." Block hung up without waiting for Tim's response.

Tim made three more phone calls, the first to Johnny Upson, his co-worker in Massachusetts, and the second to Holly. She hadn't taken a personal day that day but instead went to work for fear of being alone in the house while her parents were out. She still sounded exhausted, yet pleased he had taken the time to let her know things were alright. Tim was careful not to reveal Andrew's revelation at breakfast.

The last phone call was to the conspicuously absent Chief Galluzzo, who, along with his searches, had all but disappeared.

"So how're those searches going if I might ask?" Tim mocked. The answer was choppy, disgusting, and nearly incoherent.

"Ah, right. Tim, well, it's been some time now, and there's only two of us—Gomzi is new, and there's only so many times you can beat a path through those same woods…"

"Please, Chief, call me Mr. Russell. Tell me Chief, weren't you coordinating with Franklin and Northfield too? Weren't they assisting your department in finding my two little girls?"

"Listen, T—Mr. Russell, I hear the sarcasm in your tone, and frankly…"

"Well, maybe I should ask the newspapers what they think of the effort put forth in finding them, Chief. I don't know about you, but you haven't closed the investigation, and no one else has either. You're all trying to let it die on the vine. But I'm not gonna let you. You start those searches up again, or you're going to hear about it if it's the last thing I ever do. I bet there are a lot of folks who would *love* a cushy job like yours."

CHAPTER 57

Mildred left the girls asleep as she was in no mood to hear the wrong thing come out of Vivian's mouth right about now. To settle her anger, she hunted, for they would be hungry when they woke—and while she did, she laid more bait even though the police searches had inexplicably died down recently. All the while, Mildred brooded over who the newcomer could be. She'd killed him—it was a near medical *certainty*, and yet he'd popped up behind her holding the one weapon with the potential to end her existence. He was unpredictable—and last night was too close for comfort. *It couldn't be an accident.*

It was unnatural for him to be in the house, and yet, there he was, and there he stayed. There was odd defiance to his presence as if he hadn't a care—this wasn't just one of the townies who had gathered in the field.

He was here for her. A degree of paranoia crept in. The more she thought about it, the more she suspected Thomas Pike. But— *weren't he and Elmer gone forever?* If they weren't—*Oh, if they weren't—well then, that would change everything.*

Suddenly in the distance, she heard dogs. They were back after all, after their unexplained break—closer than ever. She could feel pressure mounting from so many different sides—all kinds of pressure: The dogs, *"Andrew,"* and on top of all that, the *Vivian rebellion*—all working hard on wearing her down, tiring her out. But she could not—*would not*—lose again. She refused to lose every single phase and every single aspect of every single chapter of her sad and overextended life.

It would be easy to return to the house that night and simply finish them, but that would not be a job well done. She had not had time to set things up correctly the way she envisioned. It would be anticlimactic to show up mid-day and simply snap necks. Tonight might not be a good night either—they would most likely be over-prepared for her, and the dog would not be sedated.

More than anything, she was rattled, unsettled—off her game and in a word, exhausted. And the girls would need to eat soon.

It was better to rest and think, if her anger would subside, just for a night. Maybe Vivian would keep her mouth shut, and an evening with the girls would be a welcome distraction from her pain. Perhaps a different emotion could have a turn, at least for a few hours. Rest, think, and strike at a time when Tim and company weren't so ready. Keep them guessing. They must be tired too.

CHAPTER 58

Thomas Pike had been waiting for the right moment to reveal Mildred's location, and this, he recognized, could be the night. Mildred had been on a rampage of late—on the offensive nearly every night. It was dangerous to split up the living people at a time like this because there was safety in numbers—but Thomas knew Mildred was tired now, so he contacted Andrew's mother once again.

CHAPTER 59

Tim raked a small section of lawn before letting Neptune out, then followed him around for five minutes very carefully until he peed. He didn't want there to be any "treats" left for him ever again. Luckily Neptune did his business quickly—*good boy*. Now the dog was in his strategic spot halfway down the hallway, and Tim and Andrew even rigged four bell-tripwires near the bottom of the stairwell as an extra-added measure. Tim put the shotgun right in the bed with him where Holly used to sleep, and all were asleep by midnight.

At 12:20 am, Andrew began a very detailed dream of he alone walking through Tim's meadow, through the grove, and into the deep woods. There were no breaks in the dream. From time to time, his mother appeared by specific landmarks, like a stone wall or a fallen oak. Andrew felt as if he were floating just above the forest floor as the dream seemed to pass at twice-realtime. This was not only a dream—but a map.

Suddenly Andrew awoke. The bedroom was dark when it should be illuminated by moonlight. It took him a second, but very soon he realized it was because the windows were blocked by someth—

It was *mother*, inches from his face, staring him down.

His heart skipped a beat and lagged before pumping again.

His body was trying to heal but, once again, would go sleep-deprived. *I must be a candidate for a heart attack*, he thought, but Mother didn't seem to care.

Quietly he rose and dressed as she waited impatiently, and when he was ready, she followed him past Neptune and down the stairs. He was careful not to ring any of the little bells strung on the fishing line. In five minutes, they were out the front porch door and walking briskly toward the woods. As he crossed into the grove, mother disappeared, but he kept on the route he'd been shown as he realized what his mission must be.

CHAPTER 60

Mildred read the Book to herself in an attempt to relax, but it wasn't working. The girls were still artificially sleeping because her mood had not changed as she'd hoped. The possibility of Thomas Pike lurking in the shadows of her life opened a can of worms in her head, and the crippling anger would not die down even for a second. She was so tired, yet so restless—this was madness. Putting the Book down, she stood, stepped out into the night to try and walk it off.

CHAPTER 61

Andrew marched on through the woods as quietly as he could, but he felt oddly detached from his body. It reminded him of some of his less-than-stellar days at UNH when he drank too much. No matter how badly he abused himself, there was still a little voice in his head, reminding him he would pay the next day. A sober Andrew—a sliver of conscience trying to help—but most often failing.

This was dream-like, but not a dream at all. Andrew was conscious enough to know that if he turned his ankle, he was going to fall—which he did twice. He also felt the cold much more than he would in a dream, and he even had to clasp his hands over his ears at one point to warm them up.

CHAPTER 62

Mildred had already thinned out the local wildlife surrounding the den, as she didn't want hungry coyotes around the sleeping girls while she was away. Occasionally she might see a deer, but most often, they smelled her long before she smelled them and kept clear. But now, curiously, came a crunching sound that caught her attention.

She stopped walking to focus on the direction it came—and waited. It approached—whatever it was, and she realized that its path was near dead-on headed for the coyote den and the girls. How many legs? *Crunch, crunch, crunch, crunch… Two* legs. *Could it be? It can't be.* She called the knife.

CHAPTER 63

Andrew continued his lonely trek through the dark woods, surprisingly unafraid. His mother appeared from time to time to keep him on track and provide direction, but otherwise, he felt like a passenger riding on his own shoulder. If Andrew turned back, his mother would punish him as she did when she crashed his car—so he chose to leave the driving to others— *decision free*. It would probably hurt where he was going (*it would most definitely hurt, let's face it*), but it was entirely out of his hands.

Or maybe it *wouldn't* hurt this time. Another theory popped into his head—an assumption that made a lot more sense than sending the troops on a suicide mission—Mother may just want him to remember this walk because it was completely off the beaten path. Memorize it, and then bring the mob.

He found himself always having to take his hands off of his cold ears to part branches. He stepped over streams and marshy areas. Just when he thought he was losing his way, he'd see her again, up close in the darkness, next to a different memorable landmark. He logged them in his mind the best he could: Stonewall, a wall of roots, crisscrossing pines, deer skull. Finally, he looked up after passing through an unusually thick cluster of saplings to see his mother in a small clearing, one finger to her lips, pointing to two spruce trees with twin half-buried boulders beneath them—nearly invisible in the darkness.

Andrew stepped forward slowly and cautiously, sensing that this might be the end of the journey. *Where was Mildred? Were the girls alive or dead?* He hadn't yet noticed the camouflaged entrance between the boulders to the den beneath and turned back to his mother for more direction.

She was gone.

Suddenly he was alone. The auto-pilot dissolved away, and any sense of protection disappeared with it. Now, all of the decisions were his again, and he had no clue what to do. His stomach swirled as he began to cope with the fact that he'd been unceremoniously dumped in the face of danger—in near-total darkness. All of the sounds of the forest—or the suspicious lack of them—perked his ears. He didn't dare move—frozen with fear and indecision—just two boulders under some trees, about fifteen feet away.

To stomp and crunch his way to them now seemed foolish. He hadn't cared about the noise until now, snuggled beneath a security blanket that had just been ripped off the bed. He didn't have to care, and all of a sudden—he did. *Mother…is this about Tim's daughters, or my sins back in Sugar Hill? Does it always end with punishment from now on?*

CHAPTER 64

Tim awoke to a knocking on the front door. He looked at his watch: 6:17 am. *Who the hell is that?* He woke up quickly and grabbed the shotgun, which still lay where Holly used to, and on his way down to the front door, he glanced in on Andrew—who was missing again. The kid was—*a good kid*—but troubled or cursed—*whatever*. Where the hell was he *now*? Did he try to leave again? Tim peeked out the sidelight window next to the front door and saw the silhouette of a gigantic man blocking out the morning sun. Suspiciously, he cracked the door.

"May I help you?"

The man said nothing but held out a business card. Tim hid the shotgun behind his back as he reached for it—and as he did, he realized the man's hand was easily twice the size of his own. Tim read the card:

Here's your new bodyguard, Russell. His name is Koji. He's an ex-sumo wrestler from Japan. Sorry, he doesn't speak any English, but that might be a good thing if everything you say is true-haha. I'll call you when I get a chance. —Jordan

What the fuck, thought Tim. *Does this man even know what he's here for?* Tim revealed that he had a shotgun, but was sure to point it at the floor, then he stepped aside and motioned for the giant to come in. Koji eyed the gun respectfully and understood that it was not meant for him.

"Can I get you any—" Tim quickly remembered that the man didn't speak English. "Never mind, I forgot you don't—" he caught himself again. *What to do?* Tim decided to bring the man to the kitchen and see if he wanted some coffee or something to eat. On the walk through the house, he wondered if the man lived in the United States or if he had flown directly from Japan. *Do they drink coffee? Or is it tea? I don't have any tea in the house. Shit. And breakfast? I have no idea. I'll worry about that as soon as we find Andrew. Damn you, Jordan.*

Tim turned around as he crossed into the kitchen and noticed that the ex-sumo had already found Jordan Block's movie camera that had been left by Mark, the previous bodyguard. *This guy's all-business*, Tim thought and put the shotgun safely in the drawer.

Koji stepped into the kitchen and scrutinized the room, checking the porch entrance as well as the sliding glass door on the way to the side entrance. When he finished his inspection, he stood in the breakfast nook where he could see both doors, put the camera on the floor by his feet, and crossed his hands just underneath his ample belly.

Tim pointed to the coffee maker, which was still switched off. He took note and frowned. Should he be worried about Andrew? *Yes, most likely.* Unfortunately, there was no time for that right this second—the new guest—or employee (?)—required his full attention. Tim clicked the machine on and continued to gesture frustratingly, tipping an imaginary cup to his lips, pantomiming a coffee drinker. Koji stared blankly for nearly ten seconds before giving one shake of his head.

Then Tim repeated the process with the refrigerator door open. *Eggs?* No. *Toast?* No. *Pancake mix?* Tim didn't bother to look over at Koji after picking up the box of Aunt Jemima. Suddenly he felt choked up. Tim looked at the expiration date on the package, realizing the last person to touch this particular box must have been Olivia. That was over a year ago when the house was brand new to them, and they were over for their very first visitation weekend.

So much had happened since then. Sheila was gone. The girls—were gone—*for now*, he quickly reminded himself. And Holly—and Johnny—and Thomas. And maybe even Andrew, who didn't have a working car anymore and was nowhere to be seen. It might be down to just him, Koji and Mildred—and Koji might not even know the real reason he was here. Changing the subject, he casually wiped the tear that had threatened to run down his face and forged ahead.

"Okay, I don't know what you like, Koji, but *hellllp yoursellllf.*" He spoke overly loud and slow as if that would make it any easier for Koji to understand. He accompanied his little speech with a long sweeping gesture toward the open fridge door, and Koji got it, confirming this with one nod of his head. With that, Tim relaxed a tiny bit. They were communicating, at least—as much as they could for the moment.

Now, where the hell was Andrew?

Just then, he heard the sound of Holly's car coming up the driveway. *Holly—thank God! Excellent timing*, he thought.

He went out to greet her but had to wait an extra fifteen seconds as she backed up and turned her car around to face the road. *This place is no good for her*; he lamented. Tim was so immersed, so committed to seeing things through; he didn't even entertain the thought of escape anymore—he almost didn't care about anything else. The emotion, the fatigue—the commitment—was a heavy load. *Was he getting sloppy?*

Holly opened her door and climbed out. She was happy to see him but wore the same look of concern she had on her face the day she'd moved out. He couldn't blame her for a second. He watched as her eyes left his face and went straight to Koji, who had followed Tim out of the house carrying the movie camera.

"Is that the new bodyguard?" she asked. Tim nodded.

"He showed up ten or fifteen minutes ago. *Not a lick of English!* I'm not even sure he knows what he's signed up for. All he did was hand me a note from Jordan, who said he'd call when he gets a chance." Holly rolled her eyes.

"Great. So what's he doing? Just following you around?"

"Kind of. He's only been here for about twenty minutes. I've been playing charades with him trying to find out if he wants something to eat."

"Yeah, well, it looks like you might need to do some grocery shopping. He's a big boy. Does he like donuts? I brought some." Holly opened the back door and pulled out a box and a small tray of coffees. There were three cups.

"Where's Andrew? Still asleep?" Tim was just about to mention him.

"No! He's gone again! I have no idea where he is."

"Cut it out." Holly looked Tim in the eyes and knew he wasn't joking. 'Where could he go? Is his bag still here? Did he sleep in his bed?"

"Honey, I don't know—I just woke up. The doorbell woke me up. Koji. I looked in his room for a quick second and saw his bed was slept in but empty. And I've been pantomiming ever since. I don't know." Tim was stressed. Holly looked stressed. She sighed.

"That's why I hate this place. I left for a while, and I missed you, and I felt some of my courage coming back, and then I pick a sunny morning to—come back, and..." Holly couldn't finish her sentence.

"I hear you. I'm glad you came, though. Welcome back."

"I'm not sure I'm 'BACK-back,' I don't think I can stay here, I..."

"I get it. That's fine. Don't worry. I didn't mean 'welcome back' to stay overnight, I just meant—well, thanks for coming to visit." Suddenly, Koji began speaking rapidly in Japanese. Holly and Tim looked his way, and then toward what he was looking at.

Andrew came stumbling out of the woods at the corner of the driveway. His shirt had a pyramid-shaped triangle of blood that began near his neck and gradually widened until the hemline at his waist. The blood was nearly dry again, just like the morning of the car crash. The stain continued onto Andrew's pants, stopping at his thigh. He must have lost a lot of blood—again. Holly gasped but did not scream this time.

Koji ran to block Andrew from further approach, but Tim called him off and ran to Andrew's aid. His stumbling ended in a hard fall, and from the looks of him, it was the last of many. Twigs and leaves were stuck to the shirt, his hair, his pants, and his hands. It was as if he had bathed in blood from his neck to his waist.

"Help him up! Help him up!" Tim barked twice at Koji, who didn't understand the words but understood the point. Holly joined in too and looked closely at Andrew's neck.

"He's all stitched up again. Tim, he's got stitches across his neck."

"Okay. Put him down. Put him down." Koji understood, and they lowered Andrew gently to the lawn. Tim ran to the house and unraveled a garden hose that probably should have been put away for the season, but thankfully wasn't. A slow trickle of water flowed from the hose as he put it up to Andrew's lips. "Are you okay, buddy? Andrew... Andrew, can you hear me?" Andrew remained unconscious until Holly took the hose from Tim and began to clean the stitches on his neck. The cold water woke him, and he slowly opened his eyes.

"I'm okay. I'm okay. Very thirsty." Holly put the hose up to his lips again, and he drank for nearly a minute. After that, he laid back on the lawn, exhausted. Nobody said a word. To assault him with questions wouldn't be helping. Tim looked up at Koji, who was diligently scanning the woods and the surrounding area for threats. *Maybe he does know what he's in for,* Tim thought. *Either that or he knows something chewed Andrew up and spat him out, and that "thing" is probably still in the woods.* Andrew coughed twice and began to sit up. Holly and Tim helped.

"I think I saw where your girls are." Tim stared aghast.

"Where. Andrew, I know you're hurting, but we have to go there—as soon as possible. We have to—can—can you—do you think you can make it?"

"Tim, look at the blood—he can't possibly—"

"No, I can't yet. I'm sorry. I saw—I don't know, a cave or something. Give me an hour, and we'll see. But first, get me inside. Get a piece of paper. I need to write things down. My head—I think I'm dehydrated. My neck hurts. I don't remember everything yet—what happened—how it happened." Holly let Andrew's own words resonate. Tim, while right to want to rush to the girls' aid would have to realize that Andrew was mortally wounded, despite whatever artificial support his mother was providing. And besides that—*would Mildred be waiting?*

"Did you see them? Are they alive?" Tim was manic.

"No. I didn't see your girls. I saw two boulders. I was shown—two boulders. She pointed to them."

"Who? Your mother?" Andrew nodded. Tim fell silent, temporarily out of questions.

"Tim—it was just a couple of boulders. I didn't see anything moving. I'm not even sure what it all meant. I—I just don't want you to get your hopes up." Tim sat back on his heels with a grim look on his face, then nodded once.

"We'll see. Let's get you inside." Tim motioned to Koji, who picked Andrew up all by himself and carried him inside the house. Tim followed with Holly close behind. Before she closed the door, she was sure to take one more look back at the woods.

CHAPTER 65

Mildred pulled the long blade out of Andrew's chest and watched him slump to the forest floor. He fell against a nearby tree and sat there upright, *undoubtedly* dead. He'd heard her at the last minute when it was far too late, and her blade had already crossed his throat. She felt a measure of relief, even if only temporary. This enigma of a man was adequately taken care of this time, and if he got back up, she'd put him back down. His strength was no match for her, despite her fatigue.

Seeing Andrew out this far, however, was bad. He, along with the dogs the previous day were signs that they were on to her, and she would have to move. They were getting closer, slowly but surely, and hiding places for living children in October were few and far between. She felt the added pressure and the burden— putting off previous plans yet again. Perhaps she shouldn't have waited so long. She felt so—heavy, so worn and beaten, though she hadn't taken any blows. It was hard to focus, and it was hard to remember her original motivations.

Thomas. Tim Russell. Holly Burns. Elmer. Betrayal. She recited the names in an attempt to rekindle the rage that might somehow get the job done and put things to rest. Recently these thoughts only made her shoulders drop, and her legs wobble. A long sleep would help. That was all she needed. *Nothing's right when you're tired.* Get the girls ready and then put them all down for a long nap. Start anew in a few years as a family. Maybe then the anger would be gone.

She left Andrew's body, where it sat for now. She had at least a few hours before the sun came up, and they came looking, perhaps longer if Andrew hadn't told anyone where he was going, and it was a safe bet he hadn't. Judging from the fact that he came out here in the middle of the night alone—like a stupid person—she might have all the time in the world.

Mildred crawled down into the den and woke the sleeping girls. They would have no idea what time it was—they'd been sleeping for days anyway. To start things off, they played some games to reintroduce the magick. As soon as they were giggling, she turned the page, where they changed clothes for an hour or so. She turned one more page and had them create sounds that seemed to come from behind them. And just as they were showing signs that they wanted to stretch their legs and go outside, she paused, deep in thought. The body was still out there, sitting against a tree. It would be the first thing they saw.

She stood to dispose of it, but they tried to follow, and when they protested, she put them to sleep again. As she climbed back outside, she looked at the spot Andrew used to sit. Her world spun, and she felt a rush of dread—*how long ago had he left?* She'd just wasted precious time.

This person had been sent to combat her—of that, there could be no doubt. Could they be on their way already? Mildred knew that revenants were not invincible and had been hunted and killed by villagers throughout their entire existence. She must act fast.

The first thing she did was wake the girls and open the Book of Shadows.

CHAPTER 66

Andrew insisted on eating even before he showered the dried blood away. Holly didn't know how he could touch food with it all over his hands, but he ate everything they put in front of him, along with two cups of coffee and two more glasses of water. Koji, who had been stoic until Andrew's appearance, was aghast at the situation but remembered to turn the camera on and take a long slow panning shot of Andrew in all of his bloody clothing.

Aside from that, Koji stayed busy, nervously glancing out the kitchen window at the rate of three times a minute. Tim couldn't help but feel a bit more at ease due to Koji's vigilance. As soon as Andrew was finished eating, they sent him upstairs to shower and lay down. Holly noticed he was no longer stumbling.

"His mother keeps him alive, right? He seems to be healing already," said Holly. Tim shook his head. "What's next? Are we going into the woods?" Tim met her eyes and nodded.

"As soon as he's ready, Holly. But—did you say 'we'?" Holly nodded.

"Yes, against my better judgment. Let's pray this is the end. Let's pray that she's not even there—wherever 'there' is. Let's pray we find your girls, and they're—alive—and—" Holly all at once choked up and stopped talking. Koji began speaking rapidly in Japanese.

あれは誰？女性。庭にいる女性!
(Who's that? A woman. A woman is in the yard!)

Holly felt the hair on the back of her neck rise. The urgency in Koji's tone said it all. Tim ran to the window.

"Shit. She's here."

Holly knew right away why Tim swore. Tim began communicating with Koji—or at least started trying. Koji recognized immediately that the woman in the driveway was not welcome on the property and hoisted the camera up then walked briskly to the front porch door.

"Wait! Koji, don't go yet. Wait!" The big man paused to look back but continued out onto the porch. "Dammit, no!" said Tim, who had thankfully brought the shotgun downstairs when he'd answered the door that morning. Quickly, he went to the drawer, retrieved it, and followed Koji outside.

Mildred stood on the lower lawn on the far side of the driveway just before the pond. She'd only just arrived. Koji had seen her as she left the woods, meandering slowly through the field—to call attention. Mildred didn't want to be in the house, where any number of traps might be set and waiting. It was best—safest—to finish this all in the open. It wasn't her first choice, but she was no longer in control of the situation. She waited too long. Things had changed.

A giant man stood between her and Tim. *A hindrance.* The big man appeared unarmed, and despite his size, she didn't give him a second thought.

Where was Tim finding this protection? It had been a while since she'd gone through his papers. Had things changed? These questions were all the more reason to get this over with.

Mildred noticed that Tim held the shotgun again—the one she could call from his hands quickly if she wanted to. Did he forget that she had that capability? Would he try to hold on tighter or something, hoping that would work? The big man pointed his camera at her, and Tim walked up behind him and stopped. Mildred couldn't see the shotgun, but that wouldn't matter.

"Don't come any closer, Mildred. Let's—"

Suddenly, the sharp report of a rifle interrupted Tim's monologue and echoed across the meadow. Mildred's right shoulder jerked forward violently as she dropped to one knee—a small grunt of agony escaping her lips. Koji turned and tackled Tim to the grass, all the while keeping his eyes on Mildred. The rifle reported three more times in quick succession, and Tim could hear at least two of the shots hit the side of the house.

"Holly! Get down!" he yelled as he struggled to free himself from the bulk of Koji's massive arms. The bodyguard resisted at first but let Tim stand when he realized that the shots were intended for Mildred. Tim looked out into the field, well beyond the pond, and saw the rifleman squeeze off one more shot. This one was not followed by the *smack* of a missed shot against the house, and Tim's first thought was *Bob Simmons*—but Bob Simmons was, of course, dead. Who else was as bad a shot, or crazy enough to fire a gun in the direction of a house?

Mildred recovered and stood again, spinning momentarily toward the meadow. On the defensive, she darted for the cover of woods. A wounded animal, she slipped between the trees and was gone. Tim's mind stretched in several directions, but the first thing he addressed was Holly.

"Holly!" he yelled again, a lump of dread rising in his throat. The shooting had gone from rapid-fire to a cease-fire, and whatever scene waited in the kitchen—was said and done. "Stop shooting! Stop shooting!—Koji!" Tim called the ex-sumo wrestler's attention and made a quick slit-throat motion followed by a gesture toward the meadow. Koji grabbed his camera and took off in awkward bounding strides. Tim privately hoped Koji understood him and wouldn't actually slit the shooter's throat—at least until they learned who he was—then charged through the porch door.

Holly nearly knocked him over as she barged out of the same

doorway, and Tim embraced her, relieved. Ed Bodwell's careless bullets had missed most everything except for the house and one lucky shot in Mildred's right shoulder.

"Are you okay?!"

"I'm okay."

"She's gone, be careful. Ran into the woods right over there." Tim pointed to the bend in the driveway. Holly looked out into the field. Koji had just barely passed the stone wall that marked the beginning of the meadow—speed was not the big man's talent.

"Is that Ed Bodwell, the vigil-guy?" Holly asked. She recognized his drunk-ish gait.

Bodwell was nearly seventy-five yards back from the bounding Koji, by the distant property line. He stumbled as he walked over the uneven ground. *Still drunk,* Holly noted.

"Ed Bodwell. Oh my God, you're right. And I told him specifically 'no guns,' not to mention 'the vigil is over—get the fuck out.'" Tim ran to the driveway, cupped his hands around his mouth and shouted:

"ED!"

"ED! Stop shooting! I told you, no shooting! You're going to kill one of us!" Ed Bodwell put his rifle down at his side and trudged toward the house, as if he had saved the day. Despite his disregard for firearm safety, Tim had to admit that he probably did. "ED!" Tim screamed one more time. Ed Bodwell heard every one of Tim's cries and finally raised his hand in mock victory.

I hear you, I hear you. You're welcome—Some of my shots were off target—but the result was I saved your ass. Yeah, yeah, a couple of bullets missed the mark, but everyone is present and accounted for, right? Don't give me any shit about 'guns,' Russell. Bodwell didn't know about Andrew, who was safely upstairs.

But he did know that once Mildred was exterminated, a few holes in the clapboards would soon be forgotten. It was time now to find her and finish her. *Track her—hunt her—put her down—* no easy task. Even the inebriated Ed Bodwell knew that his prey was merely wounded, and it was far too early to celebrate. He'd have to find the trophy and bring her home to get any credit. He saw Koji coming for him but knew the big man would stop as soon as the .45 was in his face. *Either that, or it would be self-defense, right?* Drunkenly, he triangulated a course to try and cut her off.

Let's see…she ran to the woods near the birch, and I was about… thirty yards back at the time…so that means…

He knew at least one of his bullets had hit the targeted threat. The first one even doubled her over. And then she *ran away. The "Legend of Mildred Wells" ran away. The one from television!* He'd hit her enough to scare her. Now maybe he'd get to be on the show.

Eighty-five percent sure of her direction, he set his sights for a dark patch of pines and trudged toward it, nearly twisting his ankle twice. He didn't want or need to hear any more of Tim Russell's lecture until it was over. He ran his left hand to his waist and felt the 1911 Colt—his favorite—then flipped a "concealed" middle finger at Tim Russell, for not only kicking him off the property but for his anti-gun Massachusetts state-of-mind. Also, for all of the yelling—it made his hangover even worse, especially after firing the rifle. The charging Koji meanwhile, began to earn more of Ed Bodwell's attention.

Everything was coming together nicely. The pistol on Ed's hip could blow her heart to bits—and if what they said about a revenant's heart was right—that would be *all she wrote.* That is, if *Only If You Dare* was to be trusted. He believed it was.

He approached the woods at an angle, getting closer and closer, trying to keep the dark patch of pines in his wobbly sights.

CHAPTER 67

Tim was reasonably sure that Ed Bodwell was done shooting toward the house and relaxed for the moment. He watched as the man stumbled perilously close to the edge of the woods. Bodwell was still nearly a football field away from the house but didn't seem to be coming this way. Was he considering going in after her?

"Ed! Ed! Stop! Stay away from the trees!" Ed ignored him. "ED, NO, SHE'S DANGEROUS!" It seemed as if nothing could stop the man from his predetermined path—*and did he just flip me the bird?* Tim wondered. It didn't take long to realize that Ed Bodwell was going in for the kill.

Like Death himself, a figure emerged from the forest with a long flowing black dress. Her arm was raised high over her head, holding a deadly blade, as if preparing to harvest one more soul. Mildred was fifteen feet behind Ed Bodwell, silent and all business. Ed, fatally ignorant.

She waited—trailing, but gaining, hesitating until the precise moment, and at the last second, the old hatchet from the barn swung down, collapsing Ed Bodwell in a heap. Holly gasped. Because of the distance between them, there was no sound, only the horrific visual of the killing swipe. Koji, not thirty yards from the murder, stopped dead and raised his hands in frustration.

Mildred stood defiantly over his dead body, right shoulder hunched, staring directly at the house.

CHAPTER 68

Holly couldn't see perfectly due to the distance, but it appeared as though Mildred first dropped the hatchet and then—this she knew for sure—stepped back into the woods. Mildred had disappeared again, yet that meant nothing. Backpedaling, she kept her eyes glued to the path at the bend in the driveway. If Mildred wasn't finished, she'd show up right there—far too close for comfort.

"Tim…Tim! Come back to the house. Get Koji! Let's regroup!" Tim agreed.

"Koji!" Tim yelled. The big man had stopped filming as soon as Ed Bodwell fell. Seeing Mildred in action was too much, even for a four-hundred-pound ex-sumo. She was quick, and she was quiet. Koji had underestimated her and was secretly thankful he didn't have to find out the hard way. He wasted no time in heeding the call-back. Even then, however, he wouldn't enter the house, but stayed on the front steps, exchanging the movie camera for Tim's shotgun. Tim protested, insisting he come inside, but it was impossible to explain Mildred's deadly talent.

Holly went straight for the telephone and called the police. At the very least, there was a dead or injured man out in the field, and it was best to leave the task of retrieving him to professionals—at least they weren't on Mildred's hit list. Footsteps bounded down the stairs. It was Andrew, looking as if he'd just awakened.

"What's happening?" he asked.

CHAPTER 69

"I think I can find your daughters. I feel a lot better—my head is clear now. I had another dream—a replay of my march into the woods, without the painful parts." Andrew did look a thousand times better to Tim, and the news that he might be able to take him to Olivia and Vivian was more than tantalizing—but still, he knew better.

"We can't risk it. Look what happened to you. You probably died—again. *Our* mothers are not going to show up and stitch us together as yours does. We have to wait for Galluzzo—not only to show up but to call in the proper authorities, like the Staties or the FBI or whatever. This process is going to be painfully slow and drawn out. Red tape for miles. This is going to suck."

Holly was quietly relieved that Tim's love for his daughters was not enough to push him into doing something overly macho and suicidal. Respecting Tim's decision, all four of them nervously watched the woods and the field for twenty-five minutes until Chief Galluzzo pulled into the driveway. Tim met him at his car door before it even came to a stop.

"Excuse me, Chief, but the whole freaking town is only five miles long. Why the hell does it take you a half an hour to come to investigate a *murder?*"

"Easy, Russell, you have no idea what my job entails."

"Yeah, well, the body is right out there near those trees gathering flies. Is anyone else coming, or are you going to throw him in the back of your cruiser?"

"Back off, Russell. Just back—off. You know you're on thin ice. Who is it out there in the field, do you know?"

"It's Ed Bodwell. Apparently he hid in my grove after I told everyone in the vigil to leave. He popped out of the woods, shooting about forty minutes ago—shooting toward the house. He even hit it. I've got bullet holes outside my kitchen—Holly was in there at the time. He must have been drunk."

"He was shooting at you?"

"What? No. He was shooting—at *her*." Galluzzo paused his questioning and let it sink in.

"Don't tell me..." Galluzzo wore a skeptical grin. *Pshaw. Not the "Legend of Mildred Wells" bullshit again.*

"I know where you're going with that Chief. But the fact remains you've got a body right next to that tree line. I dare you to walk out there by yourself and not think about her watching you from the woods. And don't say I didn't warn you."

"Give me a break, Russell. I don't know what's going on here, but are you serious? I've lived here my whole life and had never heard one ghost story until you showed up. Never heard of Mildred Wells either, except from Bob Simmons, right before he went nuts and got himself killed."

"Hey, don't ask me then, ask them. Ask Holly. She's from Laconia. Or ask Koji. He's from Japan. They saw her too." Chief Galluzzo ignored Tim and circled his cruiser, headed for the field.

"Are you armed? Do you have a rifle, Russell?" Galluzzo asked. Tim almost offered his sawed-off shotgun but remembered that it was illegal.

"No."

"Figures. You can't have real guns in Massachusetts, can you?" Galluzzo was referring to Massachusetts gun laws, which, as compared to New Hampshire's, were stricter. If it was supposed to be an insult, Tim didn't care.

"I guess not," said Tim. Galluzzo sneered as he adjusted his belt and strolled down the lawn toward the pond. *Tim, let him go.* The Chief arrived at Ed Bodwell's body four minutes later, and then only stared down at it. Tim noticed that he never took his right hand off of his holstered pistol and shot many looks into the forest. Then Galluzzo started a slow walk back to the house.

"Is that your hatchet in the grass out there, Russell?" *Here we go,* thought Tim.

"It was here when I bought the place. Where the hell is all your help? The coroner, the ambulance—anybody?"

"They're coming. They're coming. What's your hurry?"

"My hurry is that man right over there says he knows where my girls are in the woods, and I want to go rescue them. All of us. And we need your good New Hampshire firepower to come with us. Call who you have to call. She has them, and as you can tell, she's dangerous." Galluzzo peered around Tim to get a look at Andrew.

"Who is he?"

"Long story, but he lives in the town of Sugar Hill, up north. Owns a funeral home. He dropped by to help us out of the blue. He's—a kind of psychic I guess you'd say." Tim waited for the Chief's eye-roll. Calling Andrew a psychic was inaccurate, but it was a far more coherent story for the skeptic to believe. Sure enough, Galluzzo's body language suggested that he wasn't buying it.

"We'll check it out because you have witnesses who saw a woman. Not because you think you saw a ghost." Tim was silently exasperated with Galluzzo's ignorance—the man kept using the term "ghost," but Tim knew better than to argue the point.

"Well, she's a dangerous woman, Chief. She took out Ed Bodwell, and he was carrying a rifle and a pistol at the time."

"You all saw the whole thing? There is a ton of blood out there..."

"Yeah," Tim said. Chief Galluzzo's eyes narrowed in near-disbelief.

"What is she, a wild woman, living in the woods? What's she wearing? Is it a 'Mildred Wells' copycat?" Tim didn't want to start over with new explanations.

"Yeah, it might be that. It might be a copycat too, or even a guy in a dress. I don't know. But she's fast, and she's a psychopath, and you're going to want several guns on-hand, and maybe a few rifles, like a SWAT team, especially if he or she has my girls." Galluzzo began to move toward his cruiser. "Hey, Chief..." Galluzzo turned back to face Tim.

"What?"

"Please hurry."

CHAPTER 70

Mildred slow-walked back to the coyote den, being careful not to drip and leave a trail. Luckily she didn't have much blood to begin with, because the damage to her shoulder area was extensive—her collar bone was shattered, and while there was little pain, there was also little function. She needed an extended rest more than ever, but the pressure was mounting against her. Along with her anger was a note of fear—*they would be coming now*. Using strips of her dress, she stitched up what she could of her flesh and fashioned a primitive sling to limit the movement of the arm. As she did so, Vivian stirred and opened her eyes.

"Mommy, I'm thirsty." Mildred eyed her carefully, trying to figure out if the girl was addressing Sheila, or had finally come around. Awkwardly she poured a cup of water and handed it to Vivian, who drank deeply, finishing the whole thing. "Thank you, Mommy. Can I have more?" Mildred's heart pumped an extra beat. Vivian was clearly awake after drinking the water and looking her in the eyes. She poured another cup.

Mildred's dead lips curled into what once would have been a smile, the first in—*forever*. Using the spell, she called the Book of Shadows to her and opened it. She was so tired, yet the little girl's affection gave her a small measure of energy. But there was too much to do in too short a time. Leaving Olivia asleep, she read to them, and then made Vivian sleep again. Soon they could stay awake for as long as they wanted to. Soon—after she tied up the final loose ends.

She hadn't felt anything resembling love in over a century—nor had she loved back. The anger in her was burning itself out, but she couldn't let it go just yet. She didn't care to be hunted for the next forty years, or until Tim Russell died a natural death. To begin her new life, she would have to start clean, with no looking over her shoulder—no distractions.

With her good arm, Mildred scooped the girls up and slung them over her healthy shoulder. It was time to move.

CHAPTER 71

Due to a bank robbery in Manchester, it took nearly all day for the SWAT team to arrive. Tim knew the process would be painfully slow and that the search for Olivia and Vivian had grown old in the public eye, but he had no idea it would be this—*back burner.*

They all waited and watched as the coroner came and took Ed Bodwell's body away. Koji stood guard at the corner of the house to watch the front and side along as well as the path to the grove. Holly tied Neptune out on the lawn next to him for an extra set of "senses," but all the dog did was nap under the overcast sky.

When SWAT finally arrived, it was dusk, and the team looked exhausted—hardly up for a several-mile hike in the dark woods—but duty called, and there were lives to be saved, so nobody complained. Three state police cruisers also pulled up with dogs, rounding out the most formidable search party to date. They started with Andrew and a machete leading the way, and nearly a mile in, he made an announcement.

"Uh… You aren't going to like this, but I need everyone to shut off their flashlights, just for a few minutes. Everything looks… *different* with the lights on. It's only for a few minutes. Stay right here. I'll be alright." Chief Galluzzo, who seemed agitated with the command, murmured to Tim as Andrew walked on ahead.

"Is he lost? We've got a murderous madwoman out here, and he wants to shut all the lights off. *Wonderful.* Well, at least the good guys have their night-vision." All eight members of the SWAT team did indeed have night-vision goggles, but this was the first time they had ever used them in the field. The New Hampshire SWAT team had been founded only the year before and were relatively green around the ears. Today had been their first two calls in over four months. Andrew meandered for nearly ten minutes before coming back to retrieve everyone.

"It's this way," he stammered.

"Andrew," Tim whispered.

'What?"

"Are you alright?"

"Well, I'm nervous. I can't see a thing, and every branch I duck under, I feel like I'm going to take a knife in my liver. Other than that—cool as a cucumber." Tim thought he saw a bead of sweat on Andrew's brow and heard the stressed sarcasm. He realized he had developed a false sense of security, most likely due to the added company and the firepower around them. Andrew, the nervous point man, reminded him of the danger.

Holly squeezed Tim's hand tight while leading Neptune by his leash. There were sixteen people in all, including eight SWAT team members, four state troopers, and Koji with his movie camera. There were also four dogs, including three German Shepherds and the nearly useless Neptune.

Over two hours later, Andrew paused and had everyone turn their flashlights off again. Nerves were tense as the hour approached 9 pm. Andrew held his finger up to his lips as he stepped as lightly as he could across the forest floor. It was late autumn, however, and the leaves were deep in several spots. The effort was most likely for naught.

Finally, he gave the signal to turn their lights back on, and it wasn't another two hundred yards before their beams collectively shone on the two boulders semi-hidden beneath the two conifers. Andrew for once realized the responsibility he'd been given.

He had grown up somewhat selfish and spoiled—indeed the black sheep of the family. He's been in trouble with the law, been kicked out of college, and even played a rather large hand in getting his sister murdered. His mother haunted him for all of these reasons. Her stubborn Irish spirit lived on, within her stubborn Irish ghost.

She would—protect him, for lack of a better word. *Just as likely, she'll sacrifice me. She'll let me take the beating until the guns start blazing. I'm the canary in the coal mine, and if I die, I die. Maybe I'll get lucky, and the SWAT team will kill her before I'm dead.* No matter what happened, though—he knew it would hurt.

It would hurt like hell.

The SWAT commander understood that they had arrived at ground zero and began giving nonverbal commands, but Andrew waved them off, pointing adamantly at his chest. Dumbfounded, the commander set his men up to train their guns between the two boulders. There was no way to argue out loud.

Tim and Holly watched in silent horror as they recognized Andrew's sacrifice. He tip-toed to the boulders and crouched down, staring into a small dark hole, his machete raised. *It looks like a mouth*, he thought. *A mouth that is going to bite me in two.* After two full minutes of trying to listen for noises coming from inside, he pressed the button on the top of his flashlight.

The hole was tunnel-like, with a quick bend to the left. The light only shone on the far wall of dirt a couple of feet inside. Andrew thought for a moment of tossing a couple of rocks in, but wouldn't Mildred just wait patiently and nail him when he entered? On the other hand, would he get a startled reaction from the young girls and know they were alive?

If they were alive.

Too much thinking.

Five minutes had now passed, and Andrew felt the pressure of the crowd behind him—waiting, fingers on triggers, wondering. He tossed a rock but heard no reaction from inside. Finally, he crawled forward, craning his neck to see around the bend as soon as humanly possible.

Finally, his light illuminated the entire entrance tunnel, and he could see partially into the dark den. What appeared to be animal skins were in a pile in the corner…but nothing else. No one was here.

"They're gone. It looks like the girls were here, though." Andrew stood tall between the two boulders and held up two crude blankets sewn from what appeared to be dozens of squirrels. "This is all that's in there. It's a big enough space for three people."

CHAPTER 72

It was nearly midnight before the SWAT team, and the last police car left the yard. None of the dogs were able to track Mildred after Andrew explored the den because once again, she had killed every living thing in several directions before choosing her true escape route. The police pledged to come back first thing in the morning for a proper search.

Tim, Holly, Andrew, Koji, and Neptune made their way cautiously into the house, watching each other's backs as they went room by room to the living room, where Holly clicked on the end-table lamp, and they all sat for a minute to sort things out. Everyone, including Koji, was exhausted.

Tim was emotional—afraid, hopeful, thankful, and discouraged, all at the same time. He looked as terrible as he felt.

"Andrew—what you did—that was—that was—thank you. Thank you, thank—and he broke into tears. Holly hugged him and stroked his hair.

"Don't mention it. I just wish it—worked out. At least it seems like the girls were there recently, and we can still save them. Mildred is keeping them alive for whatever reason, and it's not too late." Tim nodded while wiping his eyes.

"She has to be close. It can't be easy traveling with two young girls in the woods. Even if she *carried* them, how far could she get in so short a time? And she's wounded too, right?" Andrew and Holly shrugged their shoulders. There were so many things they didn't know the answers to anymore, nor could they explain.

"Tim, the police will be back in less than seven hours, and you're exhausted. We should at least try to get some sleep." Holly couldn't believe she was saying this after promising herself to never sleep at the Lancaster Hill Road house again, but it was very late, and tomorrow would start very early. The circumstances warranted staying. If Mildred chose to show up between now and then, well, *I guess I have to go down swinging*. Some things you just couldn't help. The girls were close or appeared to be. There was fresh hope in the air, and no way to ignore or abandon that. Tim suddenly looked angry, as if he had something to say. Sure enough, he did.

"Andrew—what about Thomas Pike?"

"What do you mean?"

"Have you seen him? Or heard anything? Has he come at you with that damn pen of his and asked you to guess what the hell he's thinking lately?" Andrew paused for a moment. *Come to think of it; he hadn't*. Thomas Pike had been practically up his ass to get to Sanborn and had then all but disappeared. He showed up here just for the Mildred dreams, to get Andrew up to speed. That was it, wasn't it?

"No, I haven't seen him, and now that you say that, it's pretty weird that he hounded me to come here and has done almost nothing since. Today would have been a perfect time to show up and provide some guidance."

"Maybe he doesn't want to take the chance that Mildred will see him," added Holly.

"Well, that's mighty brave of Thomas, isn't it!?" Tim added sarcastically. "There are only two little girls' lives in the balance, not to mention the four of us and poor dead Mr. Bodwell. No, we wouldn't want Mildred to see Thomas—she might kill him, right? Oh, no, wait. He's already dead. I'm sick of that guy. *Fuck you,* Thomas Pike, and thanks for nothing."

"Well, maybe he's not done, and he's going to—" Holly tried to soothe him.

"Oh, bullshit. I wish… You know what? I wish I had it to do all over again. Mildred and the kid running around was no big deal. It was creepy as hell, but they minded their own business. So what? So I have to turn my back once a year when she drowns him in the pond. I could handle that a lot better than I'm handling this right now. I was going to sell the place anyway. All she did was stand in the field most of the time, and—"

"And change your daughters' clothes while they were sleeping. Don't forget that," Holly reminded him. The thought of that morning a year and a half ago when the girls woke up in old-fashioned nightgowns gave Tim pause.

"That's true. That was bad. But at least she didn't hurt them! She didn't want to kill us back then! I can't even think straight anymore. All I had to do was fix this place up and maybe sell it to a couple with no kids. I mean, several families lived here between Mildred and me, and they all survived!" Tim had snapped out of his funk, and his adrenalin drove his emotions. It would be tough to get any sleep tonight. He was angry. Angry at someone besides Mildred Wells for the first time in a long time.

"Thomas Pike pulled me in. Got me involved—made me dream things I didn't want to dream and see things I didn't want to see. That was *their* business, not mine, and it happened long before I showed up. Fix your own problems, don't just pass them on to someone else so you can go fucking 'rest' eternally. Oh, the hours I spent barbecuing his damn bones and grinding them up so we could dump them in the lake…" Andrew looked at Tim sideways.

"What the hell are you talking about, barbecuing—human bones?" Tim realized how bad that sounded and paused his rant to explain.

"Uh—never mind. It makes them brittle. Dries them out. Easier to grind up—listen, you don't have to know. It's a long story.

Thomas didn't want Mildred just to dig him back up and move their bones again. I had to grind them." Andrew rolled his eyes. *This gets weirder by the minute.*

"Do you think Thomas tricked you and then took off?'

"Absolutely. Thomas told us his side of the story via sleepless nights and bad dreams—does that sound familiar? And then he tricked us into stealing Elmer from Mildred for his selfish reasons. He stabbed Midred in the back and then stabbed us in the back too because he left us alone with her, and of course, she's pissed!

Holly was about to mention the fact that Mildred had drowned Thomas' son in the pond but was thankful she didn't have time to respond as Mildred stepped into the room.

CHAPTER 73

Mildred carried the sleeping girls over her good shoulder as she dropped every living animal from the trees. She took several hour-long misdirections, knowing that there would be dogs and that they would catch her scent rather quickly. For this reason, she was sure to pick up sticks and rocks periodically and touch them to the open wound on her bad shoulder, then discard it. At least the scent of the girls would not be left on the ground.

Her bones ached, and she dropped to a knee on two occasions. They'd be chasing her now, and that was never the plan. She could still achieve her goals—she was so close to beginning a new life. Her anger had gotten the best of her, and she had dragged the revenge game out too long and gotten greedy. After all that planning, wasting time trying to make it last—all it made her was tired.

It was time to end the game. The old drunk with the rifle had been unexpected—a margin of error Mildred had never taken into account. She'd gotten careless, thinking she was invincible—precisely the kind of thing that had gotten every other revenant who had ever lived killed.

After nearly six miles of misdirection-circles, tangents, and double-backs, Mildred headed for her new—albeit temporary—home base. She found a farm with a dilapidated barn and tucked the girls in there. The barn was no longer in use; the farmer was merely putting off the chore of tearing it down because he didn't have the time or the funds. They would be safe there for a day or so until it was all over. Then they could head north, away from the modern-day lynch mob.

Expecting to feel some relief after putting the girls down, she was severely disappointed. She didn't feel even an ounce lighter, with miles to go before she even *reached* the house. Deep down, she knew, however, that she could still take them all out very easily, even the giant man.

CHAPTER 74

Mildred waited in the hayloft of the barn for them to return empty-handed from the den. She expected the professionals to look tired and disappointed, but at least they could go home to their families. They had no idea how fortunate they were. It took fifteen minutes for all of the cars to leave. She couldn't see the front of the house from this vantage point, but she could pretty accurately guess what was going on.

They would enter the house through the front porch and then search the house. Sure enough, the turret light came on four minutes later, and she saw Tim's head come up the stairs, swivel, and head back down. The light went off, and that was her cue to move.

It took less than a minute to cross the roof of the barn, pull the nails from the turret window and let herself in. Now she would listen for their locations. It didn't matter if they were together or spread out, except for the way the job got done. There was a murmuring that seemed to be coming from the living room. Perhaps they were there. The giant man could be anywhere, however, as he didn't seem to be much of a talker. Silently, she descended the turret stairs.

Foolishly, they had left the kitchen dark, as well as the dining room. A dim glow came from the living room—which was lit by one bulb. Now Mildred could make a plan. The giant man was even in the room with them—sitting down. Was he tired? Not much of a hiker? Too bad. Too, too bad. This lapse in security would cost them everything. Before her attack, she listened in.

CHAPTER 75

Mildred stepped into the room, and Holly froze. Tim didn't see her immediately. His head was in his hands, and he was about to continue his rant—and Holly didn't have the breath to warn him. Koji, who's eyelids had grown heavy despite Tim's emotional speech, woke immediately and attempted to stand, but it was too late.

As soon as he rocked his weight forward in the chair, Mildred's knife was in his face, mere inches from his nose. For an awkward second, he hung in a half-standing, half-sitting position then fell back to save his life. Mildred was hunched, yet coiled, and the long blade was steady, holding the big man in place, forcing everyone in the room to draw a collective breath.

She stared Koji down for an extra two seconds to be sure he'd quit. Koji tucked his chin to his chest, thankful to have been spared. Tim by now had lifted his head to see the living nightmare who'd taken them all by surprise. The room was hers to do as she pleased.

It was the dinner-table scene all over again—the scene he had re-lived in his head dozens of times ever since—the scene he was ashamed of, despite her unfair advantages. Tim reflexively pulled the shotgun from behind his back and pointed it, realizing at the last second that Holly was too close to Mildred and would catch part of the blast. As soon as he hesitated, the gun was Mildred's. Neptune didn't budge.

Andrew stood against the wall across the room, fully aware of the dead woman's power. Her smell brought back vivid memories of their meeting in the forest, and of course, the smothering upstairs. He remembered the flash of the blade and the iron grip. He remembered it all and wanted no part of her—despite the fact that his machete was at his feet.

Then something caught his eye outside the window on the lawn in the moonlight—a shadow gliding on the grass. He glanced over at Holly, Tim, and Koji—but all eyes were on Mildred. The shadow stopped on the lawn and stared. It was his mother, of course, eternally disappointed, forever expecting more. She was but a silhouette in the moonlight, yet Andrew could feel her eyes boring through him. He knew at once that her wrath would be far worse than anything Mildred would inflict on him, and he'd better act.

Mildred's eyes were on Tim, who had by now realized that his time was truly up. There would be no reunion with the girls. The post-divorce life ended here—the house project had been a pipe dream in the end, a fool's errand. He'd lost—and lost it all. Everybody else lost too because he decided to move to New Hampshire. Sheila lost, Holly lost, and Andrew. Koji too. His girls, most of all. Just finish it, he said with his eyes. *Make it quick.*

Suddenly Andrew grabbed his machete and swung at Mildred's closest hand—the one holding Tim's shotgun. His dull blade arced down as she caught his movement from the corner of her eye. Unfortunately for Andrew, wounded or not, Mildred was still superior. Outclassed and outmatched, it was as if time slowed for her. Even with the bullet-damaged shoulder, she could practically dance around his best effort.

His machete chop came down from above as she deftly sidestepped and brought her own knife up. Andrew's right side was overextended, and the blade passed freely between two ribs, traveling the width of his abdomen until the bolster hit bone.

Andrew fell in a heap, wind escaping through his mouth and the gruesome gash. He was less than a minute from death, and there was nothing anyone could do. Mildred stood above him, hoping that her choice jab would be enough to slow him, at least until she could finish what she had to do.

No one dared move. *Death Personified* had shown up for work. The economy of motion, the precision, the skill. She'd barely moved, and yet she'd pinned them all down, barely making a sound. Tim stood up slowly and prepared to beg for it all to stop.

Mildred rose to her full height and faced him. Andrew's blood found her right foot and began to soak in. Several flies jumped-ship for the fresh kill.

Mildred moved slowly and steadily, watching Tim's eyes as she raised the shotgun—

—*by the muzzle.*

Tim looked at her, in shock—*what was this?* Holly, too, had no answers and held her breath.

Mildred turned her head and looked at each of them, one at a time, then sent her blade back to the Beverly woods.

Tim could only wait.

Mildred looked back to Tim and reiterated her offer of the shotgun. Tim suspected a trick, yet very slowly lifted his right hand to accept. For a quick moment, they both held the gun, and Tim wondered if it was his imagination, or if he could *feel* an agreement between them. As soon as he had the weapon, he felt her grip weaken, and the weight of the gun became his to bear.

She was toying; it had to be. Tim and Holly had partnered with Thomas Pike. *They'd stolen her son's bones*—and she'd just killed Andrew, right in front of them.

Self-defense?

Tim held the shotgun but put off any thoughts of firing the

weapon. Oddly, he had to *trust her*, if only for a moment—to see if this was indeed a bizarre act of good faith.

Tim stood, staring her in the face, trying to read her clouded eyes. His adrenalin powered him through the grisly visuals and odors and helped numb him from this strange reality as his heart beat on, trying to continue the blood flow to his head.

CHAPTER 76

Mildred hadn't anticipated the truce either. On her way from the turret to the living room, she'd hoped to hear Tim's plan to kill her. She needed the confirmation of his anger to spark her own—she needed the fire and the passion for finishing things off. She needed a reminder of their betrayal and the lack of regret. She needed to hear his angry defiance and how much he hated her for kidnapping his daughters.

But he hadn't said any of that.

He'd been duped too.

Mildred stared back, waiting to be sure Tim understood. If he attempted to fire the gun, she would have to call the knife again, and he would not find his daughters in time—if at all. The living room scene had happened fast, so fast she wasn't sure how things would proceed. Much depended on his reaction.

But from what she'd heard from the dining room, Thomas betrayed Tim, just as he betrayed her. Played him the fool. *Played them both.* Tim Russell might deserve one chance.

One.

Thomas was *The Evil* all along! Selfish Thomas. Unforgiving Thomas. Thomas the golden-boy, Thomas the egocentric "patriot." Thomas had stabbed them both in the back to get what he wanted.

Anger left her body as if a candle had been blown out. Her

head swirled as anguish dissolved—a physical withdrawal. And with it came relief, and just in time—she didn't have the energy.

And the girls.

Mothering the girls had been, in reality, a false hope from the beginning. A chance to start over and make things right. A chance to try and build a happy family like the one she had before Gideon Walker took over her life.

It would not have been fair to them. The girls would not grow physically, but they would learn as they aged, and it would be hard to convince them her decision was for them—the chance for eternal resentment was a concern.

They'd also been sleeping a lot and were too thin. They would need days if not weeks of sustenance—*before the transition*. Even if she'd murdered Tim now, she would need a long healing sleep, and the girls did not. The more she thought about it, her plan would never work. It had become a weight, a *burden…*

CHAPTER 77

Tim stood, staring her in the face, trying to read her clouded eyes. His adrenalin powered him through the grisly visuals and odors and helped numb him from this strange reality as his heart pounded on, trying to keep the blood moving to his head.

Without dropping her eyes, Mildred slowly turned and walked into the dining room. Tim noticed that she'd turned her back for a brief second but then half-turned back in the darkness. Her presence in the dark dining room assaulted his senses as she stopped, turned back to face them, and extended her left hand toward the doorknob.

"Looks like we're going somewhere, honey. Stay here. Whatever she's doing—is risky, but I have to go. Stay here and be safe. I'll take Koji."

"I'm going. Let's go." It was barely a whisper. Holly's pupils were dilated—she was in shock. Andrew's dead body lay only a foot away, and the blood had soaked down between the floorboards. Holly still stood in the middle of the red lake, a human island. Without missing a beat, she bent down and picked up the machete, which was also soaked red.

"Holly," Tim protested.

"Let's go," she whispered. Koji stood behind Holly as pale as a ghost but said nothing. Tim looked back into the darkness where

Mildred stood, and a chill went through his body. It was a scene from a nightmare.

A dead woman in the darkness of my dining room, staring back at me.

Is this a bad idea? It didn't matter, because there were no other options.

Holly squished through Andrew's blood to follow Tim and Koji. Mildred looked down at Holly's weapon and stared. An agonizing moment passed, and Holly wondered if she should leave the machete behind. Perhaps Mildred was reconsidering her offer. *Nope, it's coming with me. I know you can steal it if you want to—and that's what you'll have to do if you want it.*

Mildred turned to the front door and walked out. When she'd reached the driveway, she stopped again and waited. By instinct, they hung back, staying close to the house, a good fifteen feet from Mildred, who strangely paused again, as if reconsidering. Tim kept the shotgun down but practiced a quick-draw in his mind. Sweat dampened his flannel shirt. *She'd changed her mind. It had been a trap all along.*

Two seconds later, Neptune pushed the door open and joined the group on the lawn. Mildred turned as if she'd been waiting for him and began to walk toward the woods. *Did that just happen? Either that was a complete coincidence or the most odd-ball relationship in existence.*

They passed through the trees and up the dark path. To think that Tim would ever have to follow this phantom through a forest at night was inconceivable, yet a reality. The three of them weaved their way through trees and thickets and over marshland toward a place only God—and Mildred—knew.

She never looked back—never gave Tim a reason to raise the shotgun. Holly followed, gripping the machete tightly. She waited for the moment Mildred might stop, end her charade and attempt to kill them all, but it never came. Koji followed, bound by honor and duty, even though he knew he wouldn't be any help if Mildred changed her mind. Neptune brought up the rear, leashless and free, with a dead squirrel hanging out of his mouth.

Nearing dawn, they saw an artificial light coming through the trees. The forest was near its end, and civilization peered through the trees in the form of a sleepy farm with a repurposed streetlamp illuminating the barnyard. The house was still dark, and the rooster had yet to crow. Mildred led them to the abandoned barn, ducked through a collapsing doorway, and pointed to an old mound of hay. Tim regarded her cautiously one last time, realizing his daughters were close—and took one more cautious look at the eyes, the face—and the flies, then passed her quickly for the hay and the sleeping girls beneath it. Holly ran to assist.

"Vivian, wake up! Are you okay? Wake up!" As Tim assisted Vivian, Holly tended to Olivia. Both girls were mumbling as if waking from a deep sleep, and Tim was beyond happy. "Oh my God, you're alive. You must be freezing; you must be—"

"Tim!" cautioned Holly, cutting him off mid-sentence. Tim snapped immediately out of his ecstasy, expecting a fiendish punchline to an elaborate sham. "Where'd she go?"

Tim looked to Koji, who had hung back to keep watch. He pointed outside. Putting Vivian down, Tim raised the shotgun one more time and ran to the damaged doorway. Cautiously he stepped out barrel-first, searching the early morning farm for any sign. The trees stood dark and tall on the edge of the barnyard, swaying gently in a late October wind. The forest had swallowed her up—Mildred was gone.

Tim relaxed and stood tall again. As soon as he did, the shotgun disappeared from his hands.

CHAPTER 78

Tim and Holly woke the farmer and got help. The girls were taken to the hospital, where they stayed for two days. While Tim was still on the farmer's phone, he reported Andrew's 'murder' just in case he was truly dead this time. They were not going back to the house, and Tim told the authorities that they would be at the hospital for any questioning.

Chief Galluzzo's first question to Tim had to do with all of the blood in the living room, and the surprising lack of a body.

CHAPTER 79

Andrew, deep in a coma, dreamt. He was lying in a rain puddle. His mother looked down on him and, as always, looked dissatisfied. She said four words and four words only:

She's gone. Go home.

Suddenly he felt a hard shock rip through his chest, then fade through his extremities. His body rocked violently, and his back arched, then went still. He opened his eyes, hopelessly alone. The light was still on in the living room, and everyone—was gone. Mildred was gone too, thank God—and then he remembered the horror—how it had all gone down. A searing pain lingered beneath his ribcage.

The knife.

He sat up and looked around. It wasn't a rain puddle. It was a pool of his blood. It took him several minutes to stand, and when he did, he felt light-headed.

She's gone. Go home kept repeating in his head.

He tried to make it stop, but apparently, Mother wanted otherwise. *What do you want now?* he wondered. His car was totaled, and he couldn't just take Tim's or Holly's. He didn't know where their keys were anyway.

After a few moments of thought, he picked up the phone and called George.

Home, finally. *What would it be like from now on?*

His personal "Hotel California." He might be off-the-hook with Mother for now, but *home* didn't seem so welcoming. He'd helped Tim—somewhat, but he didn't exactly save the day. There was no possible way she was satisfied.

She's gone. Go home.

George told him that someone could come to pick him up in about an hour-and-a-half. Andrew hung up the phone, physically drained. He was hurt and hurt badly, yet he knew the healing had begun—Mother's curse would all but guarantee that. In the meantime, he limped his way upstairs and stripped. The painful shower took nearly an hour, and by the time he'd dressed and packed, George himself pulled up the driveway.

Andrew decided to call Tim and Holly later. Mother wanted him out of there. The funeral home was shorthanded, and there was other work to be done. George also needed a day off. Bills needed to be paid.

She's gone. Go home.

"Alright, mom," he murmured to the empty room. George saw him limping badly and scrambled out of the car to help.

"My goodness, what happened?! Are you alright? Where's your car?"

"I'll tell you on the road. We have to go."

She's gone. Go home. She's gone. Go home. She's gone. Go home. She's gone. Go home. She's gone. Go home. She's gone. Go home. She's gone. Go home.

As soon as they left the driveway, the chatter stopped.

CHAPTER 80

Andrew left, and the house was empty now, at least temporarily. But that wouldn't last long because of all the blood, so Thomas set to work. He couldn't use a pen to craft a proper letter, but he needed to reach out once more, and this one was important.

Mildred was worn and tired, this he knew. The whole Elmer ordeal had taken a toll on her. She was angry, and rightfully so. Her anger was caused by many things, some were his fault, but many happened before they even met. The fact that she could not rest—and the fact that she was not a ghost at all were sure signs of a cursed soul. He would most likely never know what happened to her in Beverly Farms, but perhaps it didn't matter. The results were visible. This last communication might just be the trick—if the right person found it.

The police would most likely show up—blood was everywhere, and he couldn't be sure if they'd been called or not. No doubt the authorities would slow things down—but hopefully not for more than a day or so. Tim, Holly, and the girls might come too, probably just long enough to pack their things and leave. It wasn't even Tim's house anymore, and Thomas wouldn't blame them for leaving.

Hopefully, his message—left on the bookshelf—would go undisturbed.

The shelf was still stocked with Annette Smith's collection. Tim wasn't much of a reader, not that he had the time even if he wanted to. Thomas thought for a moment about Annette Smith, the brave woman who had stayed, even after her husband Henry was slain in the grove.

If it weren't for her, nothing would have been resolved—Mildred might still be chasing Elmer's tortured ghost around the property, reliving her horrific "anniversaries." Annette had figured out how to communicate with Thomas all on her own and had been smart enough to write it all down for Tim and Holly to find. Such a brave woman—and she did it all by herself. The rest was history. Elmer wasn't tormented anymore, and there was real peace in his afterlife.

Thomas studied the top shelf and found the book he was looking for—a brown book with a leather-bound cover. The only words on the jacket read "Inspirational Quotes," and one had to look inside for any publishing information. It was a simple book, each page adorned with a famous quote and the person who said it. He'd read the book countless times over the years, waiting for Tim Russell to arrive.

He pulled the book from its spot, leaving a wide, very noticeable gap, and opened it to the page he wanted. Then he set the book down, still open, and weighed it down with the item he'd brought up from the cellar.

CHAPTER 81

The girls were out of her life now, and she didn't know how to feel. Her walk was closer to a stumble, but she didn't want to bother and dig a hole to take a long sleep. She didn't want to wake up alone again in twenty, thirty, fifty years with renewed strength and nobody to share it with. She was the last revenant—the last of her kind, a lonely existence.

It was time to end this afterlife—but it would not be a suicide this time—it was not fair to call it that. Suicide was for living people overcome by lack of hope. She'd tried that at age thirty, but she was in a bad place then and, in retrospect, should have looked for alternatives. This time, Mildred was stuck in a supernatural purgatory—she'd been brought back undead, unfairly and unnaturally.

Mildred wasn't *quitting* this time. On the contrary, she had hope. She hoped for a fair and natural death, along with an everlasting rest. To walk the earth for centuries alone was nothing but a curse.

How she would carry it out, she wasn't sure. All she wanted now was to tour the property one last time—to try and focus on the only happy years of her life—recapture them for but a second and go out on a lighter note. Maybe somewhere along the tour, she would make up her mind exactly where and how, and it would all come naturally.

She began in the grove, passing through the rows, realizing it would be the last time she ever passed through. She'd wasted many years chasing Elmer here, hoping for some sort of forced reconciliation, which she now realized had been a tremendous waste of energy.

Even though her body was bone-tired and physically damaged, she walked a bit easier as she began to let the past go. As the final row passed, she said goodbye to the grove, looking through the trees of the remaining wild forest to the meadow beyond. It was a gloomy overcast day, and yet—to her, it was beautiful. Her strides lengthened a bit as she broke through to the field. It was nearly over, and the relief of her decision gave her comfort.

As she passed the pond, she bowed her head, reflecting on the greatest mistake of her existence—an apology, of sorts. Things were different then. She'd been desperate. *What's done is done*, she thought. She left the pond area behind, looking forward to the final tour of her house.

Mildred ascended the front steps and opened the front door at the bottom of the bedroom stairs, and looked up. A lot of bad things had happened up there—a lot of angry things that didn't mesh with the brightness of her current mood...and there was blood on the stairs, giving her pause. She decided it was not someplace she wanted to explore, so she turned into the living room—to another ugly scene of which she'd been a big part.

Where was the body? It was no real surprise. Andrew was inhuman in some way—but it wasn't her concern anymore. Hopefully, he wasn't lurking somewhere. If he was, she still had the shotgun—and the knife—and she would have her final moments *in peace* even if he decided to try again.

The pool of blood was still not completely dry, and the bloody footprints that went up the stairs came from here. Surely if the police had already come, there would be signs that they'd marked the scene for investigation—but they hadn't arrived yet.

In a sort of trance, Mildred let her eyes sweep the room as she attempted to ignore the blood—One more glance at the heart of the house before she went up to her favorite place, the turret, and…

And then something caught her eye on the bookshelf. She squinted, and her shoulders tensed. An object from long ago, a distant memory, was inexplicably there on the bookshelf. It hadn't been there—not even eighteen hours before—It was *Elmer's toy drum.*

Mildred hadn't seen the drum in over a century, but she remembered it well. She remembered taking it away from him when he was a little boy because he beat it—and hit it—and beat it—until her eardrums rang.

One night after he went to bed, she hid it in the cellar, and the next day, lied about it when he asked.

Her head spun. *How in the world did that get there?* Mildred whirled and looked out the front windows. Was anyone watching? *Was it Andrew? How could he know? What else did he know? Or was it… No. Was it?*

She turned back to face the bookshelf. The drum sat on top of an open book, and the shelf above that had an empty slot where a missing book might belong. These weren't new books. These were leftovers from a previous owner and had been here for some time. Mildred crossed the room, put down the shotgun, and picked up the drum. On the book underneath, a page had been ripped out and left sitting on top, so there would be no mistaking what she should look at. It was a quote of but a few words:

"Anger is an acid that can do more harm to the vessel in which it is stored than to anything on which it is poured."
–Mark Twain

Mildred's arm twitched, and the book fell from her hand. The quote struck a nerve.

It *was* him.

He was speaking to her—directly. *Still here, Thomas?* She turned, slower this time, and looked out the front windows again. *Where?* she wondered.

Mildred left the house and ambled down the lawn, searching the field and the trees for any sign of the sender. She reached the water and paused, offering plenty of time for someone to show themselves if they genuinely cared. A quiet minute passed. The willows by the pond gently swayed.

Would it rain? It didn't matter. The moment hung in the air. She dropped her eyes, dead tired—and tired of waiting. It was time to move on before her mind began to count this last hoax as another defeat. Her energy faded ever-further, and it would take too much effort to make it all the way up into the turret.

Mildred studied the surface of the pond at her feet. She caught a glimpse of her reflection and saw what others had seen for the last century. No wonder Elmer had run away from her all those years. She was ghastly, nothing like the young woman she'd once been. It was time to end it all—again—but again, for her sanity, she repeated the thought: *It was not because she had lost hope—but because she'd been robbed of a decent death the first time.*

Mildred stepped into the pond feeling the silt squish between her toes and waded past the cat-o-nine tails and the frog's eggs until she was nearly chest-deep. She scanned the edge of the forest one final time to see if Thomas was watching, but he wasn't. Sensing it was time, she called the shotgun from the bookshelf.

It felt different in her hands now, even though she'd carried it all the way home. The reason must be, she thought, because it would serve a different purpose this time. It would send her to another existence—or, hopefully, a lack of existence at all.

Mildred turned the gun around and placed the two barrels over the left side of her chest, looking down to watch the steel bounce ever so slightly against her heartbeat and the wet fabric of her dress. Mildred watched and measured, making micro-adjustments until the barrels bounced the most.

When she was entirely sure she had the gun positioned perfectly, she let her head fall back…

…and pulled the triggers.

CHAPTER 82

The buckshot left the barrel and tore through Mildred's chest. She felt no pain as her heart disintegrated, and her lights went out. With no revenant heart to drive her anymore, the magick died, and her ancient flesh decomposed properly, as it should have so many years ago.

Falling backward, her head went under the surface, and the flesh dissolved from her bones. The bits and pieces sank, none of them lasting long enough to reach the bottom. In less than a minute, the flies were left to find new filth. Her body disappeared. Mildred Wells ceased to exist.

CHAPTER 83

Mildred woke as if from a long sleep. Her head buzzed at first and then cleared. She found herself sitting in her favorite spot—the turret—overlooking the pond and the meadow, with no recollection of how she'd gotten there. And it was quiet as if something wonderful was missing.

She felt *new*. It was her first sense of well-being since Christmas Day, 1842, just two weeks before her father died behind the barn. She had no idea how she could recollect this thought so precisely, but she was sure it was right. Her comfort now, sitting in the chair above the yard, was so relaxed that it overrode the guilt and bad memories of her painful life. None of that mattered anymore.

She exhaled, savoring the comfort—and stared into the meadow she used to haunt so pathetically.

Nevermore.

Now, the meadow was a just pretty picture to appreciate—she'd never seen it in quite this light. Even the pond was beautiful, despite its deep, dark past and ugly secrets. Death was no longer the problem. Death was no longer the end of the world. She understood now that death was just an anxious transition—*a part of life*, and she'd never have to suffer it again.

Mildred glanced down and noticed that her dress was new and clean. Her hands were pale on the arm of the chair, no longer hideous weathered mitts, worn by time, and digging. Suddenly it struck her—the thing missing from this moment. The clarity she enjoyed was partially due to the lack of *buzzing*. The hundred-year swarm of flies was *gone*, and their irritation with them.

CHAPTER 84

Tim hung up the hospital phone. Somehow Andrew had found him there and called to say he was back home in Sugar Hill.

"Guess who that was?" Tim asked Holly.

"Andrew," she replied. It wasn't too hard to guess. Neither she nor Tim were stunned when the police showed up looking for his body, and it wasn't there. Andrew's mother just wouldn't let him die—without a doubt, the most dysfunctional relationship she had ever known.

"Right," said Tim, shaking his head. "I told him I was going to have to tell the police where he was pretty soon. They have questions and won't take my word for it completely. He didn't mop up before he left." Holly nodded, understanding.

"How'd he get to Sugar Hill?" she wondered.

"An employee picked him up. You know, I was just wondering if we were ever going to see him again." Holly looked at Tim blankly, as if trying to imagine a time that they would even want to come together. *Would it be a happy occasion, or would it be a reminder of darker times?*

"Let's wait and see," she replied.

Olivia and Vivian were checking out of the hospital that day. Both girls were in surprisingly good condition. Mildred Wells had somehow taken good care of them as she terrorized everyone else on Lancaster Hill Road.

Tim and Holly went back to the girls' room to gather their things. Olivia was getting dressed into some brand new street clothes and came out of the bathroom. Vivian, who put on her clothes at a much slower pace, remained inside.

"Close the door, Olivia!" Vivian snapped.

"I AM!" replied Olivia in a huff. As soon as the door was shut, she faced her father.

"Daddy, can we go home now?"

"Uh… Well, we're going to Holly's house."

"Yay! How come? Did you paint your house inside again and it stinks in there? Or what about mom's house. Can we go there? I miss mommy."

"Well, no, honey. I sold *my* house! I don't own it anymore!" Tim avoided the more important question for now—*Sheila*. He would want to tell both girls at the same time, in a more appropriate setting than the public hospital. Olivia suddenly looked disappointed.

"What? Aw. I liked your house. It was so fun! Especially the grove. We had a lot of fun in there playing with that lady." She paused abruptly, looking as if she'd given out too much information.

"'*That lady*,' huh?" said Tim, reciting his fatherly duties about talking to strangers. *If she only knew*, he thought.

"It was okay, dad, she was nice. She showed us how to make corn dolls."

"You can't do that unless I meet them first, understand?" Olivia nodded in defeat just as Vivian emerged from the bathroom.

"Dad sold his house, and we're not going back there. We're going to Holly's house," Olivia blurted.

"What about the things that we left there? My sneakers? What about your tables and chairs, daddy?" asked Vivian.

"I'll get you some new sneakers. Don't worry about that. The man who bought the house bought the whole thing. He bought the house and everything inside." Tim looked up at Holly as he finished his sentence. Holly nodded in relief.

"Can we just get my sneakers, though? They're my favorite ones…"

"I'm sorry, honey, but we can't."

"Can I call mommy?"

"Let's get to Holly's house first, sweetie."

CHAPTER 85

In the end, she had done some things right. She'd spared Tim Russell's life, and Holly Burns's too. She'd also given Tim his girls back. Much more significantly, she'd killed an entire hoard of revenants who had fed on Beverly Farms and the surrounding community for eons—*no small feat*. These things left her feeling slightly better than a complete monster.

Her physical fatigue was gone now, but her memory was sketchy. Some things were vivid memories, but others were lost in a blur. Of course, she still remembered little Elmer, the regret of her lifetime. Regrets *plural*, was more like it. She'd mistreated him his entire life, and of course, the ending was unforgivable. Perhaps she had been unfair with him—and with others too, like Tim's girls and their mother. Or the boy in the woods with the barbed wire. *Bad things.*

Oddly, she couldn't remember what she'd done with the *Book*. It was in the coyote den, and she'd taken it with her when she moved the girls—but where—*hidden it, maybe? Was it in that old barn? Back in the house?*

She'd read from it intensely in the final days, looking for strength to see things through. She'd read it aloud and to herself, backward and forward, reciting to the girls, keeping them sedated—letting the words soak in. In the end, it kept her awake

255

and kept her going. Perhaps her insufficient memory was the cost of doing business with something so dark and powerful.

At that moment, she noticed something in the distance. Had it been there the whole time? Above the field bobbed a red kite, weaving its way back and forth across the gray. *They're in the grove,* she realized. Whoever was flying a kite was located impossibly within the long perfect rows of the spruce grove. She stood immediately and approached the turret window feeling much lighter than she used to be. Getting up was effortless and pleasant now.

Two figures left the woods and wandered out into the meadow—a tall man and a small boy. A father, helping a son with the ball of string. As soon as the boy had the kite under control, the man looked up, directly at the turret.

It was Thomas, of course—and Elmer.

He *had* waited after—all. Mildred hadn't been in a good place her entire life—and he knew it all along.

The patience on this one, she thought.

Thomas tapped Elmer on the shoulder and pointed. Elmer followed his father's finger, recognized the figure high in the turret, and handed over the spool. After what appeared to be a brief conversation—*and perhaps a moment of doubt*—the boy left his father with the kite…

…and began to walk toward the house.

A smile lit up her face.

EPILOGUE

George turned down the long driveway to Foggy Orchard, and Andrew, asleep in the passenger seat, began to stir. He'd slept the whole way home, and looked beaten, but that was to be expected. Colleen Vaughn had told George to expect as much. Andrew had showered himself somehow, but a red stain had begun to seep through his shirt. George had been instructed not to worry.

"Where are we?"—asked Andrew—"Uh, okay. *Home.* You, uh…you can just drop me off over there…" Andrew was still groggy, attempting to play host. He had no idea of the plans that had been made.

"Andrew, I'm…coming inside. I'll help you. You're injured, correct? You have blood on your shirt there." Andrew looked down, then brought his hand up to press the stain gently. He winced.

"You don't have to do that. I'll be fine, and you have a long drive back to Hull. But you can stay overnight if you li…"

"Andrew, yes, I am staying overnight. In fact, I'm staying indefinitely. I'm your new full-time employee." Andrew stared at him blankly, deep in thought, then opened his passenger-side door and got out. The two men shuffled to the house, Andrew, holding his ribs.

"Let me guess. My mother invited you to stay?"

"That's right."

"Why? I mean, why make my life easier? An experienced funeral home director like you is a godsend for me." George glanced sideways at Andrew. Perhaps it was because he'd just woken up, but the young man hadn't thought it all the way through.

"Well, maybe she wants to free you up for *other things*." Andrew stopped dead just in front of the front door to the house.

"What the hell does that mean? I...I literally died about four times in Sanborn. I took a knife through the ribs. I've got stitches all over my body. What else does she want?"

"I have no idea. You'll have to take that up with your mother."

"So, you're going to watch Foggy Orchard while I'm...doing *whatever?*" They opened the door and walked inside to the kitchen.

"Yes, that and whatever needs doing."

"Whatever needs doing? What does that mean?" George opened a drawer and produced a book, and Andrew recognized it immediately—a journal. He dropped his head in frustration. "What's that—Thomas Pike's journal again? Haven't I helped him enough?"

"No, it's not Thomas Pike's journal. It's a brand new one. You and I are going to practice communicating without talking." Andrew sighed heavily, frustrated that his punishment was not over.

"Why?" he whispered, knowing full well the answer.

"Because your mother said you are abysmal at it, and you need the practice."

"Abysmal? You two used the word *'abysmal'* in a conversation? George, how are you so good at talking with ghosts? Are you supernatural?"

"No, and I'm not from *Hell*, either. I'm a living human being, and I'd never seen a ghost before your mother. You're just really bad at this, and you need to learn." Andrew rolled his eyes.

"Doesn't she scare the crap out of you?"

"She did at first"—George paused—"but she's not angry with

me." The words were sobering. Andrew decided to change the subject.

"Okay, so you probably need a permanent room upstairs. Let's get you some sheets, towels…"

"Andrew, I'm all moved in. You don't need to do anything." With that, George put the journal down on the counter and placed a pen on top of it. Andrew was slightly shocked but barreled on in full denial.

"Dinner then. What do you want for dinner?" George pushed the journal and pen across the counter at Andrew.

"Oh, come on, let's give that a break for now. What do you want for dinner?"

George shook his head *no* and pointed to the journal.

For Josi, Karil, Ed, Addison and Olivia

Also, special thanks to my "early feedback" team:
Sherry Pratt, Erin Bergin, Laura Sterritt, Darlene Saltz,
Dawn Goodman, Ron Desjardins, Steve Hoginski, Bill
Gottlieb, Kendra Folsom, Darci Davis, & Sally Reyer

Michael Clark was raised in New Hampshire and lived in the house *The Patience of a Dead Man* is based on. The bats of the barn really circled the rafters all day and there actually was a man-made grove hidden in the forest. He now lives in Massachusetts with his wife Josi and his dog Bubba.

Follow:
https://www.michaelclarkbooks.com/
https://www.facebook.com/michaelclarkbooks/
Twitter: @MIKEclarkbooks
Instagram: @michaelclarkbooks
Reddit: u/michaelclarkbooks

One last Thing…
If you enjoyed this book, I'd be very grateful if you'd post a short review on Amazon. I read all the reviews personally and your input could very well influence future books.
Thank you!
–Mike

Printed in Great Britain
by Amazon